Where there is ma

Justice of the Arc
life to protecting the world's most vulnerable members of the psychic community. But as an ancient enemy of the Council closes in, inciting the Shadow Court and its followers around to deadly action, there's no way to avoid a world-changing war.

Worse, this final battle not only threatens millions of innocent Connecteds, it has the potential to destroy everyone close to Sara. The Magician, the Devil, the Fool, Death, the Moon, Judgment—no one is safe. Even as Sara realizes how much she has come to love her found family, she knows she could lose them in a blink of an eye.

But Sara hasn't fought this hard, for this long, to give up now. And when she combines the full limit of her abilities with her trusty Tarot cards...the game will never be the same.

Except the cards can no longer save you when you climb *The Shattered Tower.*

THE SHATTERED TOWER

WILDE JUSTICE, BOOK 8

JENN STARK

For my readers.
Ever and always.

XVI
THE TOWER.

crackled with urgency, but it was the distress in the voice on the other end of the line that put true power into my steps.

"I'm coming," I gasped, zigging out of the way of a clatter of fire and breaking glass.

The Archangel cursed something in Latin, or maybe a more ancient language than that, but though languages had recently become my strong suit, I didn't need to translate to pick up on his meaning. We were treading on sacred territory here, none more sacred as far as he was concerned—the ancient ruins of King Solomon, built atop Temple Mount in what was now the heart of Jerusalem. I was sure the streaming news services would record this assault on the Mount as yet another terrorist event, giving credit to whatever group on their short list would guarantee them the most clicks when they blasted the news across the world.

But they were wrong. They were always wrong.

The Shadow Court was behind this. A cabal of the richest, most psychically gifted humans and their allies who wanted to bring the rule of magic to every government, scientific institution, financial market, and syndicate of power in the world. That path led only to disaster, as I understood more than most. I'd dedicated my life to protecting the most vulnerable members of the psychic community, innocent Connected children, who all too often ended up as spare parts or extra batteries for the infernal machinations of their stronger, more twisted counterparts. Up to now, most of those battles had been fought in the shadows, down the labyrinthine rabbit holes of the arcane black market.

The game was changing, though. Now war was coming out in the open, putting the vast majority of Connecteds at risk of total annihilation. The Shadow Court was making their bid for ultimate power.

And I was running out of time to stop them.

I swung around the corner and jumped back just as quickly, narrowing my eyes as surprise and annoyance ripped through me. Someone was shooting at me—me! I was freaking Justice of the Arcana Council, so souped up on psychic powers that I might randomly explode the multiverse, and some asshole Connected all hopped up on technoceuticals and misplaced fanboy zeal thought he could take me out?

Not gonna happen.

I dodged another wave of bullets. Fire licked along my nerves and pooled into the center of my palms. But I didn't need to throw fire at this tryhard to knock him out. I needed to leave him in my dust.

At that moment, the operative ahead of me leapt into the air with a flip worthy of an Olympic gymnast. He was halfway into his rotation when a second figure shot out from the side, a streak of black and red. The two collided, and a wild, feral scream of sheer delight filled the alley, audible above the explosions and nearly making me stumble.

I knew that voice. I also knew the flash of jagged silver blades their owner wielded, cutting down the operative midair. My erstwhile attacker still managed to throw something, but clumsily and under the barrage of sharp pointy things. The projectile shanked awkwardly to the right, where it struck the wall. A radiating spike of electrical charge lit up the entire side of the building before the wall was reduced to ash.

"Damn," I muttered, leaving the hapless operative to face Sariah and her knives as I raced on.

Her laughter rang out after me, a disconcerting mix of my voice and her uninhibited pleasure. Caught somewhere between being my mirror self and my twin sister, Sariah had recently taken on a new job. As the Night Witch, she embodied the avenging warrior that, as Justice, I could never be.

Sariah's overall job satisfaction was very, very high. I suspected that was a performance problem waiting to happen, but not today.

Another turn, and I saw him. Archangel Michael, the Hierophant of the Arcana Council, as pale as new-fallen snow, his great wings flickering over him. His wings were invisible to ordinary Connecteds, same as his entire form wasn't visible to ordinary humans. But no one had ever accused me of being ordinary.

He also wasn't looking at me, but staring off into the distance. I whipped my head to the right, trying to pierce the smoke, but I only picked up the vaguest sense of fighting, loud, angry voices, the clash of disparate groups coming together. Part of the distraction, or an ancillary outcome of chaos in the streets? I thought I saw a flash of movement heading toward the battle scene, and a cool chill rushed over me. Death, I figured. As one of the Council's premier badasses, Blue was no doubt close to the action on a night like this.

Either way, Michael needed to keep his eye on the prize.

"Yo!" was all I could manage as I raced up to him. At the last minute, he turned, blinking at me with wide eyes as if he was surprised to see me here. Then he stepped aside, his hand lifting as one of the heavy stones shifted away.

"It's about time," he groused, recovering his disapproving attitude in record time. "If any one of those other operatives had gotten here first, I would have been bound by the Lord to give him access. Do you know what a catastrophe that would have been?"

"Yeah, yeah. Sometime today, angel boy. What am I looking for?"

"Thin golden tiles, probably no larger than your hand. They are remnants of celestial pavement."

I screwed up my face in surprise. "Pavement? Like, from streets? Won't they be heavy?"

"Pavers from the streets of heaven, or so the ancient books would have people believe," Michael confirmed, ignoring my grimace. "However many you can find. All of them have power, and they work together, but their manner of use is unknown to me. They were also never supposed to be found here."

I snorted. "Yeah, well, if you don't want something to be found, try getting rid of it, not hiding it."

With that mini TED talk, I stepped through the break in the rocks, sensing more than hearing the illusion of the heavy barrier of stone being rolled into place behind me. I turned back, hesitating a brief moment. I could still see the Archangel, and the sounds of explosions from the street beyond remained faintly audible.

As Michael turned once more, presumably to watch Death stalk through the battle scene two streets over, I blinked. The usually so-pale-he-was-practically-translucent Hierophant now rocked the full Technicolor treatment. Color suffused his face, rendering his skin a burnished bronze, his eyes stormy blue, and his hair shockingly dark and curling around his ears. His wings also flared with iridescent color, all the shades of the rainbow—some so beautiful, I couldn't describe them.

Human, I thought with unexpected alarm. Michael looked human to me for the first time since I'd met him at the end of his several-thousand-years-long sabbatical in the depths of Hell. What did that mean?

As if sensing my scrutiny, the Archangel glanced back toward me sharply, all the color leaching away from him, leaving him the Invisible Man once again.

"Go," he ordered, his voice crackling through my earphone. "And don't ask for help. Solomon was no idiot, despite his weaknesses. He would have made tasks impossible for two people to solve, requiring only one to go through the trial. A group of marauders would be separated and picked off one by one until the worthiest survived. In life and in death, the greatest trials must be faced alone."

"You guys should put that on a billboard," I said drily, but Michael didn't answer. I suspected he'd finally zipped out of the chaos to return to his ivory tower in Vegas. Protector of humanity or not, he definitely wasn't much on socializing.

Resolutely, I swung around, peering into the darkness. "You're here, right? I gave you enough time to get in?"

The response was a match being struck. A flicker of light emerged far down the space, a line of similar twinkling lights appearing all in a rush as a straight line toward me, giving my eyes a chance to adjust. One of the denser-looking shadows moved, and the Magician of the Arcana Council stepped out, surveying the space with a curious eye.

"As always, Miss Wilde, your sense of timing is impeccable," he murmured, turning back to me with a smile so satisfied, so genuinely happy, it took my breath away.

Armaeus Bertrand had walked this earth for more than eight hundred years. Nearly all his life had been spent leading the Arcana Council, a group of humans turned Tarot-based demigods who operated at the very pinnacle of psychic abilities. For some of us, those abilities showed up as heightened speed, strength, or discernment. Others had precognition capabilities; still more could generate fire or manifest thoughts into things. The Magician could perform all those tricks—*and* he could wield true magic.

As for me? I wasn't sure exactly where my magic topped out, but I definitely hadn't yet hit the glass ceiling. I was pretty sure bad things were going to happen when I did, but based on the shitstorm going on outside Solomon's temple this morning, anything I did could only help.

Right?

Armaeus extended a hand to me, his golden-black eyes sparking with interest, his face alight with curiosity. The son of a French Templar knight and an Egyptian priestess, he had bronzed skin and exquisite cheekbones and jawline, thick winged brows, and a fall of heavy black hair that curled at his shoulders. In a flash, I thought of the transformation that Michael the Archangel had gone through.

I took the Magician's hand, not trying to hide my thoughts from him. I felt his gentle touch on my mind as his fingers curved around my own.

"I have been remiss in not delving into the past of all the Arcana Council members before now to understand their weaknesses and points of vulnerability," he murmured, his tone pitched as low as the ceilings in the shadowy stone-lined corridor. "But Michael is an anomaly unto himself. The Archangel spent nearly six thousand years in self-imposed captivity, appearing to true believers in visions and dreams, but never in person. Since he emerged from captivity, he has taken on the redemption of certain demons, as well as a keen awareness of the horde in all its permutations. Otherwise, he has not strayed far from his Council domain. Yet he was willing to volunteer for this mission before I asked for his assistance."

"Yeah? And all that affected his skin tone?"

The Magician chuckled. "I have no idea, Miss Wilde. But

it is a subject that deserves close study. Perhaps when all this is done, I shall undertake that study."

A tremor rolled through me that Armaeus didn't miss. "This cycle of struggle will end, I promise you. The Shadow Court's efforts to throw magic out of balance, destroying the low-level Connecteds to elevate the high-level Connecteds and place them in positions of power, can no longer be allowed. Magic itself is in danger. We will eliminate the threat of the Shadow Court once and for all."

"Well, we'd better. I'm not going down because of these asshats."

The Magician stiffened, his hand tightening on mine as he peered ahead down the corridor. "Ahead of us, there is a change in the pattern of the hewn stone."

"Two different hallways?" I suggested, glancing to the wall. "Two different periods of construction? A false front?"

"Some light," Armaeus murmured, his voice dropping further to mutter a swift enchantment. The corridor brightened, and I could see what he meant. We stood at the opening of a hallway featuring smooth walls and rounded columns. It was narrow and short, but beautifully crafted. About ten feet ahead of us, the wall changed to what looked like plastered brick, vibrant colors mixing not in any sort of artistic way, but as if portraying an explosion of light and color. It wasn't ugly, exactly, but it was jarring.

"A trap?" I pressed. "It looks like a trap to me. Because even we are stopping to look at it, and we know better."

"It could be a trap—or it could be a directional sign designed to look like a trap," the Magician mused. "Solomon delighted in solving the unsolvable."

"That's great. You two should bro it out sometime. We're barely thirty feet into this crypt, though. Would he really put out a major clue this early? I think he'd want to trip up the fools too awestruck for their own good."

"Trip...up," the Magician echoed.

We both came to the same conclusion simultaneously and took off at a dead run, leaping ahead as a rush of spikes shot out from the base of the wall we'd been admiring. The last one was a bare six inches from the backs of my calves, so while I would have preferred to catch my breath, Armaeus tugged me on. Sure enough, we'd hardly gone five feet more when another set of thick bars shot down from the ceiling, cutting us off from the corridor behind us.

"Well, that's one way to ensure that your hunting party gets cut down early," I said, blowing out a heavy breath.

"Michael's warning," the Magician agreed. "And a second warning as well. We'd do well not to spend too much time admiring our surroundings. That trap was triggered by our sustained weight on that section of floor. Had we continued walking swiftly, I wonder..."

"Don't wonder," I assured him. "Something else would have happened, equally bad."

We joined hands again, for no good reason other than that it felt right. I didn't try to bank a rush of quiet joy as the Magician glanced toward me. "It's been too long since we have hunted together, Miss Wilde."

I grinned at him. "You always say the nicest things."

We crept forward, tensing at every murmur in the stone, which fortunately didn't happen much. Though I thought I heard the occasional haunting sigh, like wind moaning through high trees, the sound was faint, and maybe a trick of the ancient rock walls. There was very little dust, no cobwebs to speak of, and the walls and floor in this section were pristine. I drew my fingers along an edge of stone, tracing the scalloped carvings. "How was this place never found?"

"There is nothing to say that it wasn't," the Magician returned. "It hasn't been found by modern technology because its wards against magic are very strong. The only way someone could make their way in was through a back door of sorts—a door Michael clearly knew existed."

"Yeah, agreed." Whether it was temples or tombs, there were always too many overseers who would be willing to wall up the unfortunate workers inside to keep the secrets of the king safe. Solomon might have been revered as ruler, but that didn't make him any less of an asshole when it came to personal security.

I slanted Armaeus a glance. "Do you think the Ark of the Covenant is down here?"

He smiled, his teeth flashing in the flickering light.

"I have read the same articles that you have, Miss Wilde," he said wryly. "But I find it more interesting what Michael told us to look for. I suspect the Ark, if it still exists, if it *ever* existed, is a treasure too great for him to reveal to us. He is still governed by the laws of his own god."

"Yeah, well—he wants us to look for paving stones, like loose rocks from the streets of heaven. And he doesn't know what they're supposed to be used for. Hello, that's weird."

Armaeus nodded. "I don't believe he's lying, though. Which makes it all the more interesting."

"Hold up," I muttered as Armaeus's parade of lights suddenly stopped reflecting off walls and flooring. They continued out in a graceful arc, and I caught a glimpse of stone about twenty yards ahead, but not right in front of us.

"Miss Wilde?"

"Um, is that some kind of pit?" I asked, remembering the

giant pothole from the streets of Jerusalem. "Seems like a bad place for it."

"A well of sighs," Armaeus corrected me.

I heard it then, another moaning rush of breeze, and rolled my eyes. "Right. If you tell me next that only the penitent may pass, I'm totally out."

Armaeus didn't respond, and I reached into my pocket and ran my finger along the edge of my deck of Tarot cards. Since I'd first started out as an artifact hunter, even before I'd met the Magician or knew of the Arcana Council's existence, I'd used Tarot cards to help direct me wherever I needed to go. There was enough light to pull a couple, so I continued to fan through them as I followed the Magician's lead. He knelt down and peered over the edge, exhaling in soft surprise. My FOMO on spooky shit glowing in the dark being strong, I did the same.

The moment my head cleared the edge of the pit, a thunderous wall of sound exploded upward, smacking me full in the face and slamming me back into the far stone wall.

My cards went flying.

2

"Sara."

Everything was all wrong. The Magician's voice was high, strident, and filled with an emotion that didn't fit with my knowledge of his calm, cool, and collected demeanor. He also used my name. Why was he using my name? That didn't make any sense. He called me Miss Wilde unless I was... I was...

Where was I?

"You hit your head." Armaeus's words broke through my mental chatter. "The back of your head, against the wall. You are only now reviving. We are in Jerusalem, in the underground passageways of Solomon's temple. Where we are safe. Well, we were safe, except now you won't open your eyes. I would very much like it if you would open your eyes, Miss Wilde."

The hint of exasperation that had crept into Armaeus's voice was strangely cheering. I decided I could handle just about anything as long as his voice was there and I could feel the touch of his hand on mine, which I was gradually beginning to register, and the comforting weight of his presence beside me. I opened my eyes briefly—then screwed them shut again.

"There's something behind you," I whispered urgently. "Floating things."

"The patrons of this establishment," the Magician agreed laconically. "Apparently, they haven't had this much entertainment in some time. I am informed that you are a pagan goddess, but that King Solomon was a tolerant king, for all that he served the one true god. Your presence here honors the guardians of his crypt."

I managed a squint again, focusing on Armaeus. "If I'm a goddess, what are you?"

"Merely your humble servant," he said, self-deprecatingly placing a hand on his chest as a grin lurked at the corners of his mouth. "Why else would I have been so concerned at your collapse?"

"Right," I grunted. I pulled myself higher against the wall. The Magician could talk a good game all he wanted, but he'd been worried. It was arguably a little touching, since I'd been in far worse straits than a knock to the head. Then again...

I shifted my gaze to the hovering forms behind him, unable to pick out specific features on these guardians. They were vaguely humanoid, wearing long robes and hooded cloaks, their faces lost in the shifting shadows beneath peaked cowls. "So these are priests?"

"Acolytes," Armaeus confirmed. "Young men and old who were promised entry into the priesthood in return for their service as guardians. Their sighs are their only allowed expression of dismay at the...unfortunate turn of events that found them shut away without the completion of the ceremony."

"Acolytes..." I muttered. Well, these dedicated servants

had definitely gotten the wrong end of this deal. Annoyance rippled as I glanced back at the Magician. "How come you didn't get knocked onto your ass?"

He winked but sighed in sonorous relief. "I am but your humble servant."

I didn't miss the heavy inflection to his tone. He wasn't repeating that for my benefit, but for the benefit of the hovering ghouls behind him. He still didn't know how to play this yet.

Something else finally dawned on me—the cards. I'd been groping for them when Armaeus had moved forward to the well of sighs, and now a thick pile of them rested by my right thigh, several more scattered on the ground. The Magician noticed my attention, and gestured. I decided not to pick them up, in case their arrangement mattered.

Instead I glanced down, then peered more intently. The closest card was the Hierophant, not at all surprising given that we were in the temple ruins of a king dedicated so absolutely to his god. But it was the cards around him that gave me pause. The Seven of Cups, the Five of Pentacles, the Ten of Swords, and the Nine of Swords. Rarely did I find a collection of cards so miserable all in succession. I tended to give readings at least some level of a hopeful spin, but these cards taken all together spoke of despair. Confusion, loss, abandonment. That was the legacy of this place.

"Can these guys talk?" I asked, glancing back to the Magician. "Have they said anything at all other than...super-expressive moaning?" An indignant groan lifted from somewhere deep in the well, and I winced.

"There's clearly nothing wrong with their hearing," Armaeus observed.

Another issue hit my battered skull. "Um, where are the remains of people who've been down here before? We didn't see any bodies in the corridor, and there's nothing here either. I have to imagine there were at least a few casualties over the years here at the pit of pouting."

"I've given that some thought," the Magician said. "While you were sleeping."

I lifted my brows. "Was I out that long?"

"Four minutes, thirteen seconds," he confirmed. "Long enough for me to review every piece of information I have ever collected on the temple of King Solomon and its inhabitants. You will be gratified to know that Solomon did not have a stable of acolytes in his employ, beyond these worthy souls. There's absolutely no record of such in the biblical record. He did have, of course, a robust working castle and plenty of servants, but this random group of apprenticed priests is not mentioned. However, in a certain Middle Ages treatise concerning the history of Solomon, largely regarded to be apocryphal, there was a reference to the breath of God."

"Right. So you're basically saying that *Raiders of the Lost Ark* was based on the scientific record."

He smiled. "Truth is often stranger than fiction, but in this case, they appear to align somewhat more closely than usual. More likely, though, there are tenders of this crypt who come to collect the bones of the unwary."

I slanted another dubious glance at the cards. "I don't know, bones are kind of scary. Why wouldn't they leave them lying around as a warning?"

"Arguably, because that would mar the beauty that King Solomon sought to employ. Much like he took the voices from his own priests, leaving them to do nothing but sigh."

"So dude *was* an asshole," I muttered.

"Also of note, my ability to illuminate the corridor beyond the well of sighs appears to be impaired. I also could workers, or both. If any artifact hunters or their sponsors in the arcane black market had ever discovered this ruin and successfully escaped this maze, a rumor would have gone out. I would have heard about it."

I sent him an amused glance. "You never once thought that maybe you should investigate the possibility of the ruins of Solomon's temple being located in the heart of Jerusalem? Given your background, I'd think that would have been one of your primary targets."

The Magician's smile was rueful. "It is exactly because of my origins that I did not. Religious artifacts have their own peculiar resonance, and some, over time, pick up the elements of true magic. But mostly their power lies in activating the innate ability of humans who have no idea of their Connected strength—or what they would call their faith. Such tools are not my province, and they hold no worth for the unfaithful, so they're also not the province of my enemies."

"So you can't use them and the bad guys can't use them." I squinted at him. "Why are we down here, again?"

"Because Michael suggested it," Armaeus said. "I suspect we will find a treasure that surpasses our understanding."

With that, he gestured me ahead, his expansive wave drawing my attention to the walls of the corridor. The Magician was right. This was different. Jade, malachite, quartz, and obsidian had been inlaid into the marble in elaborate, intricate patterns. Oceans gave way to forests, mountains gave way to starry skies, each mosaic linked together with citrine-colored stones that undulated along the bottom of each image, a lazy river of gold.

"The force that ties all of Earth together," the Magician murmured. "The energy of creation."

"Right," I muttered as a new wave of moans lifted high

behind us. I shot a glance back, but there was no one there. "Do we have company?"

"If not behind us, then it's possible something will be waiting for us. That cry could well have been a warning."

"For us or for the bad guys?"

The Magician didn't answer. Instead, he picked up his pace. As we turned a sharper corner than the previous gentle curve, the Arcana Council flare hovering in front of us winked out and dropped to the floor with a clatter. Absolute and utter darkness fell around us like a cloak. We stopped.

"Ummm... Another flare?" I whispered, but Armaeus pulled out his own tool from some hidden pocket I couldn't see in the dark. With a quick scratching movement, new light sprang up. Then I could see he held a flint-strike lighter in his hand.

"It would seem neither magic nor technology is acceptable for the moment, but rudimentary tools are. Another card, Miss Wilde?"

I stuck my hand in my pocket and pulled out a single card from my Tarot deck. In the light from the tiny flame, the image was clear. The Fool.

The Magician nodded. "I suspected as much."

He took my hand and tugged me forward until his toe nudged against the metal cylinder of our flare. He leaned down and picked it up. Then, stretching forward another bare foot or so, he dropped it. It went a long, long way without making a sound. Finally it clanked against something solid, and then sounded like it rolled away, or maybe I imagined that. Armaeus turned to me, his eyes bright in the firelight.

"A leap of faith is required, it would seem."

"You know, just once I'd like to have a date with you that doesn't involve falling into a black hole," I groused.

The Magician's laugh was soft and warm as he snapped off the flint and stored it back wherever he'd found it. Then he wrapped me in his arms—

We jumped.

3

The journey to the bottom of the pit was swift, cold, and ended with a thud.

Wrapped as I was in Armaeus's embrace, he took the brunt of our crash landing, his knees buckling as he turned us both to drop into a rough tumble down a bumpy, oily slip and slide that ended with us smacking against something both harder and colder at the end: the floor. I lay on my back, catching my breath, as Armaeus flopped beside me, his arms going spread-eagle as his chest heaved.

"I find it curious that my speed, strength, and reflexes were not affected by the magical dead zone. By all rights, they should have been."

I rolled over to one side. My whole body felt like a shaken can of cola, nothing in its right place and my energy fizzing over, desperate to escape. "Yeah, well, by all rights, you should be eight hundred years old. You're doing all right for an old man."

But Armaeus didn't seem satisfied with that. "My strength and my speed remain," he muttered. I sensed him sitting up, though I couldn't pick out much at this point, what with the chambers decorated in Nouveau Gloom.

"No flint here," he said, and the rustle of his clothes indicated that he had regained his feet. I flapped my hand vaguely upward, reassured when his strong fingers closed around mine and he hauled me up.

"There will be torches down here," he continued. "We should use the tools left to us."

"You sure about that?" I sniffed the air curiously and ran my hands down my thighs. "There was some goop on those bags we landed on. Felt like oil to me. I'd say maybe we should be careful about the whole lighting-of-fire idea."

Without releasing my hand, Armaeus turned and leaned back, grunting a little as he pulled on one of the bags behind us. "Oilcloth," he confirmed. "And the bags appear to be stacked neatly. Why bags and not casks? Even weatherized cloth ages more quickly than wood and certainly stone."

"Maybe they didn't think they'd be down here all that long? What's in them anyway?"

The Magician pulled one of the bags out of the stack and released my hand briefly to rummage through it. "More cloth inside," he reported. "Vestments, it would seem. Ceremonial robes. I believe there was something like that mentioned in the article detailing King Solomon's treasure."

"Oh, great. I went to the crypt of the Ark of the Covenant, and all I got was this lousy T-shirt?"

The Magician chose not to respond to that, which to me indicated a marked lack of creativity, but instead he found my hand again and tugged me away from the pile. "This room will not be large," he said, and I agreed based on how his voice seemed to rebound off the space around us rather than disappear into the gloom. We moved forward, my boots making a satisfying thud on the floor. Marble tiles, maybe. It was too smooth to be cave rock.

It took a few steps for us to reach the first wall, and the Magician huffed in satisfaction. "Sconce and torch," he said.

Once again, he pulled out his low-tech lighter, and with a quick flip of his thumb, a burst of light sprang up. The Magician leaned forward while I flinched away from the retina-searing flare, and a second later, the torch caught fire against the wall.

I continued blinking rapidly against the light while the Magician strode quickly around the space, lighting additional sconces.

The room he revealed wasn't as impressive as I wanted it to be. There were the crisscrossing bags of what appeared to be more clothing, as the Magician had indicated, and a few other open cases. One appeared to be made out of solid gold, another silver—and a third was wrought in bronze. All were distressingly empty.

"Seriously? Other grave robbers ransacked the cases, but they didn't go through the bags?"

"They went through a couple of them," the Magician corrected, standing on the other side of the pile. He nudged a couple of sacks with his foot, then squatted down to peer more closely. "But they saw the same thing we did. Plain vestments, and nothing sharp or hard to excite the interest. There's no gold or precious metal or weapons in these bags."

"What a rip-off," I muttered, walking over to a third case, this one wrought of bronze but equally empty. "They cleaned the place out. We promised those ghouls some tools." I gestured to the clothes. "I don't think a wardrobe update is going to cut it."

"It might explain why previous hunters were not able to alleviate the acolytes' plight, but it's possible we're not seeing the full picture." The Magician turned slowly to scan the room. "These symbols on the walls aren't Hebrew. Or not exclusively Hebrew. This language is Akkadian."

He ran his finger through the air, as if tracing the faint carvings. "Conflict," he murmured. "The prayer in Hebrew reads of violence and retribution. The line of Akkadian reads of hope and possibility."

"Were they carved at the same time?"

"Unknown," the Magician said. "And then there's this third line. Can you read it?"

I straightened. Given my recently acquired skill with language, I should've totally been able to translate the chiseled stone. But as I peered at the dashes, dots, and jagged lines of the hieroglyphics the Magician pointed to, I pursed my lips. "So they should be Egyptian or something like that, but I've never seen any of this before. It looks like abstract art, not a line of script."

"Don't think of what you know. Think merely that all languages are available to you. Spoken, written, imagined. On this plane and any other."

His words were hypnotic, and I let my eyelids droop as I read the long line of script beneath the row of angry Hebrew and more gentle Akkadian. "Time," I murmured. "The passage of time, the reassurance of change. Sort of like time passes, shit happens, on repeat. Not super helpful."

"Not as yet, no," the Magician agreed. Pursing his lips, he scanned the room. "If there is a key, it isn't hiding in the prayers of the faithful or in the vestments of their priests. These cases were not meant to be closed."

I peered down at the ornately carved boxes, but he was right. The open lids were permanently cast in that position, the buckles and trim merely window dressing.

"Do you think there was ever anything in there?"

"No way to tell." The Magician passed his hand over the large open golden case. "I'm feeling no energy signature, no spark of magic of any kind. But the magic of the Hebrew god might not be something I could detect."

I raised my eyebrows as I looked at him. "Seriously? Why not?"

"Because I have never encountered him face-to-face, or her, or whatever form such an entity chooses to take. I have addressed demons, which are his creation, and every once in a while they resonate with an energy that I cannot combat. I do a good job of not letting anyone know that, but it doesn't change the fact that it's true. And then there's Michael, who remains an enigma despite my best efforts to penetrate his thoughts."

I thought of Michael staring at the carnage while he opened the back door to this place, and the faint, almost human cast to his skin. "Yeah, he needs a shrink."

Armaeus gestured to the walls. "There are four exits from this room, each positioned at one of the cardinal points. Which direction would he consider to be the one true way?"

"You gotta go north," I said. "The North Star was still a thing back then. I don't know if Solomon was a conquering king, but if he traveled at all, he would have used the North Star."

"Perhaps. Nevertheless, start with the south and then continue to the east entrance. See if there's anything there, but don't step inside."

He handed me a torch, and I obligingly went to the openings he indicated, the southern one inlaid with copper, the eastern one with jade. "Nice trim work, but there's nothing down these corridors that I can see," I offered.

"Nor this one," he said, from the western door. "Though

"Observe..."

I squinted my molecules down at the water's base, and with it rapidly receding, I could see how the chamber worked. The tiles of heaven had shifted off their moorings in the floor, revealing graded holes. The water drained out like a bathtub on steroids, and within a few minutes, there was nothing but wet pocked stone beneath us.

But the show wasn't over. The golden tiles, which I could now see were no thicker than a saltine cracker, lifted off the floor, bending and curling as they fluttered up into the sky. I blinked, the image striking me as oddly familiar, but I couldn't understand why.

Then I got it. *The Moon,* I thought to Armaeus. *They look like whatever the hell is falling from the Moon in the most traditional Tarot decks.*

"As if from heaven," Armaeus agreed. I felt the pull of his energy and gratefully heaved out a huge sigh as our bodies coalesced once more on the floor of the chamber. The celestial tiles remained hovering, and when Armaeus lifted a hand, the ones nearest to us flipped over in midair. He gave me that knowing Magician look, which was a clear indication that I should do the same.

I arched a brow as I lifted my hands, palms up.

"It can't be that easy," I said, but, as if defying my words, the tiles floated to us, then settled in our hands in two slender stacks.

"What part of that do you assess as being easy?" the Magician asked a little wryly. "Your skill at drawing the card to give us the vital clue? The manner with which I ultimately identified the correct course of action? Our arguably somewhat exclusive ability to render ourselves no longer of this world but still within it, showing that our abilities surpass that of normal humans?"

That drew me up short. "These tiles were meant for people who can fly?"

"Not fly. There was not enough space or oxygen for that. We had to reduce ourselves to our most basic, smallest form."

"Well, yeah, but so can Ant-Man."

Armaeus pursed his lips. "I suspect Ant-Man wouldn't have used Tarot cards to discern the proper method to find the tiles in the first place."

"Well, maybe he should use Tarot cards. Maybe he would have gotten out of the quantum realm faster if he had."

But Armaeus was no longer paying attention. He turned toward the very ordinary-looking doorway into the chamber, and folded the tiles close to his heart.

"You see how they conform to your palm?" he asked quietly as he moved toward the exit from the chamber, though I got the impression he was talking more to himself than to me. "How are they used? What do they do?"

"In point of fact, the Archangel was decidedly not helpful on that score. He was all 'don't ask questions, just go pick up these celestial pavers before anybody else does.' I suspect he had not one flipping clue, but he was hoping you would."

"As always, your discernment is your gift, Miss Wilde," the Magician murmured. By now, we were walking back up the steep spiral, heading out the way we came. I cocked my head, but of course, this deep inside Solomon's basement, I couldn't hear any of the war going on outside. Had the battle in the streets finished? Had somebody won? Had everybody picked up their guns and gone home?

The next sound I heard was a little more familiar, but

these things turn into freaking Tarot cards, I'm out. The first deck hadn't even been in play during Solomon's time."

"So far as we know," the Magician said, and I laughed.

"So far as we know. Who says the twenty-first century cornered the market on disinformation and fake news?"

A strange gleam shimmered across the celestial tile as I chuckled, but the tiles displayed no further reaction. We left the chamber by way of Armaeus Air, poofing back to the corridors above. Almost instantly, we heard the rising chorus of moans from the pit of ghouls.

Not ghouls, I chided myself, but the honorable wannabe priests of King Solomon. Who looked like ghouls.

The moan they issued as we approached sounded every bit as despondent as it had when we had first entered this area of the crypt.

"Shouldn't they be cutting that out?" I asked. "We come bearing good news."

"They should, unless they know something we—"

The attack was brutal in its efficiency. Holes in the wall that I hadn't seen the first time through emitted thin metal rods honed to vicious points. Armaeus and I were completely blindsided. Juggling the vestments and daggers as we were, me with my nose stuck in my cards of gold, we were turned into Arcana Council pincushions in less than a blink.

"Go!" Armaeus grunted, lurching forward toward the pit. I followed him, but with every step, the pins dug more deeply into my flesh, ripping my skin and burrowing into muscle and sinew. I could feel the poison ripping through us, setting me alight from the inside out in completely not a good way.

"*Jesus,*" I muttered, and the Magician laughed, the sound a little forced.

"A few hundred years too early for that, but I concur. Secure the tiles, Miss Wilde."

I unlocked my gripped fingers enough to shove the celestial pavers into my deepest jacket pocket, and by the time we reached the well of sighs, I didn't bother asking what we should do. There was only one choice. We tipped over our offerings for the priests, then sacrificed ourselves to them.

We landed not with a thud, but onto the floor of a bouncy house of spooks.

I plunged right through the first three before enough of them got together to slow my progress. As I flailed, I could see that the Magician had been similarly hammocked, the ghouls reaching for the bags of vestments and knives. Not greedily, not with laughs of glee, but with a soft, moaning reverence that heightened into a wail as the clothing spilled out among them, rendering them more corporeal in a flash. But corporeal wasn't really the best situation for hanging out in a pit.

The ghouls seemed to realize it at the same time, and a mighty surge of them pushed up and out of the hole, half of them coming back to grab the stragglers, and a good third of those hanging around to pull Armaeus and me out as well. They held us, not letting us touch the floor, which was okay since that would have driven the pins deeper—especially the spiffy new ones I could feel driving through my feet. How we'd managed to get pinned on the soles of our feet when we'd been running, I wasn't quite clear. Maybe when we'd fallen inside the pit?

The moans kicked up another notch, becoming a full-on song, and I hissed in pain. Whatever frequency they were hitting, it was reacting with the pins in my body.

"Are they doing that on purpose?" I gritted out. "Aren't they happy that we brought them what they wanted?"

"It's the final test, Miss Wilde," the Magician returned, his voice doubly strained. "I cannot dissolve. Whatever magic is fueling this final assault, it is not mortal, it is not immortal. It exceeds both. I cannot defeat it."

"Well, I sure as hell can." I swung my gaze wildly over to him, and there was no doubting the pallor to his skin, blood now welling up where the pins had dug into him. And though five different priests now stood on either side of us, every involuntary shiver I gave shoved at least one more rod deeper into my flesh.

Fury rolled through me. I wasn't wet anymore, my exigency was great, and I didn't care if I ended up with buns of melted steel. I surged toward Armaeus, imagining his extraordinary library deep in the heart of his Vegas stronghold. He seemed to be faring worse than I was, so he needed to get back to his center of power like, right now.

"Armaeus," I shouted, and he looked at me with eyes as black as midnight. He opened his mouth, and I could see electricity firing deep in the back of his throat.

"It is the unmaking," he whispered.

Then I burst into him, and the two of us went up in flames.

5

The journey from Solomon's temple to the Magician's library was instantaneous, but not precisely painless. We materialized at the far back of the chamber, past the overstuffed shelves that served to create a complex maze into the space, and next to the Magician's cauldron and pit. Because no self-respecting Magician would be without a pit of his own.

Unfortunately, the pins we'd been stuck with came along for the ride, and when I landed heavily on my side, rolling away from Armaeus, I felt them sinking deeply into my flesh. I'd never been a fan of the idea of acupuncture, but this was definitely not the way to try it for the first time.

"Pain," Armaeus moaned, and I forgot my own discomfort, jerking my gaze toward him. He had managed to stop shy of the floor and was now levitating three inches above the surface, but while he didn't suffer a deeper embedding of the pins, he was practically vibrating.

"I should pull these out of you, right?" I asked, hesitating because he hadn't already done so. "That's the fastest way for you to heal?"

"I had thought the tiles would be triggered to assist us," the Magician said, and opened his hand to allow the thin metal plates to fall from his slight height. They crashed to the floor of his library, completely unimpressed with our dilemma. I tugged my own tiles out of my jacket pocket and let them tumble to the floor. Mine slid across the stone surface, reuniting in a tidy pile with the ones Armaeus had collected, but they didn't do anything further.

"Okay, so, that was a fail. What are these things good for?" As I asked the question, I focused on the pins lining my arms and hands, letting my eyes go slightly unfocused so I didn't hurl. I was bleeding from about fifty-seven different places.

With a gentle push of my mind, the pins popped out, but hovered in the air. Not waiting for the Magician's permission, I forced my attention to other parts of my body, able to get the majority of pins out with the first wave, while the second released the more deeply embedded rods. The wounds closed with a strange, tightening feeling as the needles were ejected, but again, the narrow rods didn't crash to the ground like the tiles had. Instead, they hung, quivering in space.

"Fascinating," the Magician said, drawing my attention back to him. He hadn't bothered to depuncture himself, and I lifted a hand, only to have him wave me off with a twitch.

"Why?" he asked, and as if in response, the needles I had liberated from my body jerked to attention—and nailed him.

"*Jesus!*" I lunged for Armaeus, who arched with a shout of genuine pain as the entire set of thin spikes drove completely into his body, the wounds closing up again, but this time with the needles on the inside.

"What the hell are you *doing*?" I cried.

The Magician remained hovering in place, but as I lurched toward him, I discovered I couldn't get any closer. He had thrown up some sort of force field around his body, blocking me. I knew I could break through it, but given what he'd just done to himself, I wasn't sure I should.

"Surrender," he practically moaned, making me squint at him harder. But before I could demand an answer, he stretched almost luxuriously, betraying no further discomfort.

"The final test of Solomon's temple was that we carry more than we had planned from his sacred place. Slender rods of purest silver, gold, and bronze. When you removed these needles, they did not lose their fire. They remained active. Continuing to seek."

"And you thought it would be a cool thing to let them seek their final resting place inside your body?" I scanned Armaeus's form with my third eye, flinching a little at the bright glow beneath his skin. Nevertheless, I'd healed him enough times to know that he didn't require that sort of attention from me right now. "How is it you're not bleeding from the inside?"

"The rods remain within me, but not in their original form," he said, breathing out a long, satisfied sigh. "They are a tracing of power, the deep magic of creation and destruction. Though they would have destroyed an ordinary wizard, they would not have destroyed you."

"Yeah, well, I wasn't really up for any heavy metal poisoning this morning," I retorted, experiencing absolutely no regrets that I had taken a pass on getting pinned. "You're going to be okay with all that inside you? Because even if you're not in pain now, it doesn't look too comfortable."

"I have surrendered to the will of a magic born millennia before me," he said almost reverently, and I rolled my eyes.

"Okey doke. Once you finish nerding out, maybe we should figure out what to do with these tiles."

Armaeus sat up, still hovering a good three inches off the floor, and dismantled the force field around him enough to extend his hands toward the tiles. I absolutely expected the celestial pavers to shift into some new position with that move, but once again, I was destined to be disappointed. They remained inert, not reacting at all despite the Magician accessing his inner voodoo doll.

"Interesting," the Magician said again.

I rubbed a hand over my brow to beat back the headache forming there. "You know, maybe we should get the Hierophant back here. Maybe he'll know what to do with these things once he sees them up close and personal."

"Perhaps," Armaeus agreed with decidedly less enthusiasm than I was looking for. He looked at his hands, holding them about six inches apart, and my stomach turned as tiny pins extended from his skin, though he betrayed no discomfort.

"Oh, so now you're Wolverine?" I didn't bother trying to hide my dismay.

He ignored me as he focused on his palms. Beneath the intensity of his gaze, the pins began to quiver, then light shot between them, creating a zigzag of electricity that shimmered and sparked as it wove together. In the space of time it took me to gasp, an image appeared in Armaeus's hands. A battleground of rushing bodies and looting, with fire and bright lights in the distance flaring against an inky night sky. Despite myself, I leaned forward.

"That's not Jerusalem," I said. The city was glistening from a recent rain and looked hot, steamy.

"Cambodia," the Magician said. "Siem Reap."

My brows lifted. "Why did you get served that?"

The image shifted, new attackers coming through, throwing fiery devices that looked like souped-up Molotov cocktails. And then, in the distance, I saw the gorgeous towers of the Buddhist temple Angkor Wat, lit up by the fires that burned before it.

I refocused on the newcomers and jolted with recognition and mounting horror. The man leading the rabble was someone I knew. Big, bulky, and looking like a poster child for Island Giant Boot Camp, Rangi was a deeply tanned South Pacific warrior who wore his scars like badges of honor. His bald head gleamed in the firelight, and his heavy body moved with surprising grace through the crowd. Maybe not my favorite person in the world, but Rangi was someone I'd worked with and respected. More importantly, he was the head of the House of Wands, one of the four houses of magic that helped protect the interests of Connecteds when the Arcana Council was too unbiased for their own good.

"What the hell is he doing?" I demanded as Rangi threw another device into what looked like a modest storefront in downtown Siem Reap. Glass shattered silently in the image, and flames leapt up.

"I asked to be shown the truth that I most needed to know," Armaeus said, only slightly awed. "And this was the response."

I stared at him, then at the pins vibrating cheerfully from his palms. "I'm pretty sure I would have remembered in the Bible where it said King Solomon decided the fate of his people by whipping out his pin-poked hands and peering into a metal cage of truth. I don't think that's the way the story went."

"Who is to say what gifts we have been given? But truth is truth, no matter how it is delivered," Armaeus countered.

"Yeah, well, maybe. Or maybe what you're seeing is bullshit. Rangi is kind of an asshole, but why would he be attacking a city in Cambodia? That makes no sense."

"I suspect I know why," Armaeus murmured. He drew his hands farther apart to reveal the scene beyond the narrow street. Above the small, tightly constructed buildings stretched the ancient temple of Angkor Wat. It was calm, oddly peaceful above the city's destruction, but I couldn't help the feeling of creeping dread that spun through me.

"What do you know of Rangi?" the Magician asked, remarkably calm despite the destruction he was witnessing.

I scowled, pulling up the image of the ancient warrior in my mind. Though Rangi had served as the long-time head of one of the four houses of magic that Connecteds operated to keep their kind protected, he and I weren't close. "Never met a fight he didn't like, kind of prickly, and definitely a know-it-all."

"And what did he hate more than anything?"

"The gods," I said, then I looked again at the image, and my eyes widened as I picked Rangi out of the crowd, easily identifying his warriors in the mix as well.

"No," I breathed. "Tell me he's not going to destroy the temple. That temple is sacred." I had never considered myself a religious person, but something seemed ineffably wrong about destroying something so precious to those who did believe. Belief—faith—was part of what made human life tolerable. It stirred the well of possibilities even inside people who would never have thought of themselves as powerful. Sometimes that power wasn't used for good, but often...it was. And true believers should be allowed any grace they could get their hands on.

"It would appear its sacredness is a matter of opinion,"

Armaeus observed as more forces converged—city dwellers coming out to fight against Rangi and his warriors, and men in military uniforms as well.

"We have to stop him." I stood quickly, ready to burst into flame and hurtle myself half a world away. Armaeus remained hovering, but seemed otherwise unmoved.

"Who, exactly, are we stopping?" he asked. "Rangi is a warrior, and his warriors follow him faithfully. You stop this attack, they will wage another in a week, a month, a day. It is not the attack that should be our focus."

"They're going to burn down a sacred *temple*," I broke in. "I'd say that deserves some attention."

"But who is driving Rangi?" the Magician countered. "Is this attack a distraction, a means to an end, or the end itself?"

A sense of impending doom shot through me as I saw the rabble break through a stalwart line of guards and priests ringing the temple. I'd seen faces crazed with destructive intent before—was this a hint of what was to come worldwide? Was this truly Rangi's idea, or was the Shadow Court somehow behind this attack? They almost had to be.

I drew in a sharp breath as a stream of fire arced toward one of the towers. "I can't believe we are going to sit here and watch this happen," I bit out, my hands twitching with tiny sparks of repressed energy. "This isn't right."

"And I would say to you that a great deal of our work as the Arcana Council lies in standing aside and letting the world conduct its reign of terror. There will always be war. There will always be destruction. From the fall of Rome to the desecration of pagan sites around the world to the persecution of those who believe in unpopular truths, there is always something to burn, Miss Wilde, and always someone willing to light the fire."

"But we can't just—"

"There," the Magician said, leaning forward with more urgency, drawing his hands closer together. "And the string is pulled at last."

I jerked with recognition as a new figure stepped out from the tide of fighting. It was a person I knew all too well. Viktor Dal, Emperor of the Arcana Council.

Dressed like a millionaire mercenary in sleek black clothes that fit tightly to his robust body, Viktor struck a pose, his Aryan good looks evident despite the tight cap that he wore close to his head. It was nearing midnight in *Cambodia*, for freak's sake. The guy had to be sweltering. Then again, did Arcana Council members sweat? I hadn't really noticed. Either way, I didn't know whether I should be happy or sad to see him at ground zero of the temple fire.

"What's he doing there? Is he in on the destruction—is he helping Rangi? What possible gain could he have from the destruction of this temple?"

"For Viktor, there must be an advantage," the Magician agreed, remaining almost preternaturally calm. "The Emperor has never been motivated to act without personal gain. In addition, attacks such as this will draw attention to the Connecteds. Something that the Emperor has given lip service to wanting."

"If by attention you mean that they'll be hunted down and thrown in jail—which they should be if they're looting and destroying—yeah, but I don't think that kind of attention is necessarily all that helpful."

"Agreed, which is why—"

Rangi seemed to notice Viktor and turned to him, fury and a kind of mad delight crossing his face. He yanked out a dagger from a harness, flipped it in his hand, then sent it soaring across the open space. It buried itself in the Emperor's chest, clearly shocking the Council member, but not distressing him. Viktor sneered and reached up for the hilt, seeming barely bothered by it, while Rangi grinned and snapped his fingers.

The Emperor exploded.

"What the *hell*!"

I didn't wait for Armaeus's response. I didn't need to wait. I was Justice of the Arcana Council, and the Emperor might be a dickhead, but he was our dickhead. I'd been to Angkor Wat, so it was no difficulty for me to incinerate myself out of existence and reappear on the grounds of the temple still in full conflagration.

Rangi turned to me, recognizing me immediately.

"Stop!" he began, but I wasn't stopping. I flung out my hands, feeling the cuffs of Justice materialize in my palms. I was on Rangi a second later, binding his wrists and legs as he roared at me with incoherent rage.

"You do not understand—you do not—" he heaved.

"Stop this!" I ordered. "Stop it now, or I'll drop every one of your number to the ground and they'll be hauled away and thrown into prison where they'll rot in the cages that you sought to free them from, except there'll be nobody coming for them ever again."

"You are a *fool*," Rangi bit out, and behind us, the ancient temple of Angkor Wat exploded into a fireball.

The force of the explosion would have sent us flying several dozen feet, but I took it further, grabbing Rangi to me and disintegrating once again into fiery travel.

This time, our destination wasn't the nearest ditch. Instead, I rematerialized on the edge of a cold stone-and-metal hangar, the entryway to Judgment's Hall.

"You don't understand," Rangi tried again, but I didn't have any more time for him. I shoved him away from me, unsure why Viktor's death bothered me so much. I hated the Emperor through and through, but his death felt bigger, more dangerous than the simple scrubbing out of a desiccated little soul. Like some sort of neon sign flashing in front of my eyes that I somehow wasn't able to see. Was Viktor's death a larger loss for the Council than I realized? Was there more information we needed from him that now had been lost? My personal disgust for the man didn't hold a candle to my need to protect the Connecteds. Had I failed them in some way—beyond not stopping the destruction of Angkor Wat?

The doors of Judgment's domain swept open, and Gamon stepped out.

She was a small woman, deceptively so, her body encased in black military gear, her thick black hair pulled back in a braid. Her eyes were dark and assessing against her suntanned skin, and they swept over the bound Rangi and back to me.

"What did he do?" she asked.

"Destroyed a temple, killed fuck only knows how many people, and incinerated the Emperor," I announced flatly.

Gamon's brows lifted as she studied Rangi, who glared back at her. When these two had first met, they had both been in charge of their own Houses of Magic. They hadn't liked each other then, and time hadn't improved their opinions, apparently.

"What do you want me to do with him, then? Rip his guts out or throw him a party?"

"I want to know the truth," I said coldly. I looked at Rangi. "You knew the Emperor would show up to stop you. You knew he would, because you were ready for him. How?"

Rangi curled his lip. "I have no use for any gods," he practically spat. "You crossed that line. You both crossed that line." He turned his glowering face toward Gamon. "I will tell you nothing."

"Oh! Oh, well that's good, then," Gamon said, brightening. "This should be fun."

6

I didn't return to Armaeus after leaving Gamon with a struggling Rangi. Instead, I traveled to my own domain, Justice Hall, situated atop the Palazzo casino —and blending into that casino's penthouse floor, which was how, theoretically, ordinary Connecteds could contact me...though few ever dropped by to visit.

I glanced around as I rematerialized into the front receiving room of the unassuming space. It looked like the receiving room of a lawyer's office, with a desk, couches and chairs, and a wet bar off to the right. I strode over to the bar and yanked a bottle of scotch toward me, deciding at the last second to use the glass versus drinking straight from the bottle.

"What on earth—Justice Wilde!"

Before I had downed the first slug, Mrs. French rushed through the doorway that led to the library of Justice Hall. She was a plump but quite short woman who dressed with impeccable Victorian taste, from the starched collar of her gray, button-down, bustled gown to the polished toes of her black boots. Her gray hair was swept up into an impressive bun atop her head, and she stared at me with patent surprise. "I'd gotten word that you had reached Angkor Wat, but not in time to save those poor priests and their beautiful temple."

"Already?" I blinked in surprise.

Her gaze dropped to the bottle of scotch, and her mouth softened. "You can't blame yourself, Justice Wilde," she said. "The explosives had been set weeks ago, from what I've learned. The attack from the city was only a distraction. The greatest destruction to the temple came from within."

"A distraction," I echoed, though of course that didn't make me feel any better. "What do you know about who set those explosives? Was it Rangi?"

She rounded her mouth into a small O of surprise. "The head of the House of Wands? Oh my... It may well have been. We have been receiving more complaints from Connecteds regarding Rangi, particularly in southern Asia. So that would follow, it would definitely follow. But his efforts have been mostly to push low-level Connecteds to join his army. And it has been quiet. He has not sought to draw attention to himself. But if he was there, and he did this..."

"He killed the Emperor," I announced flatly. "He exploded him so completely, there was nothing for me to put back together again. I didn't know that Rangi had that ability. I didn't know anybody had that ability."

Mrs. French's ordinarily rosy cheeks went pale. "He killed... Well, I should say. Not that it couldn't have happened to a nicer person."

"That isn't the point," I sighed, ashamed that my own thoughts had gone there too. Had I tried hard enough to put the Emperor back together again? No. I hadn't tried at all, dismissing the likelihood of his survival immediately.

But had he died? Could he disappear like I did, like Armaeus?

Even as I thought of that possibility, I rejected it. The Emperor's strength was in his ability to manipulate others, to rule them. He was able to sway armies to his command with a snap of his fingers. Of course, the Arcana Council had never given him an army to rule. He had found a way to rule anyway, manipulating demons whenever he thought he could get away with it, but he had never been a threat of any great magnitude. Only on hyperspecific occasions. Like with me and my family.

I downed another slug of scotch. He'd been connected to the murder of my mother, or the woman who'd raised me as my mother, and who'd helped me muddle along in lower-middle-class obscurity in Memphis, Tennessee. I'd never known how much Viktor had to do with the men who had killed Rose Pelter, and the explosion that had destroyed my home and sundered me from the spirit that became Sariah. Something, for sure. But he hadn't killed Rose directly, and because of that, I'd had to be content with not blasting him into oblivion.

Viktor, for his part, had seemed content to rule his tiny fiefdom from his monolithic residence above the Paris casino. A thorn in our sides, but not truly deadly on a grand scale, not anymore. It was why the Magician had elevated him to the Arcana Council in the late 1930s, plucking him out of the war that was brewing in Europe, having foreseen the damage he could cause with his charisma and his manipulation magic. But who had been manipulating him in Angkor Wat?

"What do you know about..."

I let my words trail off, struggling to focus on the issue at hand. What did I really need to understand right now? How

Rangi had managed to kill a Council Member so easily? The most recent actions of Viktor—up to and including why he'd shown up at Angkor Wat? Where the Shadow Court was, the true enemies of the Connecteds, who were doubtless involved in some way with this attack, and what they were doing?

The Shadow Court wanted to put the one-percenter Connecteds into positions of power. How would an attack on Angkor Wat help their cause? Or had Rangi's attack from the village somehow forced the Shadow Court's hand? Mrs. French said the bombs that had wrecked the temple had been detonated inside it, that they'd been set earlier...

But who had set them, and why?

All these thoughts swirled together in my brain, but I couldn't wipe away the image in my mind of the Emperor's expression. He had not been surprised that Rangi had thrown the knife at him. He'd been surprised afterward, that flash of recognition that something had gone terribly wrong. He had expected Rangi's anger—and maybe even his knife. He hadn't expected to die.

But what did that mean? Had they been working together or not? They were both men cut from a similar cloth, born to lead an army. But the Emperor had sneered at Rangi. Was that because he discounted the ability of the head of the House of Wands to cause him any real damage? Or was there something more? A smug awareness that all was going according to plan?

And how would Viktor's death affect that plan?

I set both the bottle and the glass down on the side table and rubbed my temples. Maybe I shouldn't have acted so quickly to remove Solomon's prickly pear of perception powers from my skin. I could use some solid discernment right now.

"Justice Wilde, how may I help?" Mrs. French's soft plea reached me, and I shook myself back to focus.

"I need to understand what sort of requests we've been getting for Justice's help," I told her dully. "I feel like we're missing something important, that our focus has been too myopic and self-assured, and that's to our detriment. I mean, how in the *fuck* was Rangi able to kill an Arcana Council member to begin with? And maybe a more important question, how is it that Viktor wasn't ready for it? This is a man who is a master of manipulation and ordering people about. Strategy, warfare, all that. He wasn't an idiot. And he expected Rangi's blade, but not what it was packed with. What kind of magic was that?"

"Might it not have been any magic at all?" Mrs. French asked. "Begging your pardon, with the possible exception of you and the Magician, who have evolved in your abilities far beyond the others, every Arcana Council member can be killed. You all are immortal, but not unkillable. And Viktor obviously didn't have healing ability if he burst into pieces, the same as he wouldn't have healed if somebody had cut off his head."

"Right..." I muttered. "All of us can be killed, even if we live a thousand years."

"And some of you have lived longer than that. The High Priestess, of course. The Hierophant. Death." Mrs. French tilted her head, her swept-up gray hair bobbing. "What if someone killed Death? Now *that* would be a terrible thing."

I winced at the very thought. "Yeah, well. How about we never find out?"

I thought of lean, lithe Death moving through the destruction of Jerusalem, shepherding souls to the afterlife, whatever afterlife was awaiting them, anyway. She had lived longer than most members of the Council, ascending to its ranks right around the start of the Common Era. I knew that one day, she too would die. But that didn't mean I wanted it to happen today. In fact, I was pretty good with it not happening at all, ever.

Something else occurred to me. "We've lost a member of the Arcana Council. Does that change anything about our collective strength?"

Mrs. French pursed her lips. "Now, that's actually a very good question. And one I have had the occasion to study. As you may recall, Justice Abigail both served and died on my watch, God rest her soul. And of course, most of the Council members who have come aboard during the twentieth century were replacing existing members."

She said this as an obvious point of fact, and it *was* obvious, but I'd never considered it before.

"You're right," I said, sharpening my focus on her. "The Fool, the Devil, the Emperor, for sure. But there was no Judgment before Gamon. I mean, not recently, right?"

Mrs. French pursed her lips. "Well, Gamon is kind of an unusual Council member to be sure. But no, there has not been a Judgment on the Council since the 1500s, and once again, that role was rendered somewhat useless since there was no sitting Justice on the Council at the time. The two work hand in hand, you see, for maximum effectiveness. Justice can act without Judgment, but Judgment needs justice to be meted out first before she can truly act."

"And the Fool? Was there a Fool before him?"

Mrs. French smiled. "Oh yes, the Fool is a role that doesn't last terribly long among the Arcana Council. Sweet Simon was beset with his own troubles when he first joined up. He's managed to do quite well for himself, but it takes a certain curiosity of spirit to be well suited for the role of Fool, and sometimes that curiosity can get you in trouble.

And, of course, the Devil came into power at the assassination of his predecessor. That was a more direct handoff of the role, but the Devil is also not given to long tenure."

I didn't want to think about any of this, though I'd been the one to ask the question. "Well, that's all great," I muttered, unhappy with the idea of having to focus on the Council's mortality. But that didn't change the central tenet. "So the power of the Council ebbs and flows as new Council members fall off and are appointed. Some get replaced right away, some don't. It's really at the Magician's discretion."

"The head of the Council, I should say," Mrs. French corrected me. "Right now, that's the Devil, and it would be quite interesting to see who he would pick to replace the Emperor. My first thought would be that he rather didn't expect to be troubled with personnel changes quite so quickly, but then again, he is almost as inscrutable as the Magician, so perhaps he did know."

"Maybe..." I passed a hand over my forehead, as if I could comb through all the thoughts crowding to the front of my brain. Armaeus had served as the head of the Arcana Council for nearly eight centuries, then had ceded that role to Kreios when his memory had been wiped of several key moments. Now, his memories had been restored, but Armaeus hadn't returned to his leadership position. Did he know something I didn't?

I snorted. Probably. A flare of panic riddled through me, cold and jittery. I wanted Armaeus to stay safe, no matter what the Shadow Court unleashed on the world. I wanted all the Council to stay safe. But what would this coming battle demand from us?

"As for trends in our requests, I can definitely help you there, Justice Wilde." Mrs. French's bright words diverted my attention, gesturing toward my interior office. "The most marked trend that we've been experiencing this week is a significant downturn in requests at all. Rather surprising, if you ask me, given what I'm understanding about the level of unrest in Connected communities. But they're not asking for help, at least not the help of Justice."

"They're not?" A spasm of wholly unexpected dismay passed through me. Had I failed in my mission to help the Connecteds? They certainly needed protection; that hadn't changed. So why…?

Mrs. French waved me into the office. There, I saw canisters lined up along the wall. There were dozens of them, but I'd been in this room when they'd been literally overflowing into the reception area.

"We're getting some calls in, as you can see," Mrs. French explained. "But they're mostly requests for aid in rural areas, small villages, particularly an uptick in attacks on Connecteds targeted by operatives of the arcane black market, kidnappings, grievous bodily harm, and the like."

"Well, that's not new." Throughout history, the world had never been kind to those with psychic abilities. Either they were persecuted for being different, or they were coveted for the same, and it was difficult to say which was the worst fate. Humans had a long and unfortunate history of brutalizing those who were considered special, whether they were endangered animals or endangered mortals.

I had started out hunting magical artifacts to pay for the care of these vulnerable Connecteds, and now I was finally in a position where I could effect real change for them, but I hadn't. Much like the Emperor without an army to rule, I had been content to tackle small issues, specific battles. That needed to change, because one day, I was going to end up as dead as Viktor, blasted beyond recognition. Unlike Mrs. French, I didn't believe I couldn't be killed. But what was my life to stand for until that happened?

I refocused on the stacks of canisters.

"So what are they asking for? Delivery from their enemies? Retribution? The return of their loved ones if they've been stolen?"

"Well, that's the most interesting thing," Mrs. French said. "They're not asking you to do the work for them, and they're not looking to be rescued, is what I'm seeing. They're looking to be made stronger. To understand how to fight, how to use their magic to protect their own kind. These are people who believe they have some skill within them, or they wouldn't be able to contact us at all, but now, instead of clamoring for your aid, they're looking to be taught, and perhaps to be led."

"They don't know what they're asking for," I responded automatically, though my stomach twisted at her words. What had Rangi shouted at me, that I had become a god and that he did not serve the gods? He had helped me protect Earth from a very real, intense incursion of those gods. Did he now think I had allied myself with those who would be above mortal Connecteds, and who lived on an entirely different plane? What was a god if not that?

I owed it to the Connecteds to be better than that. To help them more than that—in a real, meaningful way. Ideally without the entire world catching on fire.

"Is there any mention of the Shadow Court in these requests?" I asked.

"Not as such, but of course, the Shadow Court doesn't go around announcing itself with a calling card. But I will say, there is a marked lack of sophistication in both the attacks and the pleas for help and instruction that we're receiving.

These are not missives from corporations, financiers, or governments."

I cocked a glance at her. "Did we ever get those?"

She smiled. "Oh yes, during Abigail's time. Many agencies, public and private, were quite open to, shall we say, supernatural assistance. Anything was fair game, any aid considered valuable. But such requests fell away with the close of the Victorian Age and the onset of the Industrial Revolution. Magic was in machines for decades, and now it's in technology, I'm afraid."

Even as she spoke the words mourning the passage of time, I felt a chill roll through me. Her words were truer than she realized. The knife that Rangi had wielded could have been a machine, but it was definitely aided by magic. The weapons of the Shadow Court would be sophisticated too. Those weapons wouldn't rely on raw magic alone, or at least not on the raw magic of their wielder. They needed to pack a punch no matter who used them, from a foot soldier to a high priestess—because they had a lot more foot soldiers to burn.

We didn't have as many foot soldiers, but we did have the High Priestess. And a whole lot of other high-level players besides.

I blew out a long breath. "We need to up our game."

"Well, in all truth, we should be able to utilize this vast treasure trove of information at our fingertips more effectively than we are," Mrs. French said. She pursed her lips, then pressed on. "I've been in conversation with Master Simon."

I blinked at her. "You have? Why?"

"It occurred to me that everything has precedent, that there is nothing new under the sun. And if the weary and downtrodden of the Connected have experienced something like this once before, some true threat from which there was no salvation, they would have gone to Justice for aid. Their misery would have been recorded in the tomes and annals of this library if they became, as you are fond of saying, cold cases without solution."

"Yeah, but..." I looked over at the door to the library. "That place goes on for miles, it feels like. How in the world can you go through it all? I'm not the first Justice to decide it's an impossible task."

"No, but you are the first Justice to have access to a Fool with such technical expertise as Simon's. With your permission, I should like to give him the task of cataloguing the information. He's quite at his wit's end right now, having gone through all the libraries in the known world and a few of the unknown to no avail, and he's very frustrated that he cannot get at any of the treasure trove of information locked inside Atlantis. But we do have this library, and he seems like such a nice young man."

I bit my lip. Simon could absolutely help sort through the chaos that was Justice Hall, to find clues to the Shadow Court's endgame. Why hadn't I thought of it earlier? Clearly, he'd been pressing Mrs. French for the opportunity, and knowing how guilelessly charming Simon could be...

"He's been laying it on pretty thick, hasn't he?" I asked, not trying to hide my grin. It was good to be able to smile about something.

Mrs. French blushed and drew herself up to the full height of her diminutive form, lifting her chin for good measure. "I am a respectable librarian, I will have you know, but...well, I am quite susceptible to flattery. Plus the assistants love him, so there's nothing they won't do for him."

"All right, all right, I don't know what he's going to find, but I'm open to him trying. Anything will help."

"Thank you, Justice Wilde." Mrs. French beamed. "I'm sure he'll be delight—"

Her words were cut off by a sharp knock at the door. She blinked at me and hurried for the door at my gesture, while I dropped the habitual wards that kept Arcana Council members from infiltrating my domain.

She opened the door wide, and Simon strode in, his blue eyes electric beneath his mop of dark hair that escaped his bright orange knit cap, his slender body practically vibrating with excitement. He wore a short-sleeve T-shirt over a long-sleeved T, beat-up jeans, and sneakers, and he grinned at Mrs. French, then me.

"Show me—oh! There, right? It has to be there."

Without waiting for permission, he darted over to the second exit door along the back wall of the Justice Hall lobby, flinging it open with an exhalation of pure, unfettered delight. Then he disappeared into the library, as Mrs. French turned to me, nonplussed.

"I mean, I'm sure he will be fine in there, yes? He won't get lost, or knock over any shelves, or open any cases he shouldn't?"

I snorted. "I'd be willing to bet he'll do all those things within the first half hour," I countered, while deep in the cavernous library, the Fool howled with delight.

7

I spent the next several hours rummaging through the most recent requests to Justice Hall. It was cathartic, but I also recognized it was an effort to put off getting some much-needed sleep, reconvening with the Arcana Council, and facing the reality that lay outside my own walls and library. There'd be time for all that eventually.

I sat back on my heels, cradling the sheaf of paper I'd liberated from the last canister. Its message was short and distinct: *Please help me help my village.* It could have been written in any of a dozen languages, with elegant penmanship or barely a scrawl. And these were the Connecteds who knew how to reach me. So many others may have wanted to, but didn't have the sophistication to know that the Arcana Council existed—in part because we'd worked so hard to keep ourselves hidden.

Setting the page quietly down on the table, I exited into the reception area, tiptoeing past Mrs. French dozing next to a steaming cup of tea. I ignored both the teakettle and the open bottle of scotch on the bar and continued to the far doorway of my lobby, which led to the library of Justice Hall.

I knew in a flash that the Fool was no longer here. Even Simon needed to sleep sometime.

Lights swept on as I entered the space, illuminating tantalizing rows that extended far into the shadows, rows that lengthened as I stepped toward them. I couldn't sense the Fool in these rows anymore, though I suspected he'd only left out of sheer exhaustion, and not for very long. Still, for what I needed to do, it probably was wise not to have Simon around.

Choosing an aisle at random, I trailed my fingers along the many books, archival diaries, collections of requests, boxes, canisters, and scrolls. Some of them resolved, some long forgotten, and far too many serving as cold cases that still demanded Justice, their challenges remaining relevant hundreds or even thousands of years after the complaint was lodged.

As I moved deeper into the arcane space, I found myself thinking about the priests of Solomon. We had outfitted them with vestments and tools, and they'd broken our fall when we'd been reeling with the pincushion effect of Solomon's final assault. But where were they now? I hadn't blasted a way out for them, though presumably they knew their own domain better than anyone.

Still, they'd been little more than ghosts stuck in a pit. What would they find as they crawled out of the depths after three thousand years of incarceration? Would Michael still be there to greet them? Or would their first introduction to the world be fire and death, some of them possibly getting caught in the crossfire, killed before they spent their first full day of renewed life? Why had I left them there for so long without going back? Could I return to that underground labyrinth, and did I know enough to find it again?

A new thought struck me, making me stop in the middle

of a narrow alleyway of books. Was it even my place to find it, to find them? The priests had made a very simple request of Armaeus and me. They wanted our help to get to the stores that had been promised them. We'd done that. We had clothed and equipped them. What they did from this point forward was strictly their choice, and their right to choose as humans making their way. Live or die, they hadn't sought further protection. They might not have known they could have, but then again, maybe they had.

Were the Connecteds seeking help in fighting their own battles any different?

No, I decided. They wanted to fight their own battles—and to be strong enough to do so, nothing more. How could ordinary Connecteds take out more powerful ones, like Rangi had done in killing Viktor? I couldn't shake the idea that I was still missing something important about Viktor's death.

"Death of the Emperor of the Arcana Council," I murmured aloud, lifting my hands as if I could pull the books from the shelves. I didn't hold out much hope, but a sigh creaked through the old stacks, and the books shifted and settled. Far off, a soft hollow *pop* sounded, and a moment later, a canister came whipping through the corridor of books. I didn't trust its speed or the angry crackling that surrounded it, and I puffed myself into embers as it struck me, letting it pass through and clatter to the ground. The force of its fall cracked its seal, and a door sprang open on the tiny compartment hidden along the cylinder. A tightly rolled sheaf of papers lay within the canister. Bemused, I pulled the pages free.

They were typed. The paper wasn't parchment or scraps like I had seen in so many other canisters, but simple computer printout paper.

The date was today.

I squinted down at the canister. If this thing had come in today, it shouldn't already be in the archives, it should still be stacked in my office. What was going on?

I started reading and received my answer almost immediately.

"'Look well upon the date you're reading this. An Emperor has departed the Council, leaving a hole in the world. I pray that you read this simple truth prior to the selection of the next Emperor, Justice. Perhaps it was by your hand the Emperor died. Perhaps it would have been better for me to have been that Emperor facing that death, rather than the one I face now. I alone chose this passage, to drink the cup of poison I have so carefully prepared as proof against my immortality.'"

My brows went up. Was this some kind of Emperor suicide note? It was definitely not written by Viktor. Who had been the last Emperor before Viktor? And, finally, why had I never asked such questions before, content to deal with what was as opposed to what had been?

Either way, this particular Arcana Council member had been a bit of a Chatty Cathy. The tightly written pages went on for some length about the weight of power. It was only after two more pages that I realized this Emperor had likely lived around the turn of the century in 1000 AD—never mind that they didn't have computer printers back then. He was Germanic. He spoke of King Henry II, and the shifting tides of loyalty to both the monarch and the church. He nattered for several paragraphs about how ridiculous it all was, what people were willing to believe in, what they invested their power in. How they gave away their magic to the king and to their faith, never building the temple within them.

I made a face. Once upon a time, Viktor had said much the same thing, though not quite so eloquently. Why had this particular tome emerged out of all the other Emperors' missives that I was sure were out there? I flipped to the end and stared down in surprise.

"'And so may I serve as a reminder for all Council members going forward, that they may not court a similar poison of destruction. I set this curse of death upon any Emperor who seeks to subject the will of the Connecteds to a force outside themselves. We are here to ensure the balance of magic such that Connecteds can live freely and not give their power away. There is enough of that in the world already. We must do nothing more than open their eyes to their power and give them freedom to fly. I am tired and old, and I shrug off the illusion of immortality so willingly embraced by my peers. For I must know death to appreciate life, and my soul yearns to take flight.'"

There were several other paragraphs that followed, despite the man's assertion of his eagerness for death, but my gaze stayed riveted on the phrase 'curse of death' for a long moment. Viktor hadn't wanted the Connecteds to have freedom to fly. He'd wanted to control them, to subjugate them to another's will. As a result, completely without realizing it, he'd been cursed to death for that infraction by a vengeful, long-dead Emperor—something I hadn't even known a Council member could do. What other magic lay dormant within the Council that we hadn't accessed yet? What were we truly capable of?

Note to self: never underestimate a Council member who had no more fucks to give.

I knelt again and tucked the pages back into the canister, carefully shutting the ornate door as the truth presented itself to me in clear and uncompromising terms. Viktor had betrayed the Connecteds—and the Arcana Council too. And unless I missed my guess, he'd joined ranks with the Shadow Court to be in the best position possible once the one-percenter Connecteds took power.

Had Rangi known that? Viktor certainly hadn't known about the potential death sentence he was assigning himself. He would have been smarter and protected himself otherwise. Instead, he died smug and certain in his own power. Had he died by Rangi's hand or because of this curse? And did it matter?

These thoughts plagued me, and I welcomed the bite of heat and fire as I whisked out of the library of Justice Hall and down to the Vegas Strip. It was full night, and Las Vegas Boulevard was hopping. People walked along, soaking in the frantic atmosphere, allowing themselves to be lured into casinos or bars. All under the guise of entertainment, for most of them.

Yet beneath the most jaded and sophisticated tourists, or the hard-eyed regulars that moved around and through those tourists like weary warriors surrounded by the ghosts of their fallen comrades, there was without fail the tiny spark of hope, or greed, or simple excitement about what might happen next. The foolhardy hope of entering a space where you intellectually *knew* the house was rigged against you, and yet you also knew that the house benefited by keeping such hope alive and so, there in the margins, you might make some magic.

I glanced up and to the right, taking in the tall white tower that had first welcomed me to Las Vegas, what I'd learned later had been erected without a full-time owner and then inhabited by the Hierophant. I peered up at it, its ghostly white column, pristine and desolate. Why had

Michael chosen it? Yet another question I'd never thought to ask. Those were beginning to pile up.

I pulled my attention from the Hierophant's home and scanned up the boulevard, walking the few steps it took to get a better view. I saw the glaring hole in the skyscape immediately. Viktor's domain over Paris Casino had vanished.

This time, my reaction was less anger and confusion, and more simple dismay. I had no sympathy for Viktor, but his death was a cold reminder that all of us on the Council could face a similar fate...perhaps sooner rather than later.

I turned to take in the other Council residences. Simon's glass menagerie Foolscap residence still danced above the Bellagio, the Devil's lava lamp light show flickered along the smooth lines of his home above the Flamingo, and the other domains of the Arcana Council stretched up the Strip as well—the tiny platform of the Hermit's home above Excalibur, the Magician's luxurious Prime Luxe tower of glass and steel. I didn't glance behind me to see if I could pick out the Sun's windswept domain above the Sahara casino or the Hanged Man's tower above the Stratosphere arcing with electricity. Instead, my gaze returned to the gap that had once been Viktor's stronghold—now as erased from the earth as he had been.

"I didn't expect you to be so melancholy." The drawled observation was made by a slender man stinking of scotch draped over a bench. The illusion immediately struck me as wrong, not because of the improbably good-looking drunk, but because he was sitting on a *bench*. Benches invited you to rest and watch awhile, and that wasn't the point of Vegas. It was a city of action, especially the action of spending money.

The Devil of the Arcana Council stood, and the bench

disappeared behind him, creating barely a ripple of interest as Aleksander Kreios turned and fell into step with me. With his entrance complete, he resumed his normal attire of Mediterranean playboy—from his loose cotton shirt to his sand-colored khakis, his feet clad in heavy sandals, glints of gold at his wrist and neck. He remained improbably gorgeous, of course, though far cleaner with his soft fall of tawny hair and his newly shaved, suntanned face. He regarded me with arched brows as I finished my survey, but didn't speak.

"Did you know what happened as soon as it happened?" I asked, returning my gaze to Paris Casino, which looked strangely forlorn without its Viktor topper. "Like, did you guys all get a memo?"

The Devil snorted a soft laugh. "I did, because I chose that moment to glance out the window. It was full daylight, and of course to an Arcana Council member's eyes, our domains fade from view while the sun graces the strip. But Viktor's didn't fade out, and it didn't implode like so many casinos along this Strip. It vanished as if it had never been there before. As if he had never been there before. If I'd actually been drunk, it would have been quite sobering."

Despite myself, I smiled. I'd never seen the Devil drunk. I didn't know if he could ever achieve that exalted state, never mind that he now smelled like remarkably expensive whiskey.

"I looked for records of such deaths when I returned to Justice Hall," I told him.

"Yes, after your delivery of Rangi to Gamon. There *was* a memo on that. The Magician thought I should know, though he remains insistent that he no longer wants the role of head of the Council."

"Yeah, well. Then you should know this too. I'm pretty sure Viktor was working for the Shadow Court."

Kreios only shrugged. "We all had suspected his potential for defection for some time," he pointed out. "In some of the Magician's projections. Viktor could've been used as an embedded mole, but in most, Viktor's future didn't end well. And it didn't end in his death quite so early."

"Armaeus didn't predict that?"

"Not that particular exit, no. You say you found evidence of his corruption in the library?"

"I learned more than that," I said derisively. "He was cursed by another Arcana Council member, by a former Emperor, in point of fact, who was determined to make sure that no future Emperor had the audacity to subject the Connecteds to any order but their own personal guidance. Presumably if the Connected chose of their own volition to follow some leader, no problem, but the moment an Emperor of the future stepped in..." I gestured to the unencumbered Paris Casino. "Blammo."

"An elegant end, and one which I am sure would have benefited Viktor to know," the Devil mused. "However, we cannot always know our entrances and exits in this world."

I glanced his way. Aleksander Kreios could present himself in any form, or multiple forms, on a whim. But he most often chose this current affectation of a rich Mediterranean vagabond. He hadn't been rich when he'd ascended to the role of the Devil, though.

"Do you think a former Devil cursed you?"

He smiled. "I rather hope so. Curses work their own mysterious magic depending upon who they are wielded by, and who they are meant to affect. I will tell you that the Magician believes quite strongly that death will not be the greatest challenge I'll face in the upcoming conflict, but rather one slightly more dispiriting. I have undertaken the needed steps to ensure I don't lose my memory, but apparently, it remains a concern."

I blinked at him, surprised. "Really?"

He shrugged. "It was but one of many outcomes, and the one I find least to my taste. In assuring against it, however, my future has grown murkier. As I say, we cannot choose our exits and entrances from the stage, nor our positions upon it."

We fell silent for a few minutes more, gradually passing the Bellagio and the Flamingo. I studied Simon's residence glittering above the Bellagio, smiling as the fountains started their routine dance.

"Does Simon know?" I asked. "He and Viktor had almost as much reason to hate each other as Viktor and I did."

"A fascinating question, and one which I suspect will be answered shortly. I've called a Council meeting."

I made a face. "You did? Since when?"

The Devil smiled and inclined his head as fireworks shot up from several casinos on the Strip for no apparent reason.

"Since now."

8

Neither Kreios nor I made any move to zap our way into Armaeus's conference room, though I'd been there so many times, I could navigate to it in my sleep at this point. Instead, we continued strolling, soaking up the jittering excitement of the Las Vegas night.

"The Shadow Court is going to make its move. They may already have started," I mused.

"Perhaps," Kreios agreed. "If they have, we will engage them on their own territory. I doubt quite sincerely they would try to face us here."

"But what if they do?" Another tendril of dismay slipped through me. "If they destroy Vegas—I mean, where would the Council go, whoever are left?"

"Wherever the magic is focused most strongly. When I joined, we were headquartered in Munich and left as the balance of that city's magic shifted to a focus we could not support—but also could not destroy out of hand."

I made a face. "So you left it to the Germans to figure it out on their own?"

Kreios shrugged. "Remember, the purpose of the

Council is to maintain the balance of magic. Had we remained, there is very little question that we would have been discovered one way or another. The powers behind the emerging government at that time had an acute understanding of magic and psychic strength. We would not have been able to hide for long in their backyard. By allowing ourselves some distance, we could do what we could to help, without altering the course of a history that was not ours to change."

"Except for the fact that you altered it by choosing to *not* alter it when you had that ability," I countered, feeling argumentative for the sake of it. "That was a lot of Viktor's point, I think. Why shouldn't those with the ability to effect real change not leverage that ability? Why should they stand aside and allow weaker players, players who don't have the same skill, to rule the day?"

"You are correct, of course, in your assessment of Viktor's stance on the question. Which is what led to his invitation to join the Council."

Kreios said the words mildly, so mildly that it took me a second to understand the extended meaning.

"That's *all* you did? That's the sum total of what you did to help mitigate the horror of Hitler's regime?"

"Not enough by any standard to help the hundreds of thousands of souls that were persecuted for their religious beliefs, their sexual and political orientations," the Devil agreed. "But again, that was not our primary focus. It has never been, and it can never be. The Arcana Council has not been appointed to serve as the stewards of the whole world. Our focus is solely on the Connecteds. To the extent that the fate of the world is tied up with the fate of Connecteds, things get a little more entwined. But in the case of the Third Reich, the psychics of that time were a relatively small part of the equation. In fact, those psychics who chose to fall in with the prevailing regime were rewarded quite handsomely, and are still rewarded to this day, I would suggest, though they subscribe to a different set of beliefs from most of the members of the Council. We are not here to provide a moral compass for those who practice magic, nor those who are magic. We fight for their ability to coexist in a non-Connected world."

I chewed on that for a few more minutes as we gradually worked our way to the Luxor casino, which rested at the base of the Magician's stronghold, Prime Luxe. Kreios's take on the Arcana Council's mission was a bit more benevolent than Armaeus's had ever been. Armaeus had only sought to protect the balance of magic. Kreios focused on those who wielded it. Maybe he was better suited to lead the Council.

"And if the world suddenly became more Connected?" I asked. "What then? Then we'd be working for the majority, not the minority."

"Then, as Armaeus would say, the situation would become...murkier," Kreios allowed, gesturing for me to precede him into the Luxor. "But a balance between light and dark, strong and weak, would still be the goal, in the end."

There was always something comforting about walking into the gaudy, glittering palace of the Luxor casino, with its brass and gold fixtures, its ancient Egypt references and tchotchke shops filled with the fake plastic artifacts of Vegas. I often wondered if anyone ever bought them, or if they were considered part of the décor, an expected side note to any Vegas trip. Along the large bank of elevators, it was easy to spot the single carriage designated for Prime Luxe. Unlike its brass counterparts, the door was a shiny ebony panel, and it was also invisible to any but those with advanced sight.

I looked around as we approached it. Unlike other times when I had traveled so traditionally to the Council chambers, there were no Connecteds eyeing me curiously from the corner, not quite sure what they were seeing, but knowing they were seeing something.

Instead, Kreios and I boarded the elevator without incident, whisking up and then up still farther, until at last we slowed, and the elevator opened onto a shallow foyer. Through the wide double doors, I could see the Magician's conference room. It was empty.

"Oh," Kreios murmured. "Now that *is* interesting, isn't it?"

I pursed my lips. "You know, this head-of-the-Council thing is making you start to sound way too much like Armaeus."

Kreios chuckled, but as soon as we entered the room, I saw that it wasn't, in fact, empty. The Magician and Simon sat at its far end. Had they been hidden from direct view? Or were they playing coy? The Magician looked up and smiled at me, and I got the impression that the answer was likely the latter.

"Miss Wilde," he began.

"The witch is dead," Simon interjected, his chin coming up, his thick brows climbing beneath his mop of dark curly hair, today pinned beneath a Union Jack knit cap. He wore his usual outfit of a long-sleeved T-shirt and jeans, slung loosely onto his lanky form, and he beamed at me, though without the usual boyish fervor I'd come to associate with the Fool of the Arcana Council. This smile was harder, grimmer.

"Ding, dong," I chimed in response. It ordinarily would

have seemed morbid, even churlish to delight in the death of another human. But we had both suffered in our own ways through the Emperor's actions. Our feelings were going to be complicated for a while. "Does everyone know?"

"Enough do." The voice that rang through the corridor came from deeper within the Magician's home, not the elevators. It was haughty and imperious but not angry, and I recognized it in a flash.

Eshe the High Priestess entered the conference room in her usual regalia of a long flowing toga, silver bracelets wrapped around her biceps and wrists, her feet shod in golden sandals, while jewels dripped from her ears and across her neck. She wore full makeup, with heavy-lashed eyes and wine-blushed lips, but I suspected she woke up that way.

"My surprise is that you did not strike the killing blow, Sara. I rather thought you would, I saw several instances in which you might, though those instances were, of course, not mine to share." She preened a little, while my own eyes widened. Eshe had the sight, but in a quite peculiar way. As the former Oracle of Delphi, her images were an unholy mess that only she could decipher, and sometimes not even her.

"Well, I'm sorry to blow up your office pool," I said drily. She waved that off. She and the Emperor had never been a thing, but they'd probably been closer than any two members of the Council. However, in that moment, I was reminded of exactly how old Eshe was. She had come to her seat on the Council nearly four hundred years before Christ was born. How many Emperors had she seen in her time?

I jolted, thinking about the Emperor whose words I'd read. Had she known him? She had to have. Did she know what he'd done with his whole curse thing?

"Viktor was also a fool," Eshe said, slanting Simon a glance. "My apologies."

At his shrug, she continued. "Aligning with the Shadow Court in such an open and obvious manner played to Viktor's ego but not his intelligence. He should have known better—he did know better because I told him so. And he chose not to listen to me."

In that moment, I felt I understood why Eshe was not more broken up about this particular Emperor meeting his end. When you are the Oracle of Delphi, people should listen to you. It was a thing.

The elevators flashed open again, and another member of the Arcana Council strolled into the chamber, fastidious and exact in his old-fashioned yet oddly elegant attire. Nikola Tesla, the Hanged Man, peered around the room with curiosity.

"I'd rather hoped that I would be surprised by at least one of you here, but I suppose Viktor provided enough surprise for us today." He looked at me. "You'll be wanting to know exactly how the magical dagger worked. I happen to have the answer to that, quite unexpectedly. It drew upon an energy source that I've only barely begun to test anew, though I found it once before, long ago—only to lose track of it again. A source of energy very few people understand, Viktor included, much to his chagrin, admittedly."

"Sucks for him," Simon said.

Tesla shot him a reproving glare. "The dagger wielded by Rangi was powered by quantum electricity, pulling its energy from a layer of space and time outside our own and concentrating it in a magical form."

"Right," Simon said. "You didn't discover this, my man. We've known about it since the 1920s."

"Which is when I discovered it," Tesla pointed out stiffly.

I broke in on their exchange, raising my voice to get their attention. "Wait a minute. Quantum electricity? That's a thing? And it's a thing the Shadow Court has access to?"

"Of course it's a thing," Tesla said, lifting an elegant hand to smooth his sleek black hair. He turned his aristocratic gaze on me. "And not only the Shadow Court, though, according to Gamon's interrogation report, Rangi's assault team stole the blades from a Shadow Court enclave. So technically, yes, the Shadow Court has access to it. We've encountered it before, but in rougher form. You'll recall the Nazi-era cubes the Shadow Court attempted to subvert to their aims? I suspect those had a similar energy source, but the construct simply didn't work as effectively as necessary. It happens."

Simon's eyes widened. "You couldn't make quantum electricity work either, could you, when you quote-unquote discovered it? That's why there was that box with the Wheatstone bridge in it that was stored in your hotel's vault, your supposed death ray that didn't do a damned thing."

Tesla rounded on the Fool, his narrow, almost delicate face now hot with anger. "I will have you know, young Fool—"

"Will you *stop*," I tried again, my heart trying to claw its way up to my throat. Quantum electricity, channeled into machines—this was bad. This was very bad. This could tip the balance of power definitively into the Shadow Court's favor. "How do we get our hands on these tools? Or can we make our—"

"Dollface!"

The sound cracked across the chamber, loud enough to make us all jump, but its owner was nowhere in evidence.

"Oh! I was wondering if she'd dial in." Simon turned back to his computer and swiveled the laptop around to face us. The Magician gestured, and a large screen appeared on the far wall, filling with an image that stunned everyone to silence.

Nikki Dawes, the newest member of the Arcana Council, who'd ascended to her position as the Moon only a few weeks earlier, lay back against what looked like a snowbank. She was dressed head to toe in blindingly white fake fur, from a jaunty cap and oversized mittens to a sleek white bodysuit trimmed in the stuff. Perhaps more alarmingly, she lay pinned between two enormous wolves, both of them howling their heads off, if the actions of their throats and upturned snouts and mouths were any indication. But no sound came through other than Nikki's voice.

"I've got full-on wolf white noise behind me, otherwise I wouldn't be able to dial in. It's hitting at a decibel human ears can't pick up, but let me tell you, nobody is hearing nothing but that static for miles around."

"Where are you?" I asked, and she cackled, wriggling free of the press of lupine bodies.

"We got a tip on another clan of werewolves, this one tucked up against the Alps way the hell up high. I've been all over hell's half acre looking for any remnant of the werewolves the first Moon left behind when she bolted for Atlantis six thousand years ago. Good news, we're finding a few. Torsten here and his pack have done a great job serving as ambassadors of the Moon, and of course, I'm not too shabby at recruiting either."

She tossed her dark hair, batting her smoky eyes, and grinned. I found myself grinning back. Nikki would be tough to resist in any situation, but surrounded by werewolves, she'd be damned near unstoppable.

"Is there any bad news?" I asked, and she winked.

"As it happens, yes. Some of them have gotten wind of

our arrival, and this next stop may not be quite so cordial. For the record, it's cold in the Alps, I don't care what time of year it is. Anyway, we're going in to convince them we're friendly and that they should join up to get all the special bonuses of working with the Moon. The more wolves we can recruit, the stronger we'll be for whatever the Shadow Court has planned. If all goes well, we'll have another were family to add to the fold before the night's done."

"That will take your pack to nearly three hundred," the Magician put in, earning him a wide smile from Nikki.

"Never let it be said that math was not your strong suit, Magic Man. But you're right. There are more wolves hiding out here, way more than we originally feared. So far, they're not all up for the fight, but they're still bringing a lot to the party. We're talking serious money and mad skills, not of the magical type at first, but give me a full moon with them, and I'll make all their dreams come true."

She said this last with a saucy grin, but the wolves around her leapt to their feet and sprang away, leaving Nikki looking strangely alone on the side of the windswept mountain.

"Gotta dash," she said as a new wolf appeared beside her, big and burly and bristling with attitude. "I'll check in when I can, but it may be a minute."

She was gone again before I could say anything else.

My heart brimmed over with pride, even as I keenly felt the loss of her in the room. Nikki had ascended to the Arcana Council the most recently, taking the place of the former Moon, who had met her untimely end several weeks earlier. It was getting to be dangerous to be an Arcana Council member, I thought ruefully.

"The return of werewolves in the open. That's going to

tip things in yet another direction," the Devil said, studying the Magician.

Armaeus nodded. "The blending of myth and magic with the mundane world will contribute to tensions already ratcheting up. So far, we believe Nikki's efforts to uncover these pockets of the Moon's former pack have gone unnoticed, but anyone who chooses to look will be able to see. Magic is starting to get noticed by non-Connecteds, exactly as the Shadow Court wants."

"Is that a bad thing, though?" Tesla asked, leaning forward. "Viktor deeply craved such recognition of Connected strength. It's unfortunate that it comes only after he has been ushered offstage."

"Where's Death?" the High Priestess asked abruptly, peering around. "The Hermit? The Hierophant? Why aren't they here?"

"Death has been called to transport more souls across the veil than usual," the Magician said. "The Hierophant together with the Syx are investigating several outbreaks of demonic activity."

"Demons? Excellent," Tesla put in, sounding almost gleeful. He straightened the cuffs of his old-fashioned suit. "Another nonmundane group heard from, and *definitely* one that will get noticed."

The Magician nodded. "The Hermit has been apprised of new breaks in the veil, as the gods beyond clamor for the opportunity to reenter Earth."

"Wait, what?" I said, turning on him. The Hermit was my father, though our relationship certainly wasn't close—as evidenced by the fact that I had no idea he was holding off another godly incursion. Those guys just wouldn't give up. "That's a thing? After all we did to shut them out, that's still a thing?"

“It is, but there’s nothing to fear on that count. We are not without our resources,” the Magician said, clearly unperturbed.

“Yeah, but—”

“*Behold*.” A new voice boomed across the room as a shaft of moonlight cut into the chamber, hitting the floor and exploding in a flurry of light and movement.

“Oh, for the gods’ sakes,” Eshe muttered darkly. “Is he going to do that every time he shows up?”

“I am the *Sun*,” Qadir announced as he manifested into his human form—big, bald, and muscular, in a white shirt and pants, spreading his arms wide like Mr. Clean after a beach vacation. “I have come to shine upon you all.”

9

"What have you learned?" the Devil asked Qadir after the Sun had fully formed, then glanced around the room. "I asked Qadir to see what he could find out about those individuals Simon had tagged as high-probability Shadow Court members."

Qadir smiled. "And I, in turn, can see anyone, anywhere, so long as the sun shines upon them, or the moon," he said, gesturing to the shaft of moonlight that had transported him into the room. "Because moonlight is nothing more than—"

The High Priestess sighed, and Qadir broke off, but his grin widened.

"For all your seniority on the Council, you are still so young, beautiful High Priestess," he said, his voice heavy with humor. "When you have lived so many years as I, you will learn to find new delight in the mundane."

"Perish the thought," the High Priestess said drily. "What did you find?"

"Far less of interest than I would have hoped!" Qadir

boomed. "Though perhaps what I consider to be of interest is not in play."

Before he could devolve into a description of what he might find interesting, he refocused and pointed to Simon.

"Those beacons you set upon the most powerful Connecteds on this earth who are not Council members have degraded in the quality of their wards, as you said they would. The Connecteds with true ability detected them, some more quickly than others, and so now they only remain on the moderately Connected who yet still reside in the upper tier of power. That places them squarely in a specialized group: the rich and the politically connected—who are *not* blessed with an overabundance of psychic power."

"Why wouldn't those who were incredibly powerful, or at least powerful enough to detect they'd been tracked, warn their compatriots who were lower level to remove their own tracking devices?" I asked. "It's been weeks now since we attached them."

"A very worthy question," Qadir acknowledged, then gestured expansively to Simon to take the floor.

The Fool swiveled in his conference chair, looking particularly pleased with himself. "The beacons are small and expend energy in two distinct events. The first is during their attachment, which is why so many of the highest-level Connecteds knew immediately that something was wrong and discarded them the moment they arrived. Otherwise, they can be detected when they're being used to track audio and visual. I don't keep eyes on these people twenty-four seven. That wouldn't be efficient, and at this point, we're gathering larger trends. Even from such secondary tracking, I was able to compile a ton of data, diving deeper when the risk was outweighed by the need to know who a specific person was. In about half those cases, we lost the tracking device, but it was worth it to get the network further established. Should the need arise, I can always send another tracker designed for a unique individual, a tracker more difficult to detect."

"There's also the fact that the Shadow Court, for all its far-flung net of operatives, doesn't include some of the highest-level Connecteds on Earth," the Devil put in. "Especially in the early going, Simon's beacon snagged several individuals of impressive capability who lived away from society and outside any sort of interaction with any organized religion or government. Separated from each other at this level, though in some cases, they did emerge from communities of lower-level Connecteds, who they kept around them, most likely for the glory of being a big fish in a small pond."

I made a face. "Or they could have been protecting a group they felt responsible for."

"You are correct, Justice Wilde. Fortunately, once I fix on an individual's identity, I no longer need to trigger the beacon," Qadir explained, spreading his hands with a delighted smile. "I require only the sun."

This time, the High Priestess barely managed to swallow her groan, while Simon picked up his explanation again. "In something like eighty-five percent of Connecteds we hooked up with a beacon, there was no indication of collusion with the Shadow Court or any clandestine operatives in the arcane black market. It was like they didn't even know of their own Connected ability, despite the fact that it resonated at a fairly high level and despite the fact that they were called to that special Shadow Court meetup in Geneva where we found them in the first place. These are the people who probably explain away their abilities to natural instinct, strategy honed to a fine point, or the experience of working at the highest levels of government or business or science. They don't know they're magical because they don't call it magic."

Is that such a bad thing? I didn't ask the question aloud, but as Simon kept talking, the Magician answered it in my mind anyway.

"It is a bad thing if such magic will be used against them. They should know what they are or how they will be targeted if they will be put at risk for such targeting. It is like a family with a genetic predisposition to be sensitive to a deadly allergen. Not a problem if the allergen is never introduced to their system. Quite a bit of a problem if and when it is, and they could have been warned about it."

I considered that and was forced to agree.

Simon went on. "Far more interesting, the remaining fifteen percent started talking way more amongst themselves almost immediately after we attached our beacons to them. They sustained that contact for only a few days, then they stopped talking to each other, cold turkey. Of this group, fifty percent own multinational businesses or operate in the financial markets at an international level, thirty percent are the heads of labs or medical organizations, and the rest are in governmental roles, but not at the highest level. Not heads of state, but more like well-placed cabinet members, trusted confidants, and well-compensated lackeys."

"Which makes sense," the Devil said, crossing his arms and leaning back against the wall as if he were a modern European despot considering which small kingdom he wanted to buy today. "The highest-level Connecteds who operated in government got rid of their devices almost immediately, but this group wasn't as sensitive."

Simon nodded. "Exactly. Still, in all cases, there wasn't

more than one Connected in a single government group. I almost got the impression that they didn't know about each other prior to their recent Shadow Court mobilization, and after the events in Geneva, they started getting super chummy, until they were told to shut up. Then they all collectively turtled up. They might still be in contact with each other, but you can bet they're being careful." He pointed at the Magician. "You'd asked specifically about the movement of money. Well, your suspicions were correct. The highest-level Connecteds with financial acumen have been consolidating their positions in the medical device sector, base metals, and real estate, to the detriment of experimental financial products such as cryptocurrency, traditional utilities, and cash."

"They're preparing for a big market crash?" I asked.

"A major disruption, undoubtedly," the Magician agreed. "But while they're acting on an individual basis, they're not the ones driving the process, and they're not collaborating. They're waiting. Why would they wait?"

I was pretty sure the question was intended to be rhetorical, but Tesla waded into the conversation.

"They wait because they do not know the limits of their *power*," he insisted, waving his hands in frustration. "They wait because after all this time, they still believe they should. Money doesn't make men great. Neither does ability. The world is full of men with both. The rewards, however, go to men of action and daring who are willing to take the risk required to achieve greatness. These Connecteds you've found are operating on too small a scale. Would they still if they knew their true gifts? If they lived in a world that did not order them to hide their Connected abilities but to exalt in them?"

I peered at the Hanged Man, not knowing if I should be

entirely dismayed or a little proud as well. The Emperor had waxed long and eloquently about the need for Connecteds to own their position in society, but the Connecteds he'd cared about were the powerful ones, who ideally were rich as well.

The Hanged Man had always taken a more democratic approach to power. Even when he'd walked the earth as the mortal Nikola Tesla, he had advocated that magic, in this case, the magic of electricity, should be accessible to all. That it was a resource that could and should be within the grasp of any who wanted to draw upon it. Small wonder that he felt the same about Connected ability. He might not be my favorite person in the world, but I liked him better for his stance on this point. Tesla would fight for the rights of all Connecteds.

"What about the woman?" Eshe asked. "The one behind Jarvis Fuggeren and all his money?"

"Eleanor St. Claire." Qadir nodded, beaming at Eshe for giving him the opening. "Yes, I was able to identify her too, in the fullness of my power. I am nothing short of remarkable."

Simon snorted. "She's kind of a cipher, though. Keeps to herself, daughter of a reclusive business scion, and now owns her own companies headquartered in Paris, London, and Berlin. She shuttles between those places on the regular in a private jet, exempt from entire rafts of governmental regulations and restrictions both financially and logistically. Her work seems to be a rather mercurial mix of financial and business consulting at a very high level, available to the one percent of the one percent. Interestingly, she doesn't source all her business through strictly Connected channels. In fact, I would say it only makes up about ten to fifteen percent recently, based on the beacon activity."

"You got a beacon attached to her? She didn't notice that?"

"Weirdly, no," Simon said. "Though, not gonna lie, of all the beacons, this one has the shittiest reception. Either that or the woman is constantly surrounded by every laptop, phone, and tablet known to man. There's always a ton of electrical static to sort out to get a true fix on where she is."

"Good enough. Let's recap where we are," the Devil began, nodding to the Magician. But before the Magician could speak, Qadir raised his hand once again.

"Alas, or perhaps happily, I am not finished."

"Of course you aren't," Eshe muttered, earning her an appreciative grin from the djinn.

"It occurred to me to cross-reference the operatives that young Simon initially tracked and could still track, with the activities of the arcane black market. You will be unsurprised to learn that the vast majority of operatives on the arcane black market who engage in the buying and selling of technoceuticals and artifacts are *not* among the most powerful Connecteds."

"Well, I guess that makes sense," Simon said, once again rotating his conference chair. "If you have to rely on drugs or artifacts to stimulate your power base, chances are you don't have a heck of a lot of power to begin with. And then there's a whole bunch of people who are in the market for the grift, the buying and selling of anything for a profit."

"Exactly so. However, there was one operative completely hidden from view, touched briefly by the beacons that Simon sent out before eradicating it, whose fingers are mired deep into the loamy soil of the arcane black market."

I knew who it had to be and was glad Nikki wasn't here for this particular conversation. Of all of us, she had suffered the most at this person's hand, and yet none of us had suffered as much as I now feared others had.

"Dixie Quinn," I said, picturing the self-styled den mother of the Las Vegas Connected community. With her trademark Southern drawl, soft pink cowboy hats, pink scarves and boots, and bright white minidresses, she definitely had looked the part of the person she'd portrayed herself as—astrologer and owner of the Chapel of Everlasting Love in the Stars. Her facade had cracked over time bit by bit, until now she was quickly escalating up the ranks of the Arcana Council's Most Wanted Evildoers list...and might possibly be working for the one remaining missing member of that long-ago first Arcana Council, the Star.

Either that, or she was the Star herself, which I still couldn't quite believe. Dixie was bad...but I didn't think she could pull off pure evil. I didn't think she was capable of that level of focus, if nothing else.

Qadir nodded.

"Obviously, this is a supposition, and as I said, the operative remains hidden. But a woman of strength, cunning, beauty, and means has been pulling the threads of the arcane black market for many years now, it would seem. Whether it is the woman you believe you have known all this time or if she is the front for another, stronger entity, I do not know. But she seems to be driving the human traffic that pulses through the arcane black market like an angry virus, and she is not Eleanor St. Claire. We have been able to rule that out—well, I have. Because, you see—"

"Fucking Dixie," I muttered as Qadir congratulated himself on his sleuthing with a delighted smile. But I could only focus on Dixie Quinn.

We'd seen that kind of trafficking right under our noses, but had followed practically any other possibility that sheared us away from the sweetly smiling Southern belle. And it had been her all along. It didn't matter whether she was the Star in the flesh or a front for that ancient Arcana Council member, Dixie was Connected. She had at least some measure of power, whether native or augmented, and she was human...or at least, I was pretty sure she was human. There were enough Connected asshats in the world, she didn't need to become one of them.

The Magician tapped his finger on the tabletop. "Intriguingly, there is an eighty-six-point-seven-percent chance that the Star is, in fact, Dixie Quinn, that she has survived all these years in a series of guises that enhance her already immortal state with a veneer of unique and varied beauty. Each of the Council members is given shrewdness, mental agility, and, of course, physical speed and stamina, but not all are given additional levels of magic. Qadir has the sight wherever the sun may touch..."

"And a glorious sight it is," Qadir agreed.

"Kreios can discern the true desires of anyone he focuses on and understand the secrets they don't want to share, as well as create powerful illusions to distract and delight or strike terror in the hearts of those he deems deserving," the Magician continued.

"An ever-expanding list." The Devil nodded. "Eshe can scry the future. Tesla can give himself over to the ether, flowing through circuits of power to be everywhere and nowhere at once."

Tesla tented his brows with interest. "Considering the Council wrenched me out of that exalted state, I'm pleased you still remember that. For all that you have subsequently tethered me like a lodestone to this plane."

The Magician inclined his head. "The Hermit has the ability to both guard and mend the veil between the worlds, powerful magic for a man who was once a simple artisan. Gamon has been blessed with extreme strength and a cold-blooded discernment."

Simon snorted. "I think she pretty much had that before she came on board."

The Devil turned to him with a slight smile. "Whereas you, Simon, have not yet embarked on your greatest adventure."

"Oh, give me a break," the Fool protested, spreading his hands. "I've been a little too busy to go on a Mormon mission trip, okay?"

I blinked, staring hard at Simon. He was the Fool, arguably the smartest among us. Especially when it came to tech, he was the puzzle solver, the tinkerer, MacGyver with magic. Was he destined for some greatness I didn't understand yet? What was the Devil implying? I mean, he couldn't be saying…

"What's your point, you guys?" I heard myself asking, my voice harsher than I intended. "You're saying that some of us have powers and some of us don't, beyond strength and speed and long life, is that it? Where does that get us?"

The Magician fielded this question, unperturbed by my outburst. His gaze was almost gentle.

"My point, Miss Wilde, is that it is not a matter of having or not having Connected abilities such as the throwing of fire or the ability to disappear and reappear. It is that we all have some abilities we do not know of, a hidden Connected potential that even at our exalted levels, we do not always choose to plumb. Viktor was the Emperor, a master of manipulation, leadership, and strategy, but he grew distracted in the final weeks and months of his life with a new project, a new pursuit. One that he thought the Shadow Court could help him attain."

"What in the world could someone possibly want more than riches and immortality?" the Fool asked, genuinely perplexed. "It's not like the guy was out to save the world."

"The greatest power in the universe, I suspect," the Magician replied. "Not the power to save the world...but to remake it."

10

Nobody knew how to drop the mic quite like the Magician. We stared at him in silence for a long moment, then Tesla leaned forward.

"That's possible, in truth?" he asked. "A world in which electricity could flow from dimension to dimension, unimpeded by politics or the constraints of technology that most human beings are too feeble to understand?"

"A world where divining the future was as natural a part of government as summoning armies and building cities?" the High Priestess murmured. "A return to the glory days of old?"

The Fool grinned. "A full-on Scarlet Monastery? Freaking sweet."

The Magician didn't look at any of them directly, but fixed his gaze on a far-off horizon only he could see. "To remake the world as you feel it should be is truly the action of a god."

"Viktor would have enjoyed trying that project on for size," Simon agreed a little sourly. "The Shadow Court must've looked like his express ticket to being King of the Universe, and he probably wasn't the only one who thought so. I bet all the Shadow Court's top-level people are going to sleep at night with dreams of godhood dancing in their heads."

I thought about the celestial tiles, likely still stacked in the Magician's inner sanctum. Was that their purpose? To remake the world? Surely that wouldn't be something any god would have allowed his people.

"Speaking of gods, has somebody been keeping an eye on Hera and Zeus?" Eshe asked abruptly. "They haven't been whining about how poorly they've been treated for a while. When they get quiet, I worry."

"It's a worry you will not have to deal with for long," Kreios said. "With Viktor's death, the Lovers have come to the conclusion that this world is no longer safe for gods or Council members. For all their exalted status in the pantheon, they are not world makers—or re-makers, for that matter. They wish merely to enjoy the adulation of their subjects and live according to their own pleasures. They have asked to be returned to beyond the veil, and I have granted them that wish. The Hermit is now assisting them through a particularly frayed section of the veil, and they in turn will use their godhead strength to reinforce the barrier, so that no other gods attempt to cross into Earth at that seam."

"They left?" Eshe protested faintly, sounding a little dumbstruck. "You let them go? That weakens the Council. Why did you do that?"

Kreios shrugged. "According to Armaeus, there was at least a seventy-four-point-three-percent chance that they would be swayed to join the Shadow Court, and in so doing, elevate the Shadow Court's likelihood of achieving cataclysmic human destruction to a surprising ninety-four-point-three percent."

"So you got rid of them before they could potentially join the Shadow Court, and ergo potentially wreak havoc on Connecteds?" Simon asked, and even he sounded a little shaken. "What is this, *Minority Report*?"

"The decision was ultimately theirs to make," the Devil put in. While he was right, something still rankled about this rapid reshuffling of the Council. It felt too rushed, too chaotic, in the wake of the Emperor's death. "When Armaeus came to me with his assessment, after I asked for it, it made sense to eliminate the potential threat and shore up our position at the same time. In war, as Viktor would have been the first to tell us, the strength of your troops is not nearly as important as their reliability. The greatest magic in the world will not serve you if it can suddenly be turned against you without warning."

"Do I sense an underlying threat in your words?" the High Priestess asked, which was ironic since there was no doubting the threat in hers.

Kreios smiled. "Not at all. You will note there was absolutely no expectation on our part to lose the Lovers from our fold. Hera and Zeus held similar abilities to Viktor. They could manifest whatever form they desired, and they were master manipulators as well. They had to be, given their line of work. And to the Magician's point, they could potentially have found a greater magic within them, given the time and inclination. It seemed prudent not to allow them that opportunity, especially considering the potential for their shifting loyalties and their own preferences. But if they had chosen to join with the Shadow Court, that, of course, would have been their prerogative, much as it was Viktor's choice."

"No," Eshe said, startling me. "No. There's something you're not telling us, something important. Viktor changed sides, or at least that's how it seems, and he's now dead. You can't tell me that's mere coincidence because I'm thinking it's statistically improbable."

She turned her attention to the Magician, who smiled a little smugly. She didn't miss the expression.

"I'm right, aren't I?" she demanded. "I've been living in this theater of possibility for going on eighty years, and that's since we moved to Vegas. You're not the first Magician I have dealt with, Armaeus, but you are arguably one of the subtlest. And Kreios here is far too amused by the loss of both the Emperor and the Lovers. We may not all be friends here, but we are allies. What is it you're not telling us?"

Armaeus turned to look at the Devil, who inclined his head almost regally. The change of their power dynamic struck me again. The Devil and Magician may have swapped roles, but the two of them were acting entirely too squirrelly. To Eshe's point, what was it they weren't telling us?

At least the answer to her immediate question was forthcoming.

"While it is true that the loss of any Council member is keenly felt in the loss of their strategy, collaboration, boots-on-the-ground capabilities, and general strength in numbers," the Magician explained, "the loss of their magic as an element of the Council's strength, as a cohesive unit, does not appear to be a foregone conclusion. We sensed, but did not know, that Viktor had transferred his loyalties to the Shadow Court. If that were the case, we should have felt the loss of his magic, his strength, immediately. We did not. It was only with his death that his resonance disappeared, and yet even then, I sensed no weakening in the fiber of the

Council. There are two possibilities, at least, for this. The first is that there will *never* be a lessening of the Council's strength as an entity. Unless it is destroyed, a kernel of magic, a binding force shall always remain, waiting to be rekindled."

I lifted my brows. That was a little advanced for me to wrap my head around, but I could see the advantage.

"The other possibility is that it takes some time for the effects of a Council member's departure to be felt. So the rapid addition of Council members these past few years, the return of the Hierophant, the recovery of the Hanged Man, the return of the Moon, the creation of Judgment, Justice, the Lovers—"

"We lost the Empress," the Fool pointed out. "But now that I think about it, that didn't seem to affect much of anything either."

The Magician favored him with a smile. "It did not. The magic the Empress brought to the Council was vaudevillian in nature, but at its source, raw and quite ripe for development. She did not want to put in the time to advance it through her own work. Of course, she is not the first Connected to fall prey to that failing, but when she left our number, the essence of her raw magic remained to be tapped as needed by any of us, so long as we work within the Council's framework."

Kreios gestured with a lazy sort of indolence, as if there was nothing to worry about. "Which brings us to this conclusion. We have more than enough strength to counter the actions of the Shadow Court, at least from what we have learned about their capabilities so far. To date, we have waited for them to act so that our response remains measured and balanced. With the explosion at Angkor Wat and the recent disruption in Jerusalem, however, it would seem the Shadow Court is moving closer to launching its war. We don't know exactly what form their opening attacks will take. We need to learn this. We also need to understand the extent of collusion between the Star and the Shadow Court. If they are working together, that...changes things. Dramatically. But above all else, we must be ready to fight."

"Fascinating," Tesla murmured, and he nodded solemnly. Even Simon narrowed his eyes, twirling his pen over his knuckles as his brain dove down labyrinthine paths I could only guess at. Time to reel this back into something I could understand.

"So what's next?" I prompted. "Viktor's dead. Surely that caused a ripple if he went over to the dark side. Rangi so far hasn't spilled, or Gamon would already be here, but I think he's going to net out as hating everyone."

"Everyone who pretends to be a god," the Magician agreed, nodding.

"Right. So I'm thinking Rangi's not in love with the Shadow Court either, although at least they give lip service to the idea of the Connecteds taking power. Only the top Connecteds, but still."

"His warriors have all dispersed," Simon said, jabbing his pen at Armaeus. "After the destruction of the temple, they totally split, and responsibility for the attack is being assumed by some bunch of local yahoos looking for instant fame."

"Okay, so where does that leave us?" I asked. "I mean, we can't wait anymore, right? Shouldn't we be doing something proactively?"

"That time is coming," the Devil agreed. "We still need to understand what Viktor's role was with the Shadow Court. Was he there to stop the destruction of the temple or to take ownership of it? With his deep Connected abilities, was he to become the new face of the Shadow Court, the power behind the throne as well as the throne itself?"

Eshe sighed, flipping her long hair back over one bared shoulder. "I should've spent more time pumping him for information at the end, but to be fair, I felt he was doing the same to me. He was certain I had arcane knowledge of the Shadow Court and its origins. He had convinced himself they were the truer path to power, the better choice for greatness. Not that they will win, but that they *should* win."

"The perfect race," the Magician said thoughtfully. "It remained an overriding passion of his."

I grimaced, remembering the group of Connected children who had borne the brunt of Viktor's obsession, taken from their families and hidden like potential weapons, against the time when he could figure out what to do with them. Armaeus had limited the damage Viktor could do by bringing him aboard the Arcana Council, but he certainly hadn't eliminated it.

"Yeah, it would have been better if we'd known that he was going in when he did. I could at least have tried to bug him," Simon groused. "But now...I mean there's nothing left of the guy."

There was a long chagrined moment. And then the Magician spoke again. "Well...not precisely."

We all turned to him in surprise and, for me at least, maybe a little horror, but Simon straightened, his face brightening.

"Seriously? You got to him in time? I didn't see you on screen."

"Neither did I," I said. "And I was right there."

Armaeus inclined his head. "I confess I was too late to save Viktor, a truth to puzzle through another time. But the essence of him, the pieces, to use Simon's terminology, they are not altogether lost."

He withdrew a small vial from his jacket pocket, and I stared, not missing the gleam of gold that swam inside the beaker.

"What is *that*?" I asked. "Eau de Viktor?"

"In a sense." Armaeus tilted the vial. "It's not enough of Viktor to recreate him. He was, in the end, human, despite his elevation to the Arcana Council. Immortal but not unkillable, and yet he had gotten so close to godlike splendor that he was left shocked at his own eradication."

I snorted. I could totally see that, that Viktor's last overriding reaction was surprise.

"And what exactly do you plan on doing with that vial?" I asked carefully. I had some experience with putting people back together, but there actually needed to be a person to start with, not their literal last gasp.

Kreios smiled. "To Eshe's point, it would be much more useful if we had something to go on. Viktor would have made the perfect embedded spy."

As the Devil spoke, Armaeus shifted. One minute he was the smoothly elegant, Franco-Egyptian Magician of the Arcana Council, and the next he was the tall, broad-shouldered, Aryan-featured Emperor. Viktor Dal in the not-quite flesh.

"Seriously?" I protested, irritated by the almost schoolkid enthusiasm Kreios and Armaeus were radiating, like Viktor hadn't literally exploded into a skazillion pieces. "You're going to waltz into the Shadow Court's net and impersonate Viktor after Rangi just proved how vulnerable we are to the killer quantum electricity pointy things? This is your plan? And besides all that, if I was the Shadow Court and my star quarterback got put back together by the opposing team, he's not going to be tossing any balls."

The Magician looked at me blankly for a second, possibly thrown by my football reference, then his expression cleared. "But what if the question was not *should* Viktor be brought back into the fold, but should he be eliminated for what he knew? Would the Shadow Court come after him to attempt to kill him a second time, up close and personal?"

Now it was the Devil's turn to assume the Viktor guise. "And if you have knowledge that you believe I also possess and you're desperate to determine if I've shared that knowledge with your enemies, who's to say you wouldn't tell me that secret knowledge by mistake before you offed me?"

"Oh, for the love," I sighed, though at least I better understood the game now. Kreios had the ability to get anyone to talk to him. He also had the ability to create illusion. The Magician possessed that ability too, with the added skill that he could make himself into nothing at all. Together, they could pull off a newly reconstituted Viktor, no problem. As long as I was there too.

"You want all three of us to go into the belly of the beast, don't you?" I asked. "One of you guys posing as Viktor while I desperately try to fix him, and then you want to pump whoever they send to clean up the mess for information. You really think they'll fall for it?"

"The Emperor died on sacred ground, with chaos everywhere," Kreios said. "Justice of the Arcana Council showed up and immediately dispatched his killer. It would not be unreasonable that she would return to the scene to collect what she could and do what, by all accounts, she has continued to do with greater frequency of late to aid Connecteds both powerful and weak. To put them back together in a form that is greater than what they were before. What a skill that would be, eh?"

"So you *do* think they would fall for it," I answered for him. "You think we'll have eyes on us as we bring Viktor back to life, and then he'll be attacked by an operative with enough intel to teach us what we need to know. We'll learn what the Shadow Court is doing, exactly, when they're doing it, and how...and then we'll bail."

"It would be an interesting gambit, you must admit," Kreios said, a smile playing about his lips. "And as Viktor himself showed us, who knows how much longer we have to play the game?"

11

The Council room had cleared of everyone except for the Magician, the Devil, and me. There had been no vote and very little additional discussion about the process to reanimate Viktor somewhere near the ruins of Angkor Wat and create a plausible explanation that we had spirited the Emperor off somewhere safe and secret for the great Humpty Dumpty experiment. I still didn't like it.

"If these people are intelligent at all, and everything seems to indicate they are, they will have figured out what your skills are, Kreios," I protested. "They'll lie to you."

"And how successful do you think that will be, lying to the Devil?" Kreios asked sarcastically. "I can tell you it's been tried a great deal over time, but that doesn't mean that any mortals other than Council members have gotten better at it."

"It just seems that there should be a better way," I insisted. "One that doesn't stick three major members of the Arcana Council in the middle of danger for such little return. I mean, how much of this grand plan are you doing because it sounds fun?"

Before Armaeus and Kreios had a chance to argue that point, the doorway of the elevator flashed open. I turned, half expecting with unreasonable hope to see Nikki striding off the elevator. The reality was far more surprising.

"Sariah?" I began as she walked in with a trio of knives clinking at her waist, an appropriate counterpoint to her ensemble of black leather jacket, heavy black leggings, and slim black knee-high boots. Her hair was slicked back into a ponytail, and she wore no makeup. To the casual observer, she could have been me, save for the heavy jagged knives that she'd fashioned for herself out of a few extra cuffs of Justice. She wasn't officially a member of the Arcana Council, but she was the Night Witch, the aide of Justice, who would go wherever she was needed and do the things that Justice couldn't or wouldn't do. Apparently, her current mission had led her here.

"Where is he?" she asked without breaking stride. She scanned the room, her gaze landing on Armaeus. "You would've been the one to collect him. But have you handed him off to your sidekick yet?"

The Devil's mouth worked at the insult. "You would be familiar with the role."

"Yeah, except I actually get things done." Sariah's prickly retort reminded me not only of the fact that she had set herself at odds against the Devil, but why. As my doppelgänger twin, Sariah possessed an interesting mix of psychic abilities. She was preternaturally fast, brutal, excellent with her bladework, and happy to take down anything in her path with a level of sensory perception that didn't quite track with being human.

But her other skills were both highly specific and hard-won. Once she made close personal contact with a Connected of reasonable skill, she could absorb their abilities for a very short time and use them however she wanted. If the Connected was strong enough, they might not even notice that their psychic power had been drained, especially for such a short period while Sariah put the skill in play.

Sariah's ability had allowed her to absorb the High Priestess's channeling ability long enough to receive the image of the Devil betraying the Magician and sending him to his death. It also had allowed her to temporarily co-opt my traveling magic—and a couple of fireballs along the way. Now she folded her arms and stared hard at the Magician.

"You can't seriously be doing what Simon told me you guys were planning," she accused.

"Where did you run into Simon?" I asked. "What are you doing in Vegas anyway?"

"I've been working kinda closely with Simon to try to synthesize my abilities into something more predictable," Sariah said. "We were supposed to have a meeting today, and he was late. Turns out, he was here playing house with you guys, while you dreamed up your ridiculous plan to bring Viktor back from the dead long enough to convince his new buddies to spill their candy. How am I doing so far? Is that about the long and short of it?" She swung her gaze to the Devil. "You really think the Shadow Court's going to hand over the schematics to the Death Star? That they'll look deep into your eyes and betray the one thing that could take them down for good?"

The Devil's smile never wavered. "People have given up far less when looking into my eyes," he allowed.

She snorted and turned back to the Magician.

"What magic does Viktor have, or I guess I should say, *did* he have? He was an asshole and he got people to do things for him, I know that much. He was a megalomaniac, and a natural-born leader."

"He was all those things," the Magician agreed.

"But he was something more, wasn't he?" Sariah countered, stabbing a ragged-edged fingernail at him. "He was all ego. You've got some sort of essence of him locked up in a bottle, so why don't we cut to the chase? I ingest that, and his magic takes me over. That magic quite likely will manifest as his person, yeah? Because above all things, he's all about Viktor."

"What?" I protested in alarm. "But—" I shut up as quickly, my mind racing ahead. I made a face. "Son of a bitch, that could work."

"You could become Viktor," the Devil said, speaking the words slowly, though I couldn't figure out if he was savoring them or trying to assess their viability. "I could give you illusion magic."

"You could," Sariah agreed. "But I don't know if you even need to do that. If I'm confronted with someone whose main defining feature was his ability to project himself outward, wouldn't he project himself through me? And then you would be getting the real Viktor, not some facsimile that you have to use to pump other people for information. I could have his mind, or, more importantly, his memories."

"Simon suggested this to you?" the Magician asked.

"He did, but he wasn't sure it would work. Turns out, this whole mutant Rogue thing I've got going on isn't quite tracking with the comic books, so he's constantly having to adjust his expectations. I never had much time for reading in Hell, so I'm not up on the pop culture ramifications. But he thought it could work, though not for very long. What do you actually think Viktor knows that's of any use?"

"Targets," I offered. "Timing. Methods of attack. The

Shadow Court's top guns may not have let him into the inner sanctum of their strategic forces, but while he was no fool, his greatest skill was manipulation. They might have taken him into their confidence."

Armaeus nodded. "It's extremely likely they did, particularly if the operatives in question were not female."

Sariah's smile twisted. "What, he didn't have a way with the ladies?"

"His superpower was mansplaining," I confirmed. "Capable women were meant to be used, but they wouldn't have been equals to him. And the more capable the woman, the more she would know that was how Viktor viewed her. I doubt quite seriously Eleanor St. Claire would have put up with that attitude, and Viktor would have known that he wouldn't get far with her. He would have gone for the next tier down. Her generals, her closest aides. He would play to their vanity and their need for power. He could get pretty far with that group, I bet."

"Quite far indeed," the Magician said. He reached into his jacket pocket and removed the vial. Sariah's eyes widened as she took in the slender beaker with its twisting golden mist inside.

"That's all that's left of the guy? You didn't get any buttons or anything?" she asked, smirking with macabre humor.

"It seemed his most vital essence," the Magician said. "I would not suggest that it is his soul."

I huffed a grim laugh despite myself, but didn't need to comment on that, as Sariah was more than happy to step into the gap.

"That asshole had no soul. I mean, it's not like Death showed up to carry his ass across the river Styx or whatever it is she does. If she had, he would've been the most surprised."

"He was an atheist, but perhaps that contributed to our success as well," Armaeus acknowledged. "He had formed no impression of what he might do or where he might go in the event of his death. With someone given such a strong sense of self, there was that moment's hesitation, a choice to be made." He waved the bottle slightly. "I made the choice for him."

"We won't have much time," the Devil informed us, still studying Sariah. "Your ability to absorb power is volatile, Sariah, and by your own admission, short-lived. While Viktor in life was a dominant personality, in death, his limits are less certain."

"Well, are you ready with your questions, then?" she shot right back. "It's not like I'll probably remember anything that I say, and it's up to you guys to figure out if it has any meaning. But let me tell you for the record, this plan is a hell of a lot smarter then you dousing yourself with the essence of Viktor and having Sara here flapping around trying to save your ass, then getting hit by guards long enough for you to get any relevant information. That's a completely dumb idea. So dumb that I begin to wonder if you ever planned on executing it."

I narrowed my eyes, understanding where she was going, but the Magician interrupted smoothly.

"Let me be the first to acknowledge that your plan has more benefits. Not the least of which is it can be executed in a controlled environment. This environment."

He waved the hand that wasn't holding the vial and half the conference room was suddenly partitioned off by a low wall, beyond which now stretched an operating bay. Doctor Sells, a robust blonde of indeterminate years who served as the Council's head physician, stood in the center of the room, clearly surprised to find herself there.

"Am I needed?" she asked.

"The percentages are very low, but it is possible," the Magician allowed.

Sariah resolutely refocused on him. I could feel a tremor of fear slipping through her. She didn't like hospitals. She didn't like anything where she felt helpless. But she would still do this.

Before I could speak, her gaze shot to me, not needing any sort of psychic ability to read my thoughts. "It's faster this way," she agreed, but I still didn't think that was the reason she was volunteering for this duty.

The Devil stepped forward. "The Magician will uncork the vial, and you'll inhale its contents. We'll be right here. I'll fix my focus on you and ask the questions. The Magician will do any additional heavy lifting to make whatever is left of Viktor feel like he is in a safe enough space to respond."

I nodded. "I hadn't thought about that. Who is Viktor going to think he's talking to? We don't know who their operatives are."

"As it turns out, manifesting the illusion of the Devil you know happens to be a specialty of mine," Kreios said with a wink. "But what he sees, you will see, so we may do well to look sharp so that we'll recognize the individual when we meet him or her again."

"Let's get this over with." Sariah turned her back on Sells and her operating room and stalked the rest of the way over to the Council's conference table, unhooking her knives from her belt and laying them on the table.

"Simon suggested that I'd be better off naked in making the switch, but the knives are the only concession I'm going to make."

"Fair enough." Armaeus reached out, hesitating slightly until Sariah gave him a nod, then adjusted her so that she was at an angle to both him and the Devil. I felt the odd man out of this little triangle, and heat scored through me, warming my palms, an impotent need to offer help where none was needed.

"Oh, in that you are mistaken," the Magician said, talking in my mind. *"Your strength, your solidity is feeding Sariah's essence. Stay strong and stay angry for her."*

I could do that.

Sariah eyed the vial of Viktor dubiously, tilting it as the glittering energy swirled inside. "So I, like, suck it down?"

Armaeus nodded. "Inhale it, swallow it if you'd like, or keep it trapped at the top of your lungs, so long as you can talk."

"Talk," she muttered. "Now that'll be a trick. Good thing I have plenty of experience of inhaling without breathing."

With that, the Magician uncorked the vial, pressed it into Sariah's hands, and together they lifted it to her mouth. She deeply inhaled the contents, tossing her head back, and jerked with unexpected vigor. The Magician clamped his hand on her shoulder, shot his gaze to the Devil, and then Sariah's head came forward, her eyes blazing with the steely blue of Viktor Dal. The rest of her looked more or less the same, but her hair seemed to pull back more severely, while her cheekbones and jawline grew heavier, more angular, her body filling out beneath her clothes.

"James!" she barked as she stared into the Devil's face. "Report."

I scowled, but the Devil didn't hesitate. He spoke in a clipped Germanic accent. "You took a magic-enhanced knife to the sternum. It knocked you flat. You're fading in and out of consciousness. I'll get the others."

"Dubai? Hong Kong? Are we on schedule there?"

The Devil smiled grimly. "I'm afraid that's above my pay grade. You know that."

"Stupid," Viktor spat. "The strategy should be secret, not the tactics, not at this level."

The Devil shifted. His eyes going harder, he leaned closer to Sariah, capturing her full attention, and Viktor's as well. "What is it you most desire that is coming to pass, Viktor? What is the truth you have learned that will get you what you want?"

For a long, harrowing moment, I didn't think it would work, but then Viktor smiled, hard and cruel, transforming Sariah's face while not taking it over.

"One week, that's it. After six thousand years of preparation, it'll all go down in less than a few days. We've got explosives in every major religious center. Jerusalem has already been hit. That was a dry run. Angkor Wat was green-lighted as a second test after the House of Wands started their foolish riot. But Rome, Mecca, major cathedrals, synagogues, and houses of worship will be next—all the biggest and the best. Then come the government buildings spread out in a network. Financial trading centers. International banks. Every single major ally and enemy alike. They will all get hit, all at once, and no one will know why. The enemy is chaos, and out of that chaos will rise a defining order."

Sariah's eyes shone with Viktor's wonder, and I watched as the Devil's lips moved swiftly and without sound, as if he were receiving more information than Viktor was saying aloud. As far as I was concerned, I'd already learned everything I needed. The Shadow Court was stone-cold crazy, and we had less than a week to stop them...if we even could at this point.

"And what will your role be in this New World Order?" the Devil finally asked.

"I will rule," Viktor said, matter-of-factly. "All of Europe and half of Asia. The world will be rewritten, the maps will be remade. We will no longer be bound by those afraid of their own innate power, but guided by those whose power and might were meant to rule."

"Such chaos—there will be death," the Devil pressed, keeping his voice filled with awe. I didn't know who he seemed to be to Viktor now, but whoever it was, Viktor preened with pleasure at his tone.

"There better be death," Viktor agreed, and he became even more animated, his features beginning to take over Sariah's, to almost subsume her. "Two-thirds of the world's population will be scraped off the earth in the coming months. Those who remain will experience a Renaissance like they have never imagined, all while they are herded into pastures of our choosing. But the rule of law will be absolute, and magic will fuel that law. It will be glorious, and I have lived to see it."

Sariah convulsed, and I finally noticed the hysteria building in her eyes. At the Magician's glance, I stepped forward. As I neared, I flipped open my third eye, flinching at what I saw.

"*No,*" I breathed. Without waiting for anyone's permission, I grabbed Sariah by the shoulders, infusing my already tricked-up hands with as much heat and healing ability as I could muster. I plunged into her circuits, shocked to see that there was no longer one set of human energy, but two, the process that the Magician had introduced within her so much more successful than we could have imagined. I shoved against the Viktor energy with all my strength, forcing it back through her bloodstream, up to her heart, her lungs, through the thin membranes, and into her throat.

Sariah convulsed in my arms, then ripped herself free to choke out a gasp. Smoke poured from her throat, coalescing into a larger cloud than ever had been captured in the stoppered vial. It had form, substance, and then, impossibly, features began to form. Viktor's broad shoulders, then his functionally fit limbs, clad in the same military-cut ensemble in which he'd died. The angle of his chin sharpened and his thin, cruel smile caught the light.

With a cry of raw fury, Sariah spun toward the conference table, picked up her knives, and plunged back into the cloud.

Kreios, Armaeus, and I remained stock-still as Sariah attacked the ghost of almost Viktor, dancing through the heart of the thick, swirling mist, slicing and dicing until it thinned again, fading out completely. Then she staggered back, her lungs heaving, her hair ripped from her ponytail and plastered against her brow. She wiped her mouth with the back of her hand, then jerked her gaze toward me, her eyes wet with fury, resolve—and deep soul-shattering pain.

"That was for Mom," she muttered.

Then she collapsed.

12

I knew the moment that Sariah came back to full consciousness. She tensed, her body going on full alert, though her eyes didn't flicker open. I reached out and grasped her hand. The loose cuffs of Justice that had been draped over her wrists, which had engaged when she'd violently convulsed, now fell away completely, leaving her free.

"You fucking tied me to the bed?" she groaned, her voice a rough whisper. "Harsh."

"Apparently, having the essence of a megalomaniac shooting through your bloodstream had, as the Magician would say, some unforeseen complications," I informed her drily. "We thought you'd fainted, but when we moved to get you, you came up swinging, and as it turns out, you can pack quite a punch when you want to. You cracked the Devil before he saw it coming and set him back on his ass. Three of him, as it happened. His surprise made him split apart."

Sariah's eyes had popped open during this recitation, and color slowly flowed back into her face.

"Really? Or are you shitting me to make me feel better?"

I squeezed her hand. "Okay, you did hit him, you did knock him back, but he didn't split apart."

"Something to shoot for," Sariah said, laying her head back against her pillow. She didn't shake off my hand, so I kept my grasp firm but easy on hers.

"You thought the Magician was going to die, didn't you?" I asked her. "That's why you came hustling over when Simon told you about their plans. You thought that Eshe's prediction was going to come true, that the Devil would do something to kill Armaeus."

"I don't think he's going to know he's doing it," Sariah said, glancing away. "I keep waiting for that fear to lift, for every choice made to result in a new future. But it still hangs on my heart."

"Yeah, but you know that becomes its own problem, right? I mean, Eshe has the power of the sight, and I'm not taking anything away from that, but sometimes the sight can become a self-fulfilling prophecy, especially if you hold on to the predictions even though you've made dramatic changes to the situation they're supposed to be predicting. You don't know that she would see the same thing now."

"But I'd feel it if something changed," Sariah said stubbornly. "I'd feel it."

Sudden insight struck me. "What did you feel with Viktor in your mind like that?"

She shrugged. "He wasn't only in my mind. I felt him crawling through my skin, weighing down my bones. I felt him squeeze my heart and knock against my lungs like he was exploring a new playground that he'd never expected to get a chance to play in. He didn't care how he got there. I'm pretty sure he never actually knew he died, or had almost died. Or whatever the hell you want to call it when everything you are can be summed up as the contents of a science-class beaker. He knew it was his right to be there and to boast to whoever asked him questions. I don't know what he was saying, actually. Did it work?" Her focus came back around to me sharply. "Did he give up the goods?"

"Oh, yeah," I said. "According to Viktor, in less than a week's time, an entire network of explosions are going to go off in every major religious base and in several government buildings as well, along with scientific and financial headquarters that have been carefully vetted for the purpose. If Viktor is to be believed, some of these devices have been in place for decades. Switched out as the technology gets better, but operational and covering the entire world."

"No shit," Sariah huffed a laugh as she repositioned herself on the bed. "And do we believe him? I mean, I know that was the whole point of this little charade, but that all seems a little extra."

I snorted. "It seems a lot extra. But to answer your question, yeah, we do. Some of the locations we have our own contacts in, and in the last few hours, we've been able to verify the existence of incendiary devices similar in style to the ones we recovered in Angkor Wat."

"Did you remove them?" she asked.

I shook my head. "As it turns out, that isn't the game. The game is to figure out how to neutralize them in place. We'll never get to all the locations, and if even a third of them go off the way it's planned, you're looking at international chaos."

"Always did love me some international chaos, especially if they serve it with pancakes," Sariah murmured, her head falling back on the pillow. "Pancakes would be good right about now."

I wasn't willing to let her get off the hook quite so easily, though. "That merge seriously messed you up. I don't suppose Eshe also passed on an oracular vision for you that you were going to deliberately try to kill yourself? 'Cause I'd kind of like to know if that's going to be a thing."

Sariah smiled at that, fatigue making her features soften, and met my gaze. "No. I did get a vision of myself looking older. Like ten or fifteen years older? Walking down a street I didn't recognize. Not all that surprising, I haven't been out that long. But I wasn't expecting that."

I knew Sariah well enough that I understood her dilemma. She didn't know if I would live, but she knew she would. In this case, it wasn't the right thing to tell her everything was going to be okay, because that was the problem. "I don't think there's any such malady as anticipatory survivor guilt, you know. That's not a thing," I pointed out, as gently sarcastic as I could be.

She chuckled a little wearily, her eyelids drooping. "Well, it should be a thing. Maybe that's what I end up doing. I should go into therapy. Become a postapocalyptic life coach."

She was fading fast, but I couldn't quite let her go.

"So is there anything else? I mean...anything you want to talk about?"

"He knew," Sariah said, her eyes sharpening as she fought for focus. "Back then. Viktor knew you were getting close—I guess we were getting close—to figuring out that he was the one behind the child kidnappings we were working with Officer Brody."

Her voice had taken on a lighter, unfinished quality, as she echoed the sound of my own voice when I'd been seventeen years old, working with a brash young rookie for the Memphis Police Department, part of the department's outreach service to jolly along the local kid psychic who'd caught the community's interest as she insisted she could help find a group of lost children. I'd been the star of that show, and while my mom had wanted me to have that limelight, she'd craved some of it to shine on her as well. She put herself out as a psychic of equal ability, fishing for interest. She'd found it. The wrong kind of interest, sadly.

"Viktor didn't know whether or not Mom had any real ability," Sariah continued dully. "But he couldn't run the risk. He had two psychics after him, after all. Even though we probably weren't serious threats, we could have stupided our way into screwing up his plans. That was no good. He didn't kill Mom, not with his own hands. But he ordered it done. Like he ordered the explosion of our house done, only for that, he knocked it up a few more notches, getting some help from some operatives in the arcane black market, who said they had the spirit of the dragon upon them. They weren't bullshitting him."

"Llyr," I said quietly, flashing back to the moment the explosion had ripped across the scrubby lot where our cheap, barely-hanging-together house had sat. I'd looked back at the brightest point of the flare and had seen the ancient dragon god opening its jaws, roaring its flame.

I had run away from that fire. But a part of me, maybe the best part of me, had peeled away and run back toward it. And I'd lost her for years.

"Hey," Sariah said, and I realized it had been my turn to let my eyelids droop shut. I blinked them open now several times, grateful that the moisture building behind them hadn't fallen.

"Neither one of us was in for a joyride after that," she said. "I ended up in Hell, you ended up in an RV gang of retirees. I'm not sure which situation was worse."

I coughed a laugh, and Sariah smiled wearily as well.

"You gotta take care of yourself, Sara. I mean it..." Her

eyes drifted shut again. I watched her for a long time, then heard movement at the door.

I turned as Doctor Sells stepped inside. Behind her was the Magician.

"You obviously want to know if Sariah will recover completely, but she is a unique patient, and for me, that's saying something," the doctor advised briskly, moving forward to the monitors beside Sariah's bed and pursing her lips as she studied their readouts. "She has powerful Connected abilities, but the most powerful of those skills are borrowed."

"She can fight, and she can kill at a level way higher than normal," I countered. "She didn't get that from me. And I'm not sure that it's fair to say she borrowed those skills. They're too consistent, too much a part of her personality."

"Unless she did borrow them from you, just not recently," Dr. Sells replied, with the same kind of scientific curiosity that so often gilded the Magician's words when he tried to figure me out. No wonder these two got along so well.

"Well, nice of me to section off all the objectionable parts and give them to the other guy," I muttered, but Dr. Sells stepped past me, running a scanner over Sariah's head, her chest.

"I suspect she would say the same thing," the doctor observed mildly, then studied her screen briefly. "She's recovering much faster. You did good work to heal her. Perhaps not surprising considering your close connection."

"I didn't really heal her. I pushed Viktor out from where he didn't belong."

She pursed her lips. "That little experiment was ill-advised and far more dangerous than was reasonable. Taking on the essence of another being, particularly one that's ascended to the Council, isn't a good idea." She said this last part very slowly and distinctly, as if Armaeus and I had been called into the principal's office for misbehavior.

Armaeus winked at me.

Sells waved off any reply I might have made and skewered me with a hard look. "She did so willingly, and I know all of you well enough to know that you won't listen to the voice of reason in a moment of great need, so listen to me now so you can make better choices down the line. Don't do that again. Don't let *her* do it again, and don't think about doing it yourself. As hard as it is for you to accept it, even gods have their limits. If you're going to make a gesture, you need to make it on a grand scale—the more intimate and personal, the more likely it will backfire."

"Grand scale is more his thing than mine," I muttered, tipping my head at the Magician.

She glanced at Armaeus. "You were right to help me set up this bay. With me here, I was able to stop the formation of neural pathways that were remapping or subverting Sariah's own biology."

"You what?" I asked. "What does that mean?"

She swung her gaze back to me. "It means that you were playing with levels of power we know nothing about, or, I should say, *knew* nothing about. Sariah will rest now and will gradually forget the violation of Viktor's possession. But you've opened up a door in her mind that may not be as easily closed as we would hope. You'll need to monitor that."

I blinked in alarm. I'd done it again, apparently—healed someone into a better, stronger version of themselves…and in Sariah's case, that could have serious repercussions, because she was already put together sketchy. I opened my mouth, trying to form the questions now banging around in my brain—*what had I done to Sariah, specifically? What could I do to other Connecteds... What should I do?*—but it looked like the good doctor's time for me today was done. She glanced at her watch in the time-honored gesture of doctors everywhere, and Armaeus nodded, drawing my attention.

"We've not been idle as you've been tending to Sariah. We've developed a plan of action to forestall the Shadow Court's attack and already begun laying its groundwork. I need to fill you in."

Before we reached the door, my phone rang, the sound so unexpected that I stared down at my body for a second, confused. The phone blared again, and I finally figured out what the offending noise was, pulling the device out of my jeans back pocket and squinting down at the screen.

"It's Brody," I said, and I conjured up the detective in my mind. "He can't already know about Sariah. They can't still be that connected. This is something else."

Armaeus chuckled. "Then perhaps you should answer the phone, Miss Wilde."

"Right." I swiped the phone on and held it to my ear. "What's wrong?"

"What isn't wrong?" Brody snapped back. "Please tell me you're in Vegas or you can get back here like right now. We've got a Dixie Quinn problem."

13

The GPS coordinates that Brody provided wouldn't have sounded familiar on my best day, and the additional information left me totally clueless.

"The Bright Rock Church of God?" I protested as Brody clicked off the line and I turned to the Magician. He lifted his brows, but shook his head. He didn't know the place either.

Fortunately, Armaeus didn't have my problem with needing to know exactly where I was headed in order to get there. Whatever plans he'd made for our morning were put temporarily on hold as he swept me into his embrace and we disintegrated, appearing moments later on the stretch of hot, dusty road that turned onto a paved boulevard. That street bisected two square plots of perfectly tended grass and flowers, the landscaping dominated by a series of white-painted stucco buildings, each of them two stories tall and topped with solar panels. From the name Brody gave us, I expected there to be a church on the grounds, but it looked more like an office park.

Brody was off talking to a huddled group of mostly

Hispanic and Caucasian men and women, the majority adults except for a few toddlers clinging to people I assumed were their parents.

"What's Brody doing here?" I wondered aloud, while the Magician studied the whitewashed, terracotta-fringed buildings with interest. Even with the good detective's particular specialty within the LVMPD, an evangelical church really shouldn't have hit his dance card.

"The Bright Rock Church of God is tied to no particular sect of the Christian faith, but instead styles itself as a church for all true believers," Armaeus advised me. "It's organized and categorized for tax purposes as a religious institution, but it does no advertising, maintains no social media presence, has no set hours of worship, and is self-sustaining through donations from its membership and its energy-saving approach to building maintenance and gardening."

He waved at the solar panels and then two buildings farther away from the main set, a green silo and what might have been a greenhouse on steroids. It was too far away to tell, but I didn't doubt Armaeus. His Arcana Wiki skills were strong.

Brody broke away from the huddled knot of humanity and headed for us. His entire body projected grimdark well before I could see the set expression on his face. The Las Vegas Metropolitan Police Department detective looked like a long stretch of bad road this morning. His hair, always rumpled, stood out in spikes, clear evidence that he had been running his hands through it, most likely with exasperation. His eyes were sunken, his skin pale beneath the heavy tan that working in Las Vegas almost assured for all the members of the force. He scowled as he approached us, deepening the wrinkles that bracketed his mouth, then radiated out from his eyes in jagged spikes.

"I don't suppose either of you knows anything about this facility? Because it sure would make my job a hell of a lot easier."

The Magician lifted his hand, and I was surprised to see it held a bottle of water, which he passed to Brody as he reached us. Brody blinked down at it.

"Do I want to know?" Brody asked as he unscrewed the top and sniffed the bottle.

"You don't," Armaeus assured him. "Drink it anyway."

It was a testament to how weary Brody had to be that he shrugged and took a deep swig. I had no idea what else the bottle held besides water, but if it helped Brody's obvious fatigue, I was all for it.

As Brody downed the drink, Armaeus continued. "I'm not familiar with nor affiliated to this operation. Its doors have been open, however, for approximately fifteen years, and I presume its tax records are up to date. All that to say, I'm surprised you were unfamiliar with it."

"Yeah, interesting thing about that. Like a lot of these kinds of places, this one falls into the camp of 'don't ask, don't tell.' We don't know how they get their followers. We don't get any complaints, so we don't care. There's enough trouble going around Clark County without having to go look for it, and this is all out here right on the edge of being irrelevant. The key part of that story is *no complaints*. Concerns have been bubbling up for the last few years about this place, mostly from disgruntled family members whose distant relatives were, shall we say, sent to the church by well-meaning or not-so-well-meaning immediate family, never to be heard from again, but it's never risen to the point of contacting the authorities."

"Sent to the church?" I asked. "So this is some kind of cult?"

"From what I'm gathering, it's more of a traditional-values birthing center, an all-too popular destination for the devout to offload daughters who find themselves about to become unwed mothers. The pitch goes that they welcome in the female, mostly young, mostly uneducated, but not always. They feed, clothe, and house her, and provide top-level medical care until the baby is born, then assist her with adoption protocols if she doesn't have the means or the interest in providing adequate support for the child. It's a scenario that's played out in Christian communities—religious communities of all faiths, frankly—worldwide. I even touched base with some of my contacts at Interpol about it, given Bright Rock's reach. They know of the church, but they said unless there's a specific, verifiable complaint, churches don't rate much investigation. Generally speaking, there's nothing to look at here."

"Except that creepy building," I said, sparing another glance for the main building. "It looks empty."

"It is empty," Brody said. "Its operations have been suspended for a quote-unquote renovation, while staff and patients—or guests, as they like to call them—have been moved to an undisclosed location. But that story doesn't quite track with the handful of family members who've been trying to reach their relatives. They believe that everybody is still on-site but underground or dead...or, my personal favorite, they've been turned into ghosts."

"I begin to understand why you were brought in on this one," I said wryly, eyeing Brody.

Brody snorted. As a homicide detective of the LVMPD, he was a capable lawman in his own right, but he did carry a very particular résumé. Namely, that he'd started his career in Memphis as Officer Brody, shepherding the potential public relations nightmare of a teen psychic and her fame-hungry mother who'd pledged to help the police find missing children. I'd discovered Brody serving in Las Vegas when I first came to the city as an artifact hunter working for the Arcana Council, and over the years had leaned quite a bit on him, both for local issues and when his connections with Interpol helped me navigate some international hot water. He was good people, and there weren't enough of those willing to help the Connecteds.

More to the point, that willingness to help had brought him to Dixie Quinn's door more than a few times, and they'd eventually fallen into—and then out of—a relationship. He never talked much about it, but it'd happened.

"How does Dixie play in?" I asked.

"Not in any way that's going to make you happy." He sighed. "Apparently, according to the group assembled here, she's served as a regular procurer of disadvantaged young women in need of the Bright Rock Church's highly specific services. With the added excitement that the young women she's brought into the fold generally possess some measure of psychic ability. Depending on their family orientation, that's sometimes a very bad thing, but interestingly enough, not always. In fact, I'd say a good third of the people who make up our little gang of crusaders"—he hitched a thumb toward the huddled group who were eyeing their police escort with open hostility—"maintain that their female family members were highly psychically sensitive. Mediums, channelers, light healers, if not operational, then well on their way before they became pregnant. I've seen more TikTok videos of crystal healing than any one person should have to endure."

"How does any of that track?" I asked. "Why would

anybody trust Dixie to shepherd their daughters through a baby shop?"

Brody shrugged, the move made more impressive given the slump to his shoulders. "Gotta go with the obvious answer on this one. We may not trust her much anymore, but Dixie is a known figure among Connecteds, with a solid rep. She's female, she's got money, and she's got connections. Whether you're poor and don't know a way out, or you're well-off and want the best for your somewhat peculiar daughter and her new baby, I could see it happening."

"She's what gamers would call 'cheerful evil,'" I muttered.

"Something like that." Brody scratched his chin, raking his nails through the heavy growth of stubble there. "We'd never know about this place, we *haven't* known about this place, except they started screwing up. This whole business with the ghosts and shit, that gets people riled up in these sort of hospital situations, especially one that has religious overtones. Nobody likes a ghost, I don't care who you are."

I considered that. He wasn't wrong. "So we go in?" I pointed to the weirdly plain main building.

He smiled grimly. "We don't have SWAT capabilities to burn, and I'm fresh out of paranormal-investigator types. So yeah, we go in. Best case scenario, we see a perfectly tidy exit with a forwarding address to somewhere that makes sense. But I gotta tell you, we've already hit up all the local hospitals and birthing centers for a good hundred-mile radius. If they moved these people, they did it fast, efficient, and with a security and secrecy that's a little suspect in and of itself."

"You think they're still inside?" I asked. "But why? Why go underground?"

"I have no good goddamned idea." Brody sighed.

"You were right to call us," Armaeus said, and with a wave of his hand, he changed our outfits into sensible CSI-style dark trousers and jackets. He conjured up aviator sunglasses for all of us as well, which I thought was a nice touch. Together, we turned back toward the building, and I was able to scan the assembled group of parents and relatives from behind my sunglasses. With the added sight of my third eye, I could tell a number of them had psychic ability, some quite extensive.

"Um, is there a reason why we're not using any of these Connected boots on the ground to help search?" I asked Brody.

"No," he said. "I mean yes. There's a very good reason. Namely that these are *civilians* and this is an unsecured building. And I don't want that kind of grief landing on my head before my fourth cup of coffee today."

"Gotcha." I couldn't fault his logic, but I also couldn't deny the level of ability I was picking up across the courtyard. "They think I'm somebody official, right? Maybe I should go and say something polite and official-like."

"Sara..." Brody began warily.

I waved him off. "Go find something with the Magician. I'll catch up."

Ignoring his groan, I jogged the short distance to the assembled group, because it seemed like jogging was something that official people did. I wasn't surprised to see them break into distinct subgroups. Those without psychic ability pressed forward, eager, almost desperate. Those with psychic ability were no idiots. They hung back, knowing that something was up with me, even if they didn't know exactly what.

I kept my attention on this latter group as I riffled through the electrical signatures of the nearer group. They were simple, ordinary humans, filled with concern and anxiety—everything you would expect from distraught family members. The psychic group was different, though. They were *livid*. Not at me, but at life.

"Did you know?" One of the Connecteds, a middle-aged woman with dark hair and a weathered face, confronted me with a glare. "Did you know what they were doing in here? Did the cops know?"

I had to recalibrate quickly, having assumed she was asking me from a psychic perspective.

"No, ma'am, we did not. We tend to leave religious groups alone as long as we can, unless something is brought to our attention."

"Religious groups," she said, disgusted. "That woman is no nun, I can tell you that right now. I knew she was trouble back when I came to Vegas forty years ago."

I blinked at her. "What?"

"Dixie Quinn. She presents like she's a sweet young thing, but I don't forget a face and I don't forget an aura. Auras can shift and develop as you get older, but they always have the same basic fingerprint. And I'm really good at reading those prints."

It occurred to me that poking this particular hornets' nest might not have been my best move, but I couldn't let the conversation go. "You met Dixie Quinn forty years ago, and she looks the same now?" I clarified.

"I can do better than that," she countered, her lips curving into a hard smile. "My great-aunt met her in the fifties too. She may act like she's some low-level psychic, all 'aw shucks, I'm just here to help out the locals,' but she's no good. And when I heard my sister's grandbaby got pulled into some stupid-ass church group in Vegas, I knew. I *knew*. I couldn't stay hidden in Lake Tahoe anymore. I had to come up and see what was what. Now you're here. A cop, sure. But something more than a cop, I think."

"Yes, well...thanks." I turned my attention to the other family members, who'd finally started drawing close. "I appreciate you all advocating on behalf of your loved ones. I want you to know that we're going to do everything we can"—I slid my gaze back to the woman—"and I do mean *everything*, to get your loved ones home. Ma'am, I know Detective Brody would very much like to speak with you about your insights into Miss Quinn. She's a person of interest in this matter."

The woman snorted derisively. "Person of interest. What I heard, she married my great-niece and her husband, treated them nice as pie, helped get them set up in an apartment. Everything was fine until my great-niece got pregnant, then she practically leapt on them."

I nodded, but the sick feeling in the pit of my stomach was turning into a ball of ice. "Another piece of information that I'm sure Detective Rooks will appreciate. First, however, we'll do our part to find everyone's loved ones. You've given him names, photographs, everything you have?"

The group mumbled a collective assent, and I asked a few more questions, though my mind was churning with the reality of what I'd discovered here. Dixie Quinn had looked the same seventy years ago as she did now, living in the shadow of the Arcana Council. Dixie Quinn was orchestrating a birthing center for Connected babies. Dixie Quinn...was the Star. All the conversations we'd had flashed through my mind, all the laughter shared, the conflict. I'd thought she was a low-level Connected. A little squirrelly, but not really all that interesting. Definitely not dangerous.

But she was the Star. One of the most ancient one-time

members of the Arcana Council, who'd been playing me for a fool for as long as I'd known her.

Head spinning as I finished my conversation with the family members, I turned on my heel, stopping abruptly when I realized the woman with the dark hair had fallen into step with me.

"I can't read your aura, which makes you stronger than most folks," she murmured, low enough so only I could hear her. "Find my great-niece. I beg you."

She pressed a small square of photo paper into my hand, the kind you didn't much see any more in this digital age. But I glanced down at it, taking in the young, dark-haired Native American girl with laughing dark eyes, a wide smile, and full cheeks complete with dimples. Her eyes sparked with Connected power so strong it practically leapt out from the photograph. I glanced at the woman, startled.

"Yeah. I couldn't read her aura either," she said.

14

By the time I caught up with the Magician and Brody, they'd made it past the cheerful, inviting foyer and sitting room with its round reception counter fronted with a conspicuous absence of electronics.

"They clear the place out?" I asked as Brody searched through the cabinets.

"Honestly? I get the impression they didn't keep any electronics here at all, ever," he said. "There's no computer intake system, nothing that went to the cloud, no record of any kind. There's no Wi-Fi station in the building, and all the electricity seems to run off its own grid from the solar panels outside and the wind farm at the back of the property."

"Yeah, because being cut off from the rest of the world when you're going to have a baby isn't the creepiest thing ever," I said drily.

He snorted. "I definitely get a hinky feeling about this place, and it doesn't have to do with its stated purpose, although that's bad enough. Can you feel it?"

He asked the question to both of us, but the Magician fielded it.

"Demons," Armaeus said succinctly.

That stopped both me and Brody. "Seriously?" Brody asked, straightening slowly and shutting the cabinet. He took a second before moving to the next bank of shelves.

I glanced around, but my demon-detection system was clearly not up to standard.

The Magician nodded, his gaze fixed on a far-off, demon-filled vista. "With the recent incursion of demons that proliferated after the closing of the veil and the retreat of the gods, my study of their activities increased. This is not the first time their paths have intersected with Dixie Quinn or, perhaps better stated, the Star." Clearly he'd been listening in on my conversation outside.

"The what?" Brody asked, swiveling his glance between us. "Like, you mean, one of you guys? An Arcana Council member?"

"A long time ago." Armaeus nodded. "She's no longer affiliated with the Council, but she has doubtless remained close to us, in one guise or another, since the Council was first formed."

I lifted my hand to pinch the bridge of my nose. "Freaking great," I muttered, though I suspected Armaeus was right. Hell, Dixie probably had been following them around for centuries without them ever knowing it. From what I knew of her, she'd get a particular kick out of that—even while fuming that she wasn't getting the attention she deserved. That undercurrent of anger had never been far from the surface with her, and it was easy to see why. If she revealed who she was—she'd have been toast. She wasn't strong enough to defy the whole Council. But now? With the Shadow Court setting its sights on the Arcana Council and ready to blow up half the planet? Oh, yeah. She'd be making her move.

"Dixie has utilized demons in a manner far more involved than the witches' covens who have long held sway over their number, albeit in a very specific and targeted manner," the Magician continued. "But her use for them here is different, their impact on a larger scale. Michael's efforts with the Syx in containing the threat of demons have obscured the greater problem."

"Do I want to know what the greater problem is?" Brody asked, rifling through another drawer.

"You do. It's the introduction of the demon horde into society," the Magician said.

I made a face as Brody muttered something dark. "Like, polite society, you mean?" I asked. "I can't imagine employing demons as domestics is going to go over all that well." Then again, I'd seen demons in some pretty dark places, and Armaeus's next words tracked with those memories.

"Primarily, they'll be used for all the jobs that humans won't do and machines can't," he said. "But I suspect they also will be used for enforcement, like they are here."

"Enforcement," I echoed, looking around the cheerful space. "At a birthing center."

"Jesus, Mary, and Joseph, you people," Brody muttered. He twitched his hand to unbutton his jacket, giving him better access to his sidearm. I suspected this wasn't the time for me to point out that humans couldn't kill demons, but it certainly underscored his point.

"Okay, let's put the demons on ice for a second," he said briskly. "Where are the patients? The staff? Where are the workers? If we've got a demon janitorial detail, that's great, but where did the rest of them go?"

Armaeus turned to me. “What do you see?”

I flipped open my third eye, rendering the space around me into two layers, one that was visible to my regular eyesight, and the second a series of electric circuitry, having less to do with the power system in this building and more to do with the subtle variation of the flow of energy between all living things, the force that could be bent to the purposes of magic.

Not surprisingly, it was absolute chaos. Electrical currents skittered and jittered in all directions, gradually increasing in force the farther back from the reception area I gazed.

“Through there,” I said, indicating a set of double doors. I gestured to either side of the room, where additional corridors led away from the main foyer. “Those other hallways go to interview rooms, but there’s nothing going on there right now. All the action is through the main gates.”

“Then that’s where we go,” Brody said.

We set off, our attempts at caution seeming foolish in the dead silence of the building, but as I approached the doors, the Magician breathed out a slow, steadying sigh.

“There is darkness here,” he said quietly. “Some would say evil.”

“Well, we’re fresh out of Warrens to fight this shit, so try to be more specific if fucking demons come screaming out of nowhere,” Brody retorted. We all tensed as the corridor’s lights flickered on, apparently triggered by the opening doors.

“Interesting, they didn’t cut the power,” Brody continued, more levelly. “Maybe they weren’t planning on leaving for too long?”

“Or maybe they weren’t concerned by what we would

find," Armaeus countered. "The energy is more organized now that we're past the barrier, wouldn't you say?"

"Yeah," I agreed. But I also understood what the Magician meant about the evil. There was a sense of oppression in the quiet hallway, the weirdly echoing sound of our footsteps making the place seem abandoned. The rooms all had windowed doors, but as I looked in, I couldn't see more than the edge of the bed. I tried to push open the nearest door, but it was locked. Before I attempted my own psychic lock-picking skills, the Magician murmured a spell, and a series of snicks and clicks echoed down the hallway.

Brody lifted his brows, and the Magician smiled. "Each of us should take a room."

I stepped into the second room on the left while Brody took the room opposite me and the Magician headed farther down the corridor. The place was empty, of course, the bed made, but there were signs that it had recently been occupied. A live flower sat in a small pot on the stand next to the window, and books on child care mixed with popular magazines were stacked neatly beside the bed. I walked deeper into the room, peering around. There were clothes in the closet, tunics and soft trousers, along with a few pairs of slip-on shoes. The drawers held underwear and pajamas, all made of soft material. The room was bright, even cheerful, but as I glanced back toward the door and opened my third eye once again, I froze.

The walls were not walls. They were windows, portals. Fire flickered through one, utter darkness through another, and through a third, I spied a roiling mosh pit of twisting forms, looking like a cauldron of bodies in a constant spin cycle. I gasped and must have said something aloud, because Brody shouted from the other room, his footsteps vaguely cutting across my senses.

"*Sara,*" he shouted, but I heard his voice only dimly. A mirror on the far wall caught my attention, and the girl who stood in it was the girl whose picture I'd tucked into my pocket.

"What are they doing here?" I asked—or thought I asked. "Why are they trying to scare these girls to death?"

"Sara, tell me what you see. I can't help you if you don't tell me what you see," Brody said, sounding far more urgent than necessary. Then another figure was beside me. Not the cool, calm, collected persona of the Magician, which I half expected, but the bright, smiling young girl who had lived in this room. She was standing beside me now, her smile almost infectious as she pointed to our joint reflections in the mirror.

"You can *see* me," she blurted, sounding relieved. "I can't leave, though. I won't leave. Not while they have Jolene. Tell Mara I'm sorry, okay?"

"Where are you?" I managed, my words sounding thick and garbled to my own ears.

"I'm safe," she assured me. "I'm one of the lucky ones, useful to them. They won't get rid of me quite yet. But will you tell her? Do you promise you'll tell her?"

"Do not agree to anything," the Magician's voice sounded in the back of my head as the girl smiled at me so earnestly, her eyes wide and bright.

"No," I told the girl automatically. "No, I won't."

"Sara—Sara, who are you talking to?" Brody asked.

But I had done the damage. At my rejection, the girl's face crumpled, first in dismay, but then it went further, her plump skin flattening against her skull and then seeming to cave into it, her cheeks hollowing out, her mouth opening in a macabre expression of surprise. Her skin adhered tightly to her body, then burned away, revealing a shocking mask of metal instead of bone and sparking circuits where there should have been muscle. Then she threw back her head and laughed, a horrifying cackle. The movement of her head drew the rest of her body back in a grotesque arc, and she somersaulted through the mirror freakishly fast and was gone.

The portals all disappeared, and I found myself once more surrounded by a perfectly cheerful hospital room. I slumped, falling into Brody's arms as the Magician appeared in the doorway.

"There's more down the hallway, every room presenting similar portals into what the young women staying here would likely describe as Hell," he said. "Their sole source of safety lay in remaining in these rooms, not straying too far from their beds unless someone was with them, and avoiding the mirrors."

"A total loss of self, loss of identity, loss of the life inside them," I said, my words hushed as Brody helped me regain my feet.

"More than that." The Magician gestured down the hallway. "I'll show you."

As soon as I stepped out of the hospital room, I stood straighter and felt better. "Did all the patients see this?" I asked, trying to shake off the adrenaline surge.

"Well, I didn't see anything," Brody said, "but I'm kind of thinking that I got the better end of the deal on that. What was it?"

I outlined what I saw, and Brody's face tightened. "Kind of standard Hollywood effects for Hell, wouldn't you say?" he commented. "Probably each playing to the girls' own biases and backgrounds?"

"Almost certainly," the Magician agreed, striding past the long stream of doorways. I glanced back, trying to count.

There had to be at least thirty hospital-style rooms along this central corridor off the stubby T-top of the reception area. The doors at the end of the corridor were doubly reinforced but opened with a snick like elevator doors at Armaeus's uplifted hand.

"Operating suites," he said, and while I steeled myself for yet more horrors beyond, the mood here was much lighter. Warm, almost inviting, despite the sterility that a hospital operating suite would require.

"Is this legal?" I asked, moderately horrified despite the tidiness of the suite. "I mean, shouldn't birth be regulated in some way? Shouldn't you have licensed doctors performing them?"

"Nope. Once consent is given, there are any number of medical procedures that can take place," Brody said. "As long as nobody gets too particular about verifying data and checking licenses, it's all good."

"But you'll note the lack of portals here, and also the lack of trauma in the atmosphere," Armaeus put in. "These operating suites were never intended to be used."

"Oh, for fuck's sake," Brody muttered. "You're telling me this is strictly for PR?"

"Indeed," the Magician said. "The real action takes place elsewhere. Note the change of energy once you cast your sight to the elevator bay, over there."

I blew out a breath, clicked open my third eye again as I glanced across the room where he pointed, and my heart rate jacked. Chaos lay beyond the elevator bays at the far end of the suite—screams, horror.

"That's where they took them," I said. "There's a whole other level, isn't there?"

"In more than one meaning of the word." Armaeus turned to Brody. "You'll want to have a specialized team come out and collect the family members outside. We need them off the premises."

Brody grimaced. "I have a feeling it's going to be hard for them to be willing to go."

"Only those with true psychic ability. We'll have a representative work with them. Danae, I think."

I lifted my brows. I sometimes forgot that the mistress of the House of Swords was a witch, because Danae was such an innately powerful woman. But it did make sense to bring her in, especially since she was based in Las Vegas.

"Danae? Seriously?" Brody rubbed his jaw. "You're going all in on the demon angle, aren't you?"

"In a moment, you'll see why. Make the calls, detective." Armaeus glanced at me. "I've already summoned Danae. She understands what we're facing here, so she will prepare those family members appropriately before joining us."

Brody pulled his phone out of his pocket and turned away to make the call to his department, while the Magician continued.

"The depth of this operation is disturbing on several levels," he said, gesturing down the hallway. "The demon incursion we're facing should not be this strong. They shouldn't have been able to move this far, this fast without the Archangel's intervention."

"Well, Michael does have the Syx on the job," I said. "Maybe we should summon them?"

Armaeus tilted his head, considering. "The Enforcers have been working around the clock and are uniquely motivated to help. The price of one's own redemption, it seems, can never be too high. But I sense patterns upon patterns converging, and I fear the result."

"Once more for the cheap seats?" I asked as Brody returned to us, his jaw set, his face tight.

"I got people on the way. We've got some on scene already, of course. They reported the arrival of Danae." Brody shot a quick glance at the Magician. "She told them she was a trauma therapist, on loan from the state to help people process their emotions."

I snorted. Danae was many things, but a therapist wasn't one of them. Then again, whatever worked. "Did they buy it?"

He shrugged. "Honestly, we're up to our asses in calls this morning. We'll take any help we can get. Anyway, what were you saying when I came up? Because we've got about thirty minutes before all hell breaks loose."

"We've got less time than that," Armaeus said, gesturing to the elevator. "Brace yourself."

The doors snicked open. No elevator bay lay beyond them, merely an empty hole.

Brody frowned, then leaned over, peering down. "You think it's stuck at the bottom?"

"I think it has been effectively disabled, if it ever existed in the first place," the Magician said. "More than likely, when the young women were brought here to give birth, their transport was a little more sophisticated in some ways and quite ancient in others. They were taken below by a demon escort."

I made a face. "I'd think that probably wouldn't do too well for their heart rate readings. I've never had a kid, but I kind of think that wouldn't be an ideal situation for a woman in labor."

"Almost certainly these were not conscious births," the Magician agreed. "The mothers would have been far too traumatized. You're quite correct. I sense no panic from humans in this space, do you?"

I glanced around, but I had more than enough panic for

the rest of my race. "Sorry. Latent panic sensory identification is next semester for me."

"So we jump?" Brody asked wearily. "We're going to jump, aren't we?"

The Magician nodded. "In a manner of speaking. There is a curious ward in this room depressing my magic, but it doesn't exist in the bay. So if you would be willing to indulge me..."

Before we could argue otherwise, Armaeus wrapped one arm around each of us, then pulled us into the elevator shaft. For a single heart-stopping second, we fell...

Armaeus poofed us into nothingness.

15

We reappeared in a corridor that was mostly disorienting because it was so normal looking. Long, white walls, white tiled, with white ceiling panels that featured inset lighting and cameras. It could have been any hospital corridor, anywhere.

Brody stepped forcefully away from the Magician. "I absolutely *hate* it when you do that," he groused, but the Magician paid him no attention.

"There's no magical dead zone in play here," Armaeus confirmed. "Bear that in mind."

"We're beneath where we were, though, right?" I asked. "Like, we haven't gone anywhere but down. Why in the hell would they put a place like this underground? It looks totally normal."

"Patient management, staff management." The Magician waved off the question. "We are operating under the illusion of invisibility, though we are corporeal. The cameras cannot track us, but any infrared or heat-sensing devices could. We should assume that somebody knows we are here, if they don't know exactly who we are."

"And you seriously think Dixie is behind all this?" Brody protested. "She's seriously capable of this level of crazy?"

The Magician hesitated, then nodded, as if he was having a hard time believing it himself. Score #273 for Dixie's mad acting skills. "We should also proceed with the assumption that Dixie Quinn is far more than how she originally presented herself."

I sent him a sharp glance, knowing that he had seen what I'd seen, heard what I'd heard up top regarding Dixie.

Brody's jaw hardened. "Seriously. I fucking hate you people sometimes," he muttered, but I understood the edge in his voice.

It wasn't us. It wasn't Dixie. It was *him*. Brody Rooks, a smart cop, a good guy, an open-minded protector of the weak and vulnerable, had been used and duped by someone with stronger psychic abilities than he had. It felt like a cheat, or at least a skewing of the system. And this was why outing the psychics of the world was going to prove such a problem. Some people would embrace them, some people would reject them, but everyone who didn't have psychic abilities or didn't know how to access them would be experiencing FOMO for ESP. Nobody ever liked to be the odd man out.

"There's no one down here," the Magician murmured. "There's very little sound."

"No conversation, maybe, but there's definitely something going on down here." Brody lifted a hand. "Electricity of some sort. You can hear the hum."

There were a few doors in the hallway, all of them unlocked, leading to empty operating bays stocked with equipment and supplies. Brody ducked into one of them and rifled through plastic-wrapped equipment. "These are dated recently. This is a working facility. Clean and scrubbed down, no dust."

We headed to the end of the quarter where it teed off, with double doors on either side of the short stubby hallway. One bay of doors was surrounded by green glowing panels, the other with red.

"They haven't shut it down," the Magician pointed out. "They have to know we're here, but they haven't shut it down."

"Maybe we're not a threat yet?" I suggested. "Maybe we're not a threat at all?"

"Maybe we haven't made the turn," Brody countered. "We go one way, they react with X. We go another way, they react with Y. It's like a maze, a game. A booby trap."

"Not a game, precisely," the Magician said, tilting his head. I winced, remembering the feeling of the needles shooting out of the walls in Solomon's temple. I really hoped it wasn't *that* kind of game. "Merely a process. A moment, if you will."

He poofed out of existence again, making Brody hiss. A moment later, he was back.

"The left operating bay is empty, the right is filled with approximately two dozen women under tents."

"Like oxygen tents?" Brody asked. "Jesus, what are they doing to them?"

"I suspect Dixie anticipates us wanting to find out," Armaeus said. "And further, that she doesn't expect us to succeed."

Brody snorted. "Yeah, except we already have."

The lights went out.

The sudden darkness struck me far harder than it ordinarily could because I'd been dazzled by the bright, sterile white light that had preceded it. Before I could light up my own fireball light show, the Magician created a nimbus of white light above us, making it all the easier to see the demon horde that rushed toward us out of nowhere, dropping from the ceiling, erupting from the floor, bursting out from the walls.

"Jesus!" Brody shouted.

"*Michael,*" Armaeus corrected, his order cracking out with such authority that I wasn't surprised at the instantaneous result. Except it wasn't Michael the Archangel who appeared at the end of the corridor, but his proxy soldiers, the only beings on this earth capable of killing demons. Even witches could go only so far in eradicating demonic blight from this earth, sending them back to their infernal home. It took a demon to kill another demon, and the Syx were more than up for the job.

"*Report,*" Warrick of the Syx roared down the corridor as his five fellow warriors, demons all—some more demonic than others at this point—leapt into action.

"We need to get to the far bay and neutralize the threat," the Magician announced tersely. He made a swipe for Brody, who ducked out of his grasp and punched a demon straight in the face, sending it hurtling back, though creating no lasting damage.

"Brody," I snapped. "Don't be an idiot."

He whirled back to bark something at me, which gave the Magician the time he needed to gather us both to him again and dissolve us. We'd successfully drawn the demons out, giving the Syx something to kill, but the problem with demons was you could always make more.

We reappeared in the operating bay to find it awash with activity. All the light panels flashed red and white, and medical personnel in white lab coats rushed frantically from tent to tent, their faces hidden behind medical masks.

"*No,*" a woman's voice shouted out, and a struggle erupted on one of the gurneys. I saw the bright syringe flash, and I understood what was happening here. They were going to kill these women and their babies, no matter whether they were inside their mothers' bodies or out. It was the fail-safe solution to being discovered. And it wasn't going to happen on my watch.

"Armaeus," I snapped as a computer nearest to one of the stations crackled and suddenly burst. "A little help here."

"They're blowing the data," Brody shouted as another monitor exploded. "It's what I'd do."

The Magician whipped his head toward me, and I understood the dilemma he faced. Twenty-four women, at least forty-eight lives, while the data in this center could take us closer to the obliteration of a global threat. I wasn't completely sure what that threat was, but I was beginning to get a sinking feeling it involved the creation of a completely undocumented population of Connecteds that could be used for any manner of experimentation that Dixie and her pals at the Shadow Court could come up with.

Another woman screamed.

"Save the data," I told Armaeus. "I'll get her."

Fury whipped through me as I turned toward the bay. I couldn't wrap my arms around all these people, but I didn't only have arms to work with.

"Sara—" Brody began.

I thrust a hand toward him, willing him back. The power of my suggestion knocked him completely into Armaeus, and I turned back to the flurry of activity, the doctors of death and the women who wanted to bring life into the world. I seethed with anger at Dixie, and at the demons who guarded this place and now danced along the periphery, feasting on the human misery that was their favorite delicacy. But mostly, much like Brody, I was furious with myself. I should have seen that Dixie was a total snake in pink cowboy boots. I'd discounted her because of her fluffy blonde hair and syrupy-sweet drawl. How many people had died because I'd been too smug and self-righteous to see what was preening right in front of me?

As anger rolled through me, I felt a searing pain across my back. I shuddered as my skin split and a mighty pair of wings shot out and extended around the room, several times bigger and longer than I'd ever attempted before. My power drained instantly, but I couldn't stop. I couldn't hesitate. When the far tips of my wings touched, I collapsed them inward, capturing gurneys, flailing humans, everything I could in my grasp. I pulled it all toward me, and then I incinerated myself and everything else into motion, returning to the only place I could think of suitable for such a mess.

I crackled back into existence to a chorus of angry shouts, not the least of which was Sariah's bark of "What the hell!"

I staggered back, my wings crackling into nothingness, leaving only open fiery gashes that scored my back as Dr. Sells rushed in, a few white-suited orderlies behind her.

"Justice *Wilde*," the doctor began, her voice betraying anger but no shock. She'd been around the Arcana Council long enough not to be shocked by anything.

"These women are in trauma, possibly on the verge of death, definitely on the verge of giving birth or having given birth or babies are involved, whatever. Fix it!" I growled at her, and then I lunged for Sariah, who beat me to it by rolling out of her bed and grabbing her blades.

"Tell me there's going to be a fight," she announced, lurching toward me.

"Oh, there's going to be a fight, all right." I grabbed her and disintegrated us back to the birthing center, which was a full-on demon bloodbath.

"Excellent," Sariah breathed out, practically vibrating with menace.

Displaying moves I hadn't realized she'd developed, Sariah leapt into the fray, battling the demons that had rushed the space the moment I cleared it of humans. But not all the humans had gone, it seemed. The women in tents and on gurneys were no longer present, but human bodies littered the space, easily half a dozen. Brody was currently fighting for possession of one of those bodies, while the demon on its other side cackled and tried to yank the limp form through a fiery hole in the wall.

"It's about *time*," Brody growled as he noticed me returning, and I piled on.

With Sariah on the scene, the Syx battling the demons in the hallway, and me giving Brody support, the Magician continued doing whatever he was doing with the computer system. Brody and I managed to secure the human—who doubtless would be useful for interviewing once he recovered from his glazed-eyed horror—and spun him toward the corner of the bay, where a growing pile of groaning bodies was amassing. The doors to the corridor burst open, the fight outside spilling into the fight within, but there was a new player as well.

A woman strode forward in a long gray silk tunic and trousers, her dark eyes flashing, her black hair pulled back. She held up her hand, and a ring of white fire erupted around the human refugees. The flame instantly winked out to leave a thick pile of salt.

"I hope you're making another ring, because there's more of these assholes to collect," Brody informed her.

"I'll do you one better," Danae, mistress of the House of Swords, shot back. She lifted her hands, tipped back her head, and shouted something that sounded like half song, half chant. I felt the eerie prickling of my skin as other voices joined her, though there was no one else obviously present. Across the room, Sariah gave an exultant cry, then started calling out the same spell. As the Night Witch, she *was* technically a witch, but her facility in dispatching demons still surprised me, as did her familiarity with Danae's spell. What kind of classes had she been taking in her off time?

Nevertheless, it worked. New demons stopped entering the fray, allowing Sariah and the Syx to make short, goopy work of the ones that remained. In a matter of minutes, there was nothing left in the operating bay but pools of black demon gore and shuddering, shaking humans.

Danae turned to me. "You were right to summon me, though it required me to use Qadir to reach you so quickly. I left him with two other members of the coven to address the concerns of the Connecteds above. Where are the women?"

"Safe," I said. "As safe as they can be. I gave them to Dr. Sells, the Council's physician. I don't know what's been done to them. I assume they all have Connected ability, and their children as well. But I don't know about pregnancy or children or any of that."

She nodded. "I'll need to see them, to make good on the promise that I made to their families."

"We will take you," Warrick of the Syx announced. I looked up and realized he was the remaining member of the Syx present. He turned to me. "This battle is one of a dozen going on at this exact moment all over the world. Demons are bubbling out of every dark alley they can find. It's a distraction, but a distraction for what?"

He didn't wait around for an answer, but gestured to Danae, who stepped up to him, the two of them striding swiftly out of the operating bay. He would protect her from attack, if there were any other demons hanging around, and he would be at her side should any of the women we had recovered from this center have a demon problem as yet undiagnosed.

The Magician materialized as Sariah approached Brody, wiping off her knives.

"You think anything's hinky with these doctors?" she asked Brody as the Magician looked around with a curled lip. Armaeus breathed a new spell, and the demon gore disintegrated into mist, leaving nothing but the strangely barren operating bay, with its remaining gurneys and other equipment in various states of destruction. The doctors and orderlies who were huddled together in the far corner of the room moaned in collective misery.

"No clue," Brody sighed. "But I'm going to have to get these guys processed and interviewed. I don't suppose you could help me with that?"

Sariah grinned. "I got a visit in my hospital room from the Devil earlier today, and I'm still rocking his unique interviewing skills. I'm in."

"Miss Wilde," the Magician said quietly as I watched Brody and Sariah move toward the doctors. Technically, the doctors were part of the villains in this pageant, but half of them were crying and the other half mumbled to themselves nonstop, clearly traumatized. How much had they known about what they were doing? How much had they believed?

I turned away and focused on Armaeus. "What did you find?"

"Birthing centers of this type registered to religious organizations under the umbrella of Bright Rock have operations in twenty-five countries—many of them have been in operation for decades. It would seem that Dixie decided to forgo the dirty process of acquiring Connected humans through kidnapping or human trafficking of the kind usually employed by the arcane black market. She went straight to the source and got women to volunteer their babies in exchange for little more than medical expenses and a promise that the infants would be adopted into good homes. After their children were born, the mothers were killed...or possibly impregnated again. What happened to the children, I'm not sure, but I think what we both suspect is the most likely answer."

"She used them as fodder for experimentation, or spare parts for technoceuticals. Or...something equally terrible." My stomach tightened as my thoughts flashed to the gleaming metal skull in the demonic illusion I'd been served up in the patient room upstairs. "That can't be all Dixie. There's no way she's *that* evil."

"Oh, it gets worse," the Magician said. "We need to go."

16

The birthing centers were shut down worldwide within the next twelve hours. The Archangel diverted the efforts of the Syx to the cause, and Sariah happily joined them once she'd finished processing the orderlies with Brody.

That had proven instructional as well. Now the Devil, Simon, the Magician, Brody, Sariah, and I stood in the Arcana Council's conference room, which had been updated for the occasion with several additional screens. The images on the screens were sobering. Rows upon rows of hospital bays, the finest equipment, and the most up-to-date and sterile facilities. I almost preferred the back alley kidnappers I'd encountered so many times working the arcane black market. This level of...professionalism was so much worse.

"How did this go on unregulated for so long?" I asked as Simon spooled through the scenes.

"A long, long history of the authorities not interfering with religious organizations," Simon said. "You wrap something in enough layers of tradition and belief and people stop asking questions."

The Devil's lip curled. "I have had the opportunity to interview a dozen directors of these facilities, and they truly believed the company line, that these women and children were blessed by a higher power, and that it was their duty to dedicate them and their children for a future far beyond our current understanding. That the wrong kind of people have ruled the world for too long, and it was time that we followed a different star."

I winced, not missing his emphasis. "Where are we with identifying what else Dixie has been up to?"

"Closer than we thought," Simon said. "Nikki kind of hit the Star jackpot over in Switzerland. The last stronghold she pierced had been given a couple of healthy sips of the Dixie Quinn Kool-Aid."

"They defected to the Shadow Court?" Sariah asked, bristling, but Simon lifted a quelling hand.

"Remember, they didn't know that other choices were out there. We take for granted that everybody knows about the Council, our work for humanity, blah blah blah, but the truth is, we've been pretty quiet about how we go about our business. Things happen, people are saved, but it's all very hush-hush. Our pushback against the gods breaking through the veil hit some of these guys' radars, but that whole scene got wrapped up and time got displaced so quickly at the climactic moment, that a lot of 'em were left wondering what'd actually happened. I mean, they vaguely recalled that something bad had gone down, but they had absolutely no data detailing the experience. These people have lives and businesses and battles of their own, and they moved on."

I considered that. We'd worked so hard to keep the

disruption to a minimum when we'd removed the threat of the gods from the world, and the Council had always sought to keep the Connected, well, disconnected. Safe and separate. Meanwhile, many of the Connected had tried to go the other direction by carefully integrating into society, hiding in plain sight. Plus, from what I understood about the werewolves Nikki was slowly contacting—their powers were dormant. Without the Moon in place on the Council, their psychic abilities hadn't been strong enough to give them the confidence to step out.

"And now?" I prompted Simon.

"Nikki has proven pretty convincing." Simon grinned. "That, and the fact that we've got another full moon coming up is giving these packs pause. They're definitely onboard with getting more power."

The Magician turned to Brody. "What have you gotten from Interpol?"

"Quite a bit," Brody said, still grim, but looking surprisingly more rested. "Now that they know what to look for, they've identified supply chains of technoceuticals funneling into hospitals and labs everywhere. Robust and mainstream. Again, this isn't the drug-running operation of a few years ago. It's been ratcheted up significantly."

"She knew trouble was coming," I said. "Dixie knew what I was when I came to Vegas, maybe as soon as I freed the Devil from the Vatican. She could have suspected I'd cause her problems all the way back then. That was really the first true interaction I had with her. Maybe that's when she started putting things in motion for this final endgame."

"An endgame that involves the hyperrich, moderately Connected members of the Shadow Court...and very few others," Kreios said. "What are the financial movements of the Court?"

Simon shrugged. "They haven't been as active as you would think they should be, especially if we're nearing the end times. I mean, money's getting moved around into tangible goods, property, precious metal mines, like that. But there are some holdings that haven't made any adjustments at all. I will say they're backing out of cryptocurrency, selling their positions as quietly as possible for more tangible assets while the average investor keeps diving in deeper, taking advantage of the slight softening of the market."

"That tracks." The Devil nodded. "There is concern, anxiety among the rich, and the Shadow Court has done a good job stoking their fears."

"What about the scientific community?" I asked.

"Not a peep," Simon returned. "The Shadow Court's taking advantage of the fact the world is tied up with disasters, climate change, new viruses sprouting up and spreading like wildfire, all of it. Everyone's focusing on that."

"A shell game," the Magician murmured. "A flurry of activity to hide her final preparations. Who's moving the most money?"

"The folks at the top of the Shadow Court pecking order, not surprisingly," Simon confirmed. "Especially the Fuggerens and this new family we've found, the St. Claires. They've got stashes of cash in places that none of their allies do. On the surface, they're doing the least of all, but behind the scenes, they aren't letting any grass grow under their feet. They're totally bracing for the coming storm."

"And the Shadow Court's ties to government?"

"Not a factor, it would seem," Simon said. "The government operatives that we tagged as members of the Court still haven't reached out to each other, and none of their incoming communications are questionable at all. It's like they've been told to sit tight as a volcano is getting ready to blow."

"Another distraction?" I asked.

"The Court isn't rallying any nation's military or government to their aid," mused the Devil. "Why do they believe their coup will proceed unimpeded?"

"Remember, the operatives in Geneva ranged all up and down the ladder in terms of their level of influence," I pointed out. "Some were quite low-lying."

"And, I would suspect, they were low-lying in areas of importance to the Star," Kreios conceded. "There to gather intelligence, not act. It would be worth determining that specifically, if it matters."

He spoke this last almost offhandedly, and I looked at him sharply.

"What do you mean if it matters? Of course it matters."

"Not at this late hour," the Devil disagreed. "War is coming, and quickly. The assessment of how we arrived at this impasse will be something for the archivists to debate in the future, assuming there's anyone left to debate."

"So you're giving up?" Sariah snapped, turning on him. The now-familiar current of conflict leapt between them, and I remembered her concern about the Devil sacrificing the Magician.

Kreios shrugged, regarding her with deceptively placid amusement, though his eyes glittered at her challenge. "Sometimes the greatest achievements come after surrendering to the problem."

"And sometimes people talk a lot of bullshit when they don't have anything better to say," she shot right back, then turned to me and Armaeus. "So let me see if I've gotten this straight. The Star, Dixie, whoever the fuck she is, has been operating behind the scenes, but in the last few years, she's gotten her shorts in a twist. Probably because of Sara."

I rolled my eyes but didn't dispute the claim. It made a certain sort of sense.

"Up to that point, the Star could kind of coast along, living the way she wanted, gathering money and followers as needed. She'd seen what happened at the fall of magic six thousand years ago. She'd seen someone she thought of as her greatest ally, the Moon, flat-out run away and hide on another plane she couldn't get to. She'd seen the strength of the Council wax and wane too. Eventually, she figured out, fuck a bunch of councils, I don't need you guys. So far, so good. She started feeding the egos and maybe the magical capabilities of the Shadow Court, letting them think their megalomania was all their own making. Then came Sara and the rapid augmentation of the Council, and don't think I'm not picking up on the timing of all that," Sariah said, pointing to Armaeus with a hard jab. "You know more than you've told us."

He spread his hands. "There are easily four thousand six hundred and seventy-two potential outcomes of this conversation, let alone the subsequent acts it may engender. I learned a long time ago that discussing possible paths becomes its own trap."

To my surprise, Sariah seemed to accept his explanation. She flashed him a quick grin.

"You know what, I totally buy that. So you get a pass. That doesn't change that, for whatever reason, the Star has decided to make her move. To bring magic to the forefront and the focus of the world squarely on the Connected like, right now. Why? It's not like she has any particular love for the Connected community. I'm not buying any amount of bullshit that she wants the proliferation of magic because she's secretly some sort of great humanitarian."

"Godhead," the Magician said curtly, as if he had come to an inescapable conclusion. "If the Star sought to transcend *beyond* Council level, to become one of the gods, there is only one viable path to it."

"Through us," I said. "She needs to destroy us. She couldn't do it herself, but with the Shadow Court tying us in knots..."

"She lets them do her dirty work, they take power, and the only god left to serve is...her," Simon said, causing everyone to look at him sharply. "I mean, it makes sense, right? The fewer people you have, the more they need you and the structures you've set up. In a postapocalyptic world, people are gonna be hurting. Somebody is going to be there to pick up the pieces, and you can call that somebody whatever you want, victors, rescuers, or gods."

"It probably goes further than that," the Devil mused. "The Star may even be encouraging the Shadow Court to eradicate low-level Connecteds, for two very good reasons. First, they don't have enough power to interest her, but secondly, it's often among the weakest populations that revolution stirs."

"Because they have nothing to lose." I continued pulling this string as clarity arrowed through me. "Think about it. Who has Dixie been targeting to be part of her little club of one percenters? People with money, influence, culture, history, and when they're really lucky, magical ability. That's a group with *everything* to lose, and they know it. They'd better fall in line now or they're going to be left with a whole lot of nothing when the dust settles."

"Okay, fine, but who really would believe something seriously whack is going to happen?" Sariah complained. "I mean *we* get it, but we're up to our asses in this stuff. Who in the world would believe Dixie?"

"That's why she was recruiting," I muttered. "She needed to show them, up close and personal."

"That's exactly why she was recruiting," the Devil agreed. "Dixie Quinn, den mother for the Connecteds of Vegas, gathering the lost and the disenchanted together to celebrate and deepen their Connected ability. Only she wasn't trying to build a community of people who enjoyed each other's company. The best and the brightest were lured to Vegas to be conscripted into her own private army—or funneled into her camps for harvesting."

"And those who survived were sent off to whisper into the ears of the rich and powerful," I said. "Preparing for a day like this. Or better stated, a day about six or so days from now, if Viktor's timeline still holds. When the whole world will literally go up in smoke."

"Fucking Dixie," Sariah muttered.

17

"But where does that leave us?" Simon asked. "We have resources too. A whole hell of a lot of them. Shouldn't *we* be recruiting?"

"Yeah, we should," I sighed. It was time, despite the danger. How many people had I encountered over the course of my work with the Arcana Council who had been willing, even eager, to embrace their Connected abilities, to go to the next level? How many Connected children had I seen, lost and afraid? How many frantic parents whose children had been taken and trafficked on the arcane black market? Even the families at the birthing center, the weathered, sharp-eyed Connecteds who'd spoken to me today. They all were ready to fight for the cause.

They only needed someone to light their way.

"What's our timetable?" I asked, turning to Devil. "You said there wasn't enough time to interview all the players in this game and find out how we'd gotten here. But do we have enough time to prepare the Connecteds for this global attack of the Shadow Court? Because once we do, they're not going to toddle back into their homes and continue their lives like nothing ever happened. Everyone will know they exist. Are we—the Council—ready for that?"

"Well, you guys better be," Sariah said. "War is coming."

"This isn't about the war. This is about what happens afterward," I countered. "If the point of the Arcana Council is to preserve magic and maintain its balance, we have to understand that dragging all this into the open is going to create an entirely new global dynamic. Ridding the world of the threat from the gods was one thing. It was a defined danger to humanity as a whole. We were able to rally the forces of Connecteds who might not ordinarily agree with us and get them to contribute their strength and will to our cause. And in the wake of that, we unleashed a scourge of demons on the earth, though fortunately, most of our allies don't hold us accountable for that. But this is different. Dixie or the Star, whatever she is, may want to be a god. But she *isn't* a god. She's barely a demigod who has broken with the Council, able through long effort to sustain herself without abiding by the Council's rules. That's just one more magic asshole fighting for survival and dominance. There's a reason why we haven't obliterated the Shadow Court even though they piss us off."

"She's way bigger than the Shadow Court," Sariah insisted, and Simon leaned forward.

"In this, I gotta agree with Sariah. The Star is bad news. You saw what happened at Angkor Wat. That was legitimate destruction of a temple of faith that has existed for centuries. She can't go around blowing shit up and get a pass for all of it just because she's not a god. That doesn't make any sense at all."

"And so we who are near gods ourselves are justified in

stopping her," the Magician said. And though he didn't state it as a question, the query still stood.

The Devil straightened. "Yes," he said, surprising me. "Yes, that's exactly what we're going to do."

Sariah blinked at him, and I glanced at the Magician, not missing his soft smile. But the Devil was all business.

"Sariah, you follow the witches. More than any other group, they have a vested interest in knocking out Dixie, given that she employs demons in her work and is upsetting the covens' natural balance of control. Start with them, but don't end there. There are witches' covens that can direct you to a cabal of academies of witches and wizards in Boston. You may want to check those out too."

"Oh, I know those guys," Sariah said, grimacing. "They're a menace."

"Then they're well suited to the occasion," the Devil countered. "Simon, you've got the gamers."

"You bet your ass I do," Simon said, grinning as he swiveled to me. "Maybe you don't remember your cult-like status among the community when you gave ordinary Connecteds access to the whole freaking new dimension at Kathmandu, one long-ago adventure, but trust me, Madame Justice, they haven't forgotten. They're ready to fight."

"Those people are kids," I groaned. "Or they act like it, anyway."

"Doesn't matter," Simon said, nearly bouncing with excitement. "Even kids or the adult-challenged have a right to defend themselves if they feel they're in danger. And I don't think there's any question that they're in danger."

"Detective Rooks," the Devil said. "Interpol is the next step."

"Roger that," Brody said, but he no longer looked weary.

He looked energized. A man about to be handed a mission he'd been waiting for, for far too long. "Anything in particular you want me to tell them, other than all hell's about to break loose?"

"I trust you will find some way to convey the fact that the international drug trafficking trade is now transporting explosives," the Devil said. "And those explosives, some ingestible, some that we suspect are positioned in prominent governmental and religious structures, will be going off in a very short period of time. As a result, it might be a good time to start rounding up the usual suspects for the most heinous crimes on any pretext whatsoever. Because if those people are not able to get into the wind and to safety, they may not be so willing to pursue Dixie's endgame."

With that, Brody brightened further. "You know, that almost makes sense, which scares me more than I can adequately express. But I like it. I like it a lot."

"I thought you might," the Devil said, offering his own smile. He turned to Armaeus. "I don't think there's any need for me to explain to you what you need to do. But you'd best get to it. Time may wait for the Magician, but the sands run out for all of us eventually."

"What the hell is that supposed to—" Sariah's words were cut off abruptly as the Magician turned toward her, the two of them poofing into smoke. He returned a moment later and did the same for a protesting Brody, while Simon swiveled back to his console, cackling with glee.

"Sariah's now at Danae's stronghold, while Brody got dropped straight into the middle of a meeting in the South of France at Interpol headquarters, materializing out of thin air. That would have been worth some serious money to see."

"What about me?" I asked as the Magician returned.

The Devil smiled at me, his face suddenly looking every one of his nearly hundred years, the glamour of the European playboy slipping just a little. "To you falls the most vital task, as your powers are arguably the greatest of any on the Council. And you already know what it is. What do you really want, Justice Wilde?"

I stared at him, feeling the pressure of his unique Connected power on me. The faces of a thousand children flashed through my mind, and then the kind eyes and soft smile of the now-deceased priest who'd been so dedicated to helping them. Had I done enough to carry on the legacy of Father Jerome, the man who had given my efforts wings? Could I ever do enough?

"I want to do whatever will keep magic available to all Connecteds who wish to wield it," I finally said. "I want to keep the vulnerable from being abused by the rich and powerful, but I don't want magic to go away. We *need* magic in this world. There's no point to a world without it."

A shiver seemed to roll through the room, and though I wanted to believe only I felt it, Simon scooted back on his chair a few inches and looked around with wide eyes. "What the fuck was that?" he asked.

"That was a development that bears some study," the Magician said, his voice laced with amusement. "Miss Wilde, as I have said before, you should be careful what you wish for. Perhaps more than most, you are likely to get it."

He held out his hand, and I took it as Simon turned back to his computer and began typing furiously, simultaneously calling out orders to the other consoles.

The Magician and I crackled out of the conference room, but we didn't go far. A moment later, we were back in his library, surrounded by bookcases, standing next to the cauldron and pit that I had come to know as his innermost magical sanctuary.

"It's happening, isn't it?" I asked. "We're going to put the Connecteds at risk."

"The Connecteds are already at risk," the Magician assured me. "We are merely going to bring that fact to their attention."

"Right," I sighed. "So we know the Shadow Court is planning on blowing everything up in less than a week in their bid to become the magical power behind every public or private sector on the planet—squashing the low-level Connecteds in the process—and that the Star in her guise as Dixie Quinn has been feeding them demon support and trafficked Connecteds for long enough that, well...they may be able to pull it off. And now we're going to stop them."

He smiled. "That sums up our position quite well, I believe."

I narrowed my eyes at him. "Will you be in danger? Did the Devil making this decision for us to finally take action put you at the risk that Sariah's been afraid of? She still thinks he's going to kill you."

"What do you think?" the Magician asked, not going to his cauldron or stepping nearer to the pit as I'd expected him to do. Instead, he stepped toward me. The unexpected movement created a shiver of electricity between us. "Is Sariah's interpretation correct, or is the situation more that the Devil won't try to save me despite wishing to do so? What if he has to choose between saving me or saving you?"

Panic rippled through me at his words. They resonated with a sincerity I couldn't discount. "Do I want to know what the percentages are?"

"You might," the Magician said, and he brushed the hair from my cheek. "But I won't tell you."

He drew his hand down my cheek, and unexpectedly, my heart trembled. Tears sparked behind my eyes. Just as Kreios had, Armaeus looked far older than I'd ever seen him. Worn and weary, a man pushed past his limits, but who knew he had much, much farther to go.

"What's happening, Armaeus?" I whispered. "I don't want to lose you. I feel like I've already lost you too many times, and I don't want to do it again. I don't want to live without you."

Armaeus gazed at me as another ripple of energy flowed around us, and his smile, when it came, was grim. "My beautiful, powerful Sara," he murmured, searching my eyes as if they held the mysteries of the universe, "you should really be more careful when you make statements like that."

"I don't want to be careful," I argued. "I want to be—"

"Hush," the Magician said abruptly. "Look."

I blinked away angry tears and glanced around, then blinked a second time for good measure. All the books in the Magician's library had floated off the shelf and were now hanging suspended in midair. And not only the books. The two dozen or so golden pavement tiles that we had recovered from Solomon's temple had separated from their tidy stacks and were floating as well, shimmering with energy. While the books seemed inert, there was no mistaking the crackling energy of the celestial pavers.

"What the hell is that?" I whispered, and the Magician's laugh was soft and cautious.

"Power not of hell, if we're lucky," he said. "But a power to be feared all the same. Perhaps you should rein in your emotions for now?"

"Oh. Oh, sure," I said hurriedly. I breathed in, then out again, and watched the contents of the Magician's library return to their places on the shelves, and the golden celestial pavers drift back to their uniform stacks.

I glanced back to the Magician. “Better?”

He smiled, his gaze once more searching my face as if he too was afraid he might forget me again. “Perfect,” he murmured. Then he leaned forward and touched his lips to mine.

18

"Dollface!"

I would have recognized Nikki's furious shout anywhere, but it was particularly disorienting to hear it in the middle of the night while I was buried in a sea of satin and entangled in the Magician's arms. Her urgency was so great, I reacted without thinking, incinerating both Armaeus and myself and using the connection I had inked into my skin to find Nikki wherever she was.

We materialized in the middle of a firestorm.

Fortunately, because I had the Magician along for the ride, he was able to manifest clothes suitable for this particular party. But we still leapt for cover as flame ripped out across the open field, a shower of bullets following hard behind.

"Sweet Christmas, what is *wrong* with you people?" Nikki roared, and I poked up my head, my eyes widening in horror as I saw her clothed head to toe in gray leathers, straddling a fallen wolf on a stretch of beaten-down, frost-bitten grass. Despite the Magician's murmured caution, I disintegrated again, reappearing by them both.

"What happened?" I asked, panic and fury lighting my hands on fire and sweeping out my spectral wings in a painful rip of flame.

"Holdouts," she said. "You want to know what I think? I think Dixie got to this particular family first and did a number on them. I think we need to get our asses inside their little hidey-hole and fucking see what's going on."

"They're werewolves?" I asked. "Does that change anything?"

She snorted. "Darlin', I haven't been doing this too long, but I'm coming to realize that Weres aren't all that different from the rest of us. Most of them are just trying to do the right thing, some of them going above and beyond the call of duty to play it straight and play it strong, and—"

Her words were cut off by a new barrage of gunfire. It soared over our heads, but the message was clear: Get out.

"—and some of them are *fucking assholes*," Nikki concluded, roaring into the wind.

I dropped to my knees, my hand passing over Torsten's wolf form. He was alive, but he'd been struck several times with silver bullets.

"These wolves are using *silver*?"

"Did I mention that they were assholes? They're literally unloading an arsenal on us, and they don't even know me! How could I have pissed anyone off that much that I haven't even met?" Nikki griped, looking like she wanted to hit someone. She clenched her big hands into fists, their ice-white tips matching her white hair and frosted brows and eyelashes. No doubt about it, she had jacked the Moon's style into the stratosphere. "I'm sorry to call you, but—"

Her voice broke, and I nodded sharply, not needing her to explain more. Torsten was the leader of Nikki's newfound pack of guardians, but this wasn't just the remorse of a leader for her top general. This wolf had gotten under her skin.

"He'll be okay," I said, and that weird ripple of magic happened again, but this time, it didn't strike me as odd. Of all my abilities, my power to heal was the one that felt the most right.

I laid my hands upon the great wolf, seeking out his wounds and picking up the bits of silver that threaded through his bloodstream, heading for his heart. I stopped that craziness right away, grateful I didn't have to reorder this creature into either his natural form or something better than that. He wasn't human, and he wasn't animal. He was myth and magic, a pure supernatural being and a blessing to this earth by the mere fact of his existence. And he was *not* going to die on my watch.

A moment later, Torsten surged up, his eyes wild as he roared with fury.

"Knock it down, White Fang, we got work to do," Nikki shouted, but there was no doubting the relief in her voice. She spun toward me. "Right over that ridge is Casa Dickhead, where the leader of this little pack is sending out these baby wolves to do his fighting for him."

I peered toward where she was pointing, but through the thick alpine forest, I could only see a rooftop of a building that looked like it was built into a mountain. These guys definitely had their security game down...but Nikki was right. The barrage of gunfire was too much to scare off a delegation that wasn't shooting back. Why the show of such force?

Nikki flinched as another flurry of bullets scattered overhead, followed by yips and howls. "I'm not saying they aren't feisty little assholes, but those shooters are all approximately twelve years old in people years, not wolf. That's too fucking *young* to be put on the *front line.*"

She and Torsten turned in one movement and bolted across the open ground. The Magician materialized in front of me long enough to pull me close to him, then he dissolved us into a puff of smoke. We arrived at the front of the fortress-like chalet almost at the same time Nikki and Torsten did, the two of them seeming to have survived the volleys of additional firepower through sheer anger.

"If you would find it acceptable, Miss Dawes, I can get us inside without more fanfare?"

Nikki snorted and waved him on. "As much as you're sweet to look at, Mr. Wizard, I love you more for your mad skills. I will happily stop with the gun shit for one day."

The Magician lifted a hand. A sudden silence descended over the field, shouts of surprise and sharp barks filling the space. Even as I readied my hands to shove some serious fire into the front door, it opened.

"Explain to me again why you didn't go out with me on more work trips?" I asked as Nikki and Torsten pushed inside. The Magician and I followed immediately after. The door closed behind us, but no one rushed out to attack, and Nikki and Torsten, now in his human form, fanned out to either side, while Armaeus studied the foyer intently.

"This is the house of Augustus Brombacher," he said, sounding slightly surprised. "There was no way to discern that from outside, but his energy is practically vibrating in these halls. We have encountered the family before, but not for several centuries. Fascinating."

"You know these head cases?" Nikki asked. "I'd never heard of them, but they were close enough to the Alps that we figured we might as well take the opportunity while we had it. We didn't expect to get shot at, so brace yourself for more of that bullshit."

"There is no violence here—not inside," Armaeus mused. "There's sickness."

That surprised me, but when I flipped open my third eye, I could feel it too. The energy of the Brombacher house was stagnant, crippled. It hunched like a wounded bear in the back of its cave, holding off all intruders with roars of fury. "What happened to them?" I asked.

The house remained silent in response to that question, but only for a moment more. And then the stillness was broken visually as a young woman appeared in the doorway to the grand foyer. Pale, blonde, and slender, she seemed unreasonably poised, as if she was used to entertaining guests who had survived a dogfight to get to her door.

Across the foyer, Nikki chuckled, privy to my unintended joke. She and I had always been attuned, but with her recent ascension to her role as the Moon, that had increased yet more. I welcomed it. I couldn't fight my growing apprehension over my fellow Council members slipping away from me in the midst of the changes hurtling toward us. How would those changes affect Nikki? And how much risk had she willingly taken on to become the Moon, just because she was Nikki Dawes?

These thoughts shot by in a flash as the young woman spoke.

"I wish I could welcome you, but no one is welcome at the House of Brombacher, not now," she said solemnly. "My name is Sophia, and my grandfather is Augustus." Her gaze swiveled to Armaeus. "He was surprised to sense your entry. Surprised and ashamed."

"There is no shame in protecting your home," Armaeus returned, though Nikki snorted beside him.

"I apologize for our poor greeting, Mistress Moon, but you must understand. The ruse of strength you witnessed is all we have left. But please, you must come quickly. My grandfather has asked to see you before he..." She faltered a bit, then strengthened, her chin going up. "Before he passes."

My brows shot up at this. Werewolves are exceptionally long-lived, and with modern technology were probably able to extend their lifespans even more, so how was death a concern for the patriarch of the Brombachers? What was the sickness that hung over this home?

Without saying anything further, the girl spun on her heel and hastened off. Nikki threw me a look that told me she'd already become wary, despite her relative newness to her position. She'd probably spent more than a few hours tracking wolves through their lairs. But she headed off after the woman, and we followed.

Once we entered the hallway, lights swept on, electric sconces flickering to life triggered not by magic but our proximity. Appearing nervous for the first time, the woman started speaking.

"My grandfather will doubtless attempt to apologize himself, but I urge you not to prolong his focus on that topic. Yes, Mistress Moon, we were aware of your meetings with our distant relatives in the area. Yes, we were aware that you had been quite convincing. But you were new to us, and particularly in recent days, new has proven to be untrustworthy. My grandfather gave an audience to the Star, after all, and he has paid for it."

"He's not the only one," Nikki said, surprising me. "When did he take that meeting?"

The woman looked at her worriedly but didn't slow her fast stride. The house was enormous, far larger than it seemed from the outside. Not illusion magic, I didn't think, but a building that took advantage of its location tucked up against both mountain and forest.

"They came three months ago, though it seems far longer. A beautiful woman, human, not a Were, with long silvery-blonde hair, large eyes, and the air of the rich. They have a look."

Nicki snorted. "They do at that."

"She spoke of a new alliance, a court that would elevate those who had done all they could to maintain the purity of their line and the focus of their purpose. She told my grandfather about the Moon and regaled him with the old stories that we all already knew, but that we thought no one else knew outside our own society. How we were destined for power, for magic, but abandoned by the goddess who should have protected us. She said the Shadow Court would repay his loyalty far more richly. He listened, of course. But my grandfather is an old and proud wolf, not easily swayed by beauty or riches. And he sensed a rotten core."

"Intuition. That's probably the single biggest unaugmented ability I've found among the pack. It could grow stronger, though. You all could get so much stronger." Nikki said those words almost casually, not pushing, but also not apologizing. It didn't matter that these probably were the same promises that Dixie and her kind had made. A point Nikki drove home as she continued. "Just because she couldn't deliver what she promised doesn't make it less true."

Sophia lifted a hand, dropped it. "It doesn't matter," she said. "My grandfather didn't believe her, and betrayed his disdain. That was his undoing. He was too proud to feint and shift into the shadows as we have long done. Perhaps he wanted this to happen, I don't know. In any case, he and the

Star broke bread together, drank, and she poisoned him. His body is ravaged now, and he only wants his life to end."

"If it is his wish, then it's his wish," Nikki countered. "But we'll see."

Sophia fell silent, continuing to move quickly through the building until we reached a hallway with a door standing open at the far end, a shaft of bright light shining through it. She shot us a final quick glance. "He's quite ill." She sighed. "And still very proud."

With that, she entered the room, which not only contained a large wingback chair with the frail man that I expected, a thick coverlet over his legs, but also half a dozen other young warriors, dark-haired and bulky, their eyes quick and their manner bristling at our intrusion. I still couldn't tell they were werewolves, which made me wonder —had I seen other werewolves out in society without ever realizing what they were? Probably. I'd been so convinced they didn't exist that I never truly saw them. It was probably how they had survived so many centuries undetected.

"Monsieur Armaeus," the old man rasped as the Magician entered, and to my surprise, the Magician moved forward quickly, dropping to one knee to grasp the man's hand.

"Powerful words indeed, old friend, considering I never knew your true nature."

The admission seemed to please our host. He smiled tiredly, his watery-blue eyes focusing.

"The House of Brombacher is proud. Too proud, perhaps. But our true nature was not a tale we easily shared. We had been betrayed too many times, even by your illustrious Council. And so we kept our own counsel, you could say."

The Magician nodded, squeezed the werewolf's hand,

then stood, standing far enough away that the old man did not have to look up at him, but merely keep his head level.

The Magician turned to me. "Augustus, allow me to introduce Sara Wilde, Justice of the Arcana Council, and Nikki Dawes, whom you already know as Mistress Moon. Torsten is her most trusted general."

I hid my smile, noting how Armaeus had picked up the archaic appellation for Nikki from the young wolf. It suited Nikki, as did the fierce and forbidding-looking Torsten, who remained tight by her side. I had no doubt that if it came down to it, he could take out a good half of the room before anyone reached her.

Nobody tried.

"I trust Sophia gave you the information that led us to this impasse?" Augustus asked.

Nikki nodded. "Love chop, you're not the first to get betrayed by a pretty face. But we don't have a lot of time, so if I could..."

The younger wolves snarled and growled in defense of their master. Torsten lifted his hands in a menacing gesture as the other wolves reacted. The old man waved them all off, and Nikki went down on one knee much as the Magician had. In both cases, it was not a show of submissiveness, but of strength, honoring an old warrior who had long since passed his prime.

Nikki closed her large hands around the old man's frail fingers and stared at him. "You have the gift of discernment deep within you, and intuition, as you all do. But you have more, Augustus Brombacher. You are the storm bringer, the lightning wielder. Do you feel it?"

The old man's eyes brightened. "Those are dreams of my misspent youth, never come to fruition."

"And now you are poisoned," Nikki said succinctly,

squeezing his hand. "I can't strip away your age, but I can strip away your sickness, should you want me to do so. Should you want to wield the storm and fire."

"Don't toy with him," Sophia hissed at my side, but Augustus paid no attention to anyone but Nikki.

"You can do such a thing?" he asked, his rheumy eyes going wide. "You would do such a thing?"

"I shouldn't," she said drily. "You unloaded a bunch of silver into my team. It's a damn good thing we could duck."

"All except for the protector who would not die," Augustus nodded, his gaze going to Torsten. "My apologies for our poor reception. Only a Connected of true strength could have opened our front door as easily as you did, or survived our gauntlet of firepower. I needed you to pass that test, since I clearly didn't test the last Council member who came to our home. I could not subject my family to a second assault."

He sighed and lifted his gaze to Nikki. "Regardless of what strength you may yet be able to raise within me, know this. My family will follow you and your pack, Mistress Moon, wherever you may lead."

Nikki turned to me, and I nodded, stepping forward, drawing the attention of the proud Augustus Brombacher. He peered at me with eyes already slightly less cloudy—and slightly brighter with the fire still within him. I smiled. This wasn't going to be very difficult at all.

"Let's see what we can do," I told him.

19

As usual when I worked on a victim whose electrical circuits had been disintegrated, his magic all but destroyed, I lost all sense of time. I didn't know exactly how Dixie had poisoned Augustus Brombacher, but she'd done a damn fine job of shattering his neural pathways.

At least now, I was becoming familiar with Weres. Despite the fact they weren't human, they had lived as humans for a great deal of time, their bodies adapting to the world in which they found themselves. And so I took two paths of healing with this proud man—one path stripped away the damage to his body and the other mended his soul.

I was surprised to see how close his magic was to the surface, his Connected ability shimmered to life at my first touch. I knew a full moon and Nikki's grace would bring it into true power, and I hoped he would take that final step with her to step fully into his power. By my untutored estimation, despite his age, he would live another fifty years or more, possibly quite a bit longer. Of course that assumed there was anything left of the world to live in after the next few days.

Eventually, he slept. I backed away, stiff from my prolonged work on Augustus. Nikki stood to one side of me, her faithful guard on the other, holding me upright. I blinked in surprise at how similar their holds on me were. Torsten unconsciously emulating his goddess, or Nikki aligning herself with her wolf? I didn't know, but either way, it suited them.

"Armaeus is ready for you whenever you're up for it, dollface, but if you need to rest, you should," Nikki began, giving me a small squeeze. I could hear the excitement in her voice. Something had happened, something good.

"I'm good," I informed her and Torsten, pulling away to straighten my long-sleeved shirt, smoothing it against my heavy tights. "Whaddya got?"

"No spoilers here." Nikki winked with a broad grin. She flipped her long, icy locks over her shoulder. "We'll let him do the honors."

I let her lead me to where the Magician stood in a spacious office dominated by a large desk, but with plenty of room for seating all around. The six wolves from Augustus's drawing room were there, as well as young Sophia. Armaeus looked up as I entered, his face brightening.

"It's done?" he asked. "What have you learned?"

I smiled despite myself. The werewolves were going to prove to be a source of long-term interest for the Magician when all this was done. When a man lived eight hundred years, the prospect of learning something new never failed to delight...even in the face of war.

"He's stronger than he wants to be, frankly," I acknowledged, not missing Sophia's sag of relief. "He'd given up believing he could survive this, given up believing that he *wanted* to survive this. But when Nikki started talking to him about storm and fire, that made all the difference."

"It would," a new voice rumbled from the corner, and I turned to see an older man, elegant in his aesthetic build and style, standing in perfect counterpoint to his younger, rougher-looking clansmen. The older Were bowed to me.

"I am Wilhelm Brombacher. Augustus is my brother, the patriarch of our clan. By the ancient legends, he was born to bring the storm, and I was born to bring the ice." Wilhelm smiled, the expression of a man talking about childhood games, and I found myself wondering at the innate pride that radiated from him. This was a Connected, even if he didn't fully know how to access the deep well of his ability. How many other Connecteds out there just needed the grace of another to open their eyes to their own power? "Neither of us brought anything quite so grand, though we led our family to the best of our ability, and in our age and foolishness, we almost lost it. A sobering lesson indeed. And one which we are grateful not to have paid for completely."

Wilhelm stepped forward and held out his hand to Nikki. "Indulge an old and foolish wolf who wishes to believe that his best birthdays are not behind him."

"Oh honey, your best days are just getting started." Nikki took his proffered hand, her grin curving with delight. "I can sense that you've got ice in spades, but honestly, it's not buried all that deep. If you'd augmented with some of the technoceuticals out there, I'm thinking you would have had some serious success."

I lifted my brows. I'd felt much the same thing with Augustus, though given the state of his injuries, I'd been less certain.

Wilhelm chuckled. "You are not the first to say so, though it should be said, we did not let the Star know this.

Despite her beauty—perhaps because of her beauty—we could not trust that what we saw was real, nor what we heard. We could go only by what we felt. But there have been fortune-tellers who have come our way before, insisting that we no longer needed to hide. That others like us were beginning to emerge, our magic closer and more accessible than we realized."

Nikki nodded. "The moon waxes full in a few short weeks. If we all survive until then, we will help you access the power long denied to you and your entire pack. I don't apologize for the actions of the Moon who came before me. She was born into a different night and fled into a different dawn. But I can tell you this, Wilhelm, augmented powers or no, we have need of you."

"And we can give you more than you bargained for, Mistress Moon," Wilhelm said staunchly. "We have not been idle since the Star laid our family low. We have tracked the families that she has similarly poisoned, and, in some cases, mourned their deaths."

Nikki stiffened. "There were more?"

"Only a few, the younger families, who did not remember growing up with the same level of persecution that we did, and protected themselves even less than we did." He sighed. "We have grown too distant from one another, leaving each other at risk through simple ignorance. But no more. When you breached the defenses of our cousins, we knew you were coming, and we knew we would test you. We did not—could not know—the result of that test. This is no longer a fight from which we can flee, to hide once more in the darkness. The darkness is no longer our place. However, such precautions have served us well for these long centuries in ways the Shadow Court could not predict."

He gestured, and four screens lit up along the wall. The younger Brombacher family members stood to take their positions beside them. The youths were a competent-looking lot, dark eyed, dark haired, and fit. They waited as Wilhelm explained more.

"The Brombacher family is no stranger to riches. It became a passion of ours, a way to fight without fighting. We have tracked other Connecteds who have fought in similar ways and we know their secrets. In fact, we can give you the greatest of those secrets right now."

My heart quickened as the old man folded and unfolded his hands a touch nervously, clearly unused to leading the family so openly. His eyes flashed as he spoke again. "There was no need for the Star to poison our patriarch as if we were filthy dogs beneath contempt. Whatever you do, Mistress Moon, however you choose to lead, remember that even the lowest of your victims in the coming war have dignity."

Nikki gave him a grim smile. "You can bet your sweet fangs I understand that message. I've lived on the opposite side of persecution more than a few times."

He nodded. "Of all the members of the Shadow Court, you seek most the matriarch of the St. Claire family, Eleanor. She styles herself as being the face of her family, the figurehead, but make no mistake, she is a fierce warrior with the strength of many men. She is Connected and has tremendous skill." Wilhelm's gaze shifted to the Magician. "In another lifetime, had you found her, had she made herself known, you might have ascended her to the Council to keep her from becoming the threat she has become. But now we understand that the Star found her first, or found her family in any event, we don't know how many generations ago, and the family now serves her. Eleanor St. Claire carries forth the wishes of the Star into whatever the Shadow Court does."

"What is her endgame?" the Magician asked. "What does she hope to accomplish?"

"What so many at her station have wanted secretly or otherwise once they reached a certain exalted status," Wilhelm said. "Recognition of their superiority and the return of a defined caste system. She has already reaped the benefits of the undefined caste system of the rich. But the existence of the poor offends her, whether they are poor in Connected ability but have the audacity to practice anyway, or they are merely impoverished, their bloodline less rarified than hers. Those with the will to improve their lots have proven to be particularly troubling to her. Not because it didn't fit her narrative of what should be possible, but because they didn't deserve the right to succeed, the right to step on the field. Her family included prominent eugenicists back when that was not considered in poor taste, and they remain powerful in the secret circles that still advocate for it. I hesitate to say that any human is pure evil, having been the recipient of such broad characterizations ourselves, but if anyone deserved the title, it would be Eleanor St. Claire and her family."

"And she has friends?" Nikki asked, earning her an actual smile from the old man.

"Friends? No. She has allies and supporters, of course. But no friends, and few enemies within the Shadow Court that we have been able to find. Unlike most tyrants whose downfall is secretly advocated by those around them, nobody wants to step into her shoes. They want her to do the hard lifting for them, and they're willing to live by her terms. They believe themselves protected by their money and their status. Their pride cannot conceive of a situation where she would turn on them as well. Their bloodlines are too old, too well established. They don't understand that once the dust clears from whatever battle is to come, Eleanor St. Claire will not be content to sit upon a golden throne and rule as an equal. She will grind them beneath her heel."

"So a real charmer all around," Nikki drawled, and I watched in fascination as her sardonic comment unwound Wilhelm another notch.

"She believes she is the strongest female in the world, second only to the Star," he agreed, eyeing Nikki with speculation. "I suspect she doesn't yet know you."

"Yeah well, there's awareness and there's getting your starry-eyed ass kicked," Nikki agreed. "That tends to enhance one's understanding of the situation, but we'll get to her later. What else you got for us?"

One of the other wolves took up the tale with a dissertation on the Fuggeren family, still the second most powerful members of the Shadow Court—where their wealth now existed, how they were investing it, and where they could be found. The results surprised me.

"They're not heading to any bunkers or private islands or protected areas," I mused. "I would have thought as close as this war is feeling, that would have started happening."

"It is a curious thing," Wilhelm agreed. "But in this particular battle, you cannot give up your position of authority too soon. If you choose to hide, you miss out on the opportunity of amassing wealth. It becomes a question of knowing when to leave a sinking ship. The rats leave first because their goal is self-preservation. But imagine if they had been led to believe that there was no possible way they could fail, that their preservation was assured? Then it becomes a situation of who is able to scoop up the vast amount of bounty while the other rats flee, because those rats are likely going to die anyway and won't be back to stake their claim on what is rightfully theirs."

"These guys are really starting to chafe my chaps," Nikki quipped. "I think I was happier when I didn't know they existed."

"I think we all were," I agreed, and though Nikki's words were meant in jest, I found my attention drawn to the Magician, who was rapidly scanning the screens, his fingers flicking to drive the information forward and back again so quickly that no one noticed. He was a sponge for this kind of secret intel, but he glanced my way as I studied him, knowing what I was thinking. He had been deprived of his memories up until a short while ago, and in some cases that memory gap covered hundreds of years of information. He inclined his head, giving me a small smile.

"It is never good to not know your enemies," he said in my mind. *"For it is in knowledge that you can defeat them."*

It took a little bit of finesse, but Wilhelm eventually agreed to feed the information from the Brombachers' prodigious archives into Simon's computers back in Vegas, allowing us to cross-reference it and augment everything that had come before. When that was done, we had a better understanding of the battlefield before us.

The battlefield sucked.

"The Shadow Court has embedded operatives in every city, near every major religious installation, and presumably has access to stealth explosive devices strong enough to create chaos even if there isn't tremendous loss of life," the Magician said at the end as we stared at screens with rapidly shifting probability strikes indicated in sharp detail. "There is one piece that doesn't make sense, however. The Shadow Court and especially Eleanor St. Claire come from a long line of eugenicists. This pattern of death and destruction is not great enough to create a massive die-off event on a global scale. That does not feel consistent with her interests."

"Maybe we don't know everything the Shadow Court's got in the works?" I suggested. "Maybe it's rule the world first, kill off a bunch of people later?"

"Inevitably," the Magician agreed, "but I feel there is some other element we are missing. Some critical piece. There's simply not enough death."

"Remind me never to ask you guys to a party," Nikki drawled, though her hands were clasped behind her back and she studied the maps with equal intensity. "As much as I don't like it, though, I think you're right. Every time we've come across these Shadow Court assholes, they've been looking to make a grand statement. This statement is grand, but only in aggregate. Only if all the explosives go off at the same time, causing massive chaos. But the way this looks, it's not enough. So you blow up a few buildings, maybe you blow up a thousand buildings. This ain't 9/11, not anymore. Shit gets blown up all the time. It sucks, but it's almost become a way of life. How is this different?"

"The Shadow Court isn't informing the governments," I offered. "They've got operatives in a lot of midlevel government jobs, a few in a couple of high-profile positions, but that's almost by happenstance, not intention. They're not dealing the governments into their game. There's going to be hit after hit after hit, with nobody to blame and everyone scrambling. What would they do?"

"They would blame whoever is most convenient," Wilhelm answered. "Whoever is the enemy of choice."

"And it would need to be a big enemy for something this coordinated," Nikki agreed. "So a major power. What if this

Eleanor chick has left a trail of bread crumbs to lead them to the enemy of her choice, not theirs?"

"And what if the government entities she targeted are the ones already considered the most likely to be at fault," the Magician put in, his head tilting as he worked through the calculations. "That would result in mutually assured destruction."

I waved a hand. "Yeah, maybe. But not necessarily, depending on what kind of bombs the Shadow Court sets off. It could be step two. How are we going to know for sure?"

"That is more problematic," Armaeus said, his voice suddenly becoming certain, more absolute. He turned to me, and there was no doubting the excitement in his eyes. "But all possibilities point most favorably in one direction. If you're ready to travel, Miss Wilde, prepare yourself. We need to go back to where it all began."

20

"I am *not* going back to the Vatican," the Devil said, his words brooking no dissent. "I was highly constrained the first time around, so it's not as if I noticed a lot. I would serve no purpose in returning."

"Oh, stop being such a pussy," Sariah muttered from her position against the far wall of the Arcana Council conference room.

I bit back a smile as I scanned the room, feeling the tension build. Kreios stood at the front of the table, squared off against Armaeus, while Simon sat once more in front of his multiple laptops, peering at the stack of celestial pavers that rested on the table near him. Nikki and Torsten remained with the Brombachers, hoping she could help bring their magic into sharper focus before the next full moon.

For once, the Devil didn't spare Sariah a droll remark to counter her criticism, but kept his focus on the Magician. "Why do you feel that this is the most appropriate way?"

"Because when I stepped back and started considering the true impact of this push to elevate Connecteds to their highest possible station, when I considered Dixie Quinn and her desire to become a goddess, and when I considered that we were given heavenly tools to combat this menace at great personal risk to the Hierophant, it occurred to me that we were missing a key audience of interest in this concern. Namely, the Catholic Church."

The Devil winced. He hadn't spent a great deal of time locked up in the Vatican's catacombs, but it apparently had left an impression. I looked at him. "Straight up, when I found you in the Vatican, you were in a box. A very small box. I'm willing to believe that there was no way that you could have seen outside it."

Kreios blew out a sharp breath. "It was not for lack of eyes that I could not see outside my prison, it was for lack of a view," he said. "I was routinely subjected to the scrutiny of the cardinals who had captured me, some of whom were in direct church employ, and some of whom operated the shadow cabal that we so effectively took out."

"You mean SANCTUS," I said, perking up, recalling one of the grittier enemies of the Council who'd made my life miserable during my artifact hunting days. "But they're all gone, aren't they?"

"Their organization has been dismembered, but as with many artifacts of the church, they have not all been destroyed," the Magician said. "But your return to the Vatican serves a more pressing need. Despite exhaustive study, I still do not know what the specific effect of the celestial pavers will be. I know they are a weapon of last resort and devastating impact, but not precisely what that impact will be. We must know this before we use them. Otherwise, we may create far more problems than we solve."

"You mean in all the vast research we've assembled over

the years, these tiles have never once been mentioned? We're going only on Michael vouching for them?"

The Magician waved a hand, murmuring something in a language I couldn't quite discern. Hebrew, I assumed, as the slim gold celestial pavers, each no longer than my own hand, lifted from the table and hovered. Without Armaeus doing or saying anything further, they shifted and reshifted, coming together and breaking apart. Creating miniature designs without any apparent pattern.

"Simon?" Armaeus murmured.

The Fool stared at the pavers with keen interest a second more, then shook himself and swiveled back to his machines. "We've got three major power grid fails in southern Asia, two more in northern Russia. All of Canada is blacked out. Whoops, now they're back online. There goes Argentina, though. Annnnd...she's back."

As Simon made these announcements, the celestial tiles continued to move. With each shift, a new power grid was affected, and when the tiles changed design again, the grid came back online.

"Okay, so Solomon was able to pull electricity down from the heavens back before anyone had discovered electricity?" I asked, studying the pavers. "How does that make sense? Has anyone asked Tesla about this?"

"He advised us to consider the question in the parlance of the day," Armaeus said. "Solomon would be interested in displaying absolute power over his opponent. He had to generate the energy to make the Ark of the Covenant work. Even if the details we've all heard about ancient powers incarnating through the Ark are wrong, those myths have lasted for thousands of years. Great power was assigned to it, and that power had to come from somewhere. Electricity is the power of the modern age, but as you know perhaps better than anyone, Miss Wilde, Connected ability tracks along similar pathways as those of electricity. The neural networks of mortals, the pathways of energy between all living things. What if in the absence of actual electricity, these celestial pavers attuned themselves to that more natural, organic power structure? Displacing the magic of the time and directing it into an object of considerable prismatic force."

I nodded. All that seemed reasonable enough. "But we don't have the Ark of the Covenant. We're not going to find it in the next couple of weeks either. Unless you think that the Vatican has it?"

"Not at all," the Magician conceded. "If it did, that information would have leaked, and it would honestly be to the Catholic Church's advantage to advertise such an artifact of worldwide renown."

"They do kind of need the PR," Sariah piped up from the corner of the conference room.

"And their leadership is not as strong or as dogmatic as it once was. We live in the age of information, no longer in the age of faith and belief. In short, we would know if it had been found. But these celestial tiles make no sense without a strong enough force behind them to activate them into motion. Once activated, however..."

He gestured, and I blinked. Nothing happened. He drew his hands together, and there was the same complete lack of reaction from the pavers. They continued on their preset pattern as Simon ticked off various power grids around the world that were coming off and online.

"Your turn, Miss Wilde?" Armaeus prompted, and I waved at the pavers, willing them to move. They ignored me too.

"Once activated, they refuse to change course, regardless

of my intervention—and, it would seem, anyone else's. It is only the initial intention that matters, the path on which they are set. My information about their nature is woefully incomplete," the Magician said. "Without further clarification, I cannot activate this prismatic force in a period of absolute crisis and understand what will happen."

"Maybe we're overthinking it," I said. "Maybe the point is the show. Stories that we have regarding the Ark of the Covenant say that its primary purpose was to make whoever saw it bow down in fear of the Lord. Well, right now, watching these things do their little synchronized swimming thing kind of creeps us out. We're not about to bow down in the face of God over it, but it's certainly giving us pause. Maybe that's all the purpose is."

"Perhaps. Yet I am the one who started them, and I can also stop them." Armaeus spoke again, this time in Hebrew. "It is finished."

The pavers clattered to the table, the sound so loud and unexpected, it made me jump.

"Well, that's a nifty trick," I allowed.

"And a problem, because what happens if I'm not there to stop it? What happens if I'm killed or distracted at the crucial moment when we should stop their movement?"

"Well, I vote you don't die," Sariah put in, sending a hard look to the Devil.

"I second that," Kreios said. "Moreover, I fail to see how returning to the Vatican will help illuminate this particular problem. You've plundered their records several times throughout the centuries. They don't have any information about something like this."

"I have plundered their archives, you are correct. I have not plundered all their treasures, however, nor those in particular that they do not know they have."

The Devil stared hard at him and came to the same conclusion I did. I spoke first.

"The patterns these things are making. The mosaics in the air. You think they're replicated somewhere in the Vatican, that somebody has those designs? And maybe a secret decoder ring?"

"I think those designs are located in a sacred site behind and perhaps beneath Vatican walls," the Magician agreed. "What was to be the holding site for the Ark of the Covenant upon its return to Rome. No one outside the highest orders of cardinals and their military guard has ever seen this room or knows its exact location other than it lies beneath the grounds of Saint Peter's Basilica. Most people outside the Vatican's inner circle have never heard of its existence, as every mention of it has been ruthlessly scrubbed from the history books. Fortunately, I happen to know an excellent artifact hunter, along with an illusionist who knows more about those byways than he would like to admit."

"So you keep saying," Kreios said tersely. "What is it you know that I don't—about this particular situation specifically? I don't have time for you to recite everything you know that I don't on all the other subjects in the world."

"I know that I cannot go to Rome," the Magician said. "Also that you know the terrain, even if you don't think you do. Sara has been there, but not in this location. Her focus was more specific. And, yes, to answer your unspoken question, they'll know you're there."

My brows climbed up my forehead as the Devil stiffened. Even Simon looked up.

"How is that a good thing?" Simon asked as Kreios stared at the Magician.

"If they know we're there, and if there are any agents in

the Vatican working for the Shadow Court, they'll think we know something they don't," I said slowly. "That will tip the balance of power."

"I think it will tip it in a number of interesting ways," the Magician agreed. "Number one, the most powerful member of the Arcana Council and the head of the Arcana Council take a trip to one of the holiest places on Earth, which is an undoubted location of incendiary devices."

"Why are they there? What do they know? What do they think they know? What should we know?" the Devil continued. "You're not interested in the reaction of the Shadow Court. You're interested in those who are financing them."

Armaeus nodded. "I confess it was Jarvis Fuggeren who gave me that suggestion, albeit from beyond the grave—and not literally," he said, waving off Sariah's sudden interest. "How did the House of Fuggeren make their money? By buying and selling the allegiances of the Medici family. Who now makes up the strongest members of the Shadow Court and their distant network? Not new money, not the Elon Musks and the cryptocurrency gods. Their time may yet come, but not in this fight. This is old money, old prestige, and families who are still infatuated with the idea of gods—an infatuation that began long before the age of atheism and secularism. That is the thread I have been missing all the way through this. That is the magic that the nonmagical have tapped into since the dawn of time. Framed in a way they could accept and embrace, but magic all the same. The power of the unmoved mover. The Arcana Council making a visit to the Vatican under cloak of darkness for unknown purposes will capture the focus and attention of anyone involved in the coming battle, while we have our attention on them."

Finally, I got it.

"You'll have the complete list of Shadow Court supporters, then," I said. "Or at least be able to fill in the gaps. And you'll be seeding discord and dissent within that group, because if there was something beneath the Vatican, the Shadow Court should already have ferreted it out before now. The fact that they haven't yet means something is there they don't know about, making them look stupid—or, more likely, that something's there that they *did* know about and they didn't share the information."

"FOMO is strong with this group," Simon put in solemnly, then he grinned. "I like it. It's going to ratchet up the anxiety of some of these guys, piss others off, and at least rattle the chains of the rest. And then there's the Shadow Court and this Eleanor St. Claire, and maybe the Star who might be interested in poking their fingers into the Vatican pie to see what's what."

"If they do, they'll need to send their top operatives," Sariah pointed out. "Not hired guns."

"They'll send Eleanor herself," Armaeus said, and Sariah moved off her perch by the window.

"Then I want to go too," she said. "You can't shoot a gun worth shit, Sara, and don't even get me started on your knife skills."

The Devil slanted her a look. "I am capable of keeping Justice Wilde safe."

"Yeah, and who's going to protect your skinny ass?" she shot right back. "I'm going. You can't stop me."

For only a second, I toyed with the idea that I *could* stop her. But Sariah was her own person with her own demons, and I nodded. The Magician did not look surprised.

"Take one tile," he said to me. "If it will let you."

A tile slid across the table without the Magician making

another gesture. It landed in front of me. "Why only one?" I asked.

Once again, it was the Devil who answered. "Because nothing rendered of the Jewish god would stay with me," he said. "And Sariah would probably use it to gouge somebody to death."

"Not untrue," Sariah allowed.

I picked up the tile. It weighed next to nothing.

The Magician's smile was sharp and fierce. "This is how it will work," he said.

21

"Why can't she walk with us like an ordinary person?" the Devil griped, his exasperation plain.

I glanced over my shoulder, easily picking out Sariah in the gloom. "She feels more comfortable by herself. She always has. Particularly somewhere that reminds her so much of Hell. You could go back and talk to her if you want to, convince her you're not going to try to kill the Magician outright."

"I would, if I knew that to be true," the Devil said, sounding even more annoyed. "When Sariah first aired your concerns, I raised the issue with the Magician. He pronounced the idea as fascinating, then went on about his day. Which left me without much to go on. I think he thinks it's likely that I will attempt to kill him, yet he seems unconcerned."

"Yeah, it honestly sounds like something he wouldn't be concerned about," I agreed, realizing I wasn't all that concerned about it either. If the Devil truly tried to kill the Magician, it was either going to be part of some kind of scam, or the world was a shell game that wasn't worth playing anyway.

"While we're up, let's discuss the real reason Armaeus wanted us off on this trip. What's he up to?" I asked.

Kreios shot me an amused look, the first hint of a smile I'd seen on him since we'd landed in Rome, the three of us transported by Air Magician to a construction opening the Magician had stabilized on the perimeter of Vatican grounds. To any casual onlooker paying attention, the camera feeds cut out at precisely 3:33 a.m., for thirteen seconds. More than enough time to get us into the catacombs and to close the entrance again, albeit at a section that had been walled off since the 1500s.

"I assumed you knew," he said, not with the air of a concerned man realizing that both of us needed answers, but with the smug assurance of having inside intel. "I forget that despite all your close connection with Armaeus, I have known him longer and have the advantage that he does not seek nor need to impress me."

"You want to cut to the chase?" I surveyed the walls, not sure why they bothered me so much. Something was wrong here. The corridors were too clean, almost as if they'd been swept down recently.

"The Magician's preparations require that you cannot be aware of them," Kreios said. "Blocking your knowledge of them is only half the problem. He's also had to stymie his desire to reveal his plans to you prematurely, and in this situation, that would not be ideal. Sending you here removes the source of the temptation temporarily, allowing him to focus on his work. And two, the rest of his explanation holds, with the additional caveat of you being the most interesting member of concern to the Shadow Court. You, not him. Were he to come to make this recovery effort alone, the immediate question would be, where is Sara Wilde? Now the attention is on you and effectively away from him."

"He really thinks things are going to go down fast?" I asked. "After all these thousands of years, the Star is going to rush to action?"

"He would argue that the rush to action has already occurred, and that the Star merely executed a plan that was millennia in the making. The trigger may well have been the release of the Moon from her hidden sanctuary, or it may have been the rise of the Connecteds' interest in making a big noise. Most likely, there were several potential triggers, only one of which was necessary to start her in her game. She could equally have chosen to wait. But with emotions involved, we do not always make the wisest choices, even when we have lived six thousand years."

I glanced around the corridor as we continued moving forward. "You notice anything unique here? Or I guess I should say familiar? There has to be a reason why this corridor is so clean."

"Clean and creepy," Sariah put in from behind us. "There are no bugs out here, no animals, but the air is fresh. You notice that? Doesn't smell like your typical crypt filled with moldering bones. These may have been the catacombs at one point, but they've undergone a reno job."

The corridor curved, and we walked another hundred paces more, the occasional clinking behind us indicating that Sariah was testing the tiles with her knife. Not with any expectations of breaking through to some hidden portal, I suspected, but marking time.

Tiles. I jolted myself back into focus, then lifted a hand, a faint spurt of fire glowing at my fingertips and illuminating the artwork pressed into the walls.

But my initial hopes were dashed. "There were patterns

in the rock beneath Solomon's temple, but they're nothing like this."

The Devil peered closer. "It was a good thought, though."

The corridor continued curving, subtly at first, then with a greater angle, but not enough that it was reminiscent of the drain-style maze at Solomon's temple. The floor also remained flat, even as we passed an open passageway that angled off to the right.

"You got any sense of where we are?" I asked, squinting up at the low ceiling. "We're still on Basilica grounds, but I feel like we've actually moved away from the church, not closer. That doesn't make much sense."

"Gee, if only we had an artifact hunter with an unerring set of Tarot cards to help guide her way," Sariah drawled.

As I reached for the cards, a sound cracked across the silence down one end of the long hallway. The unmistakable slam of a door.

Sariah drew closer, a thin light gleaming at her shoulder, just enough to illuminate the side of her face. "I've been in a lot of catacombs. They don't have much in the way of doors."

"It was some distance, but definitely back toward the church," Kreios said.

"You know, there really wasn't any reason for the Magician to turn off the electricity of the Vatican's security network in such a visible way, now that I think about it," I mused. "He was putting on a show. A short show, but a show. He could have undone said show just as quickly. Do you think the Shadow Court doesn't know about his ability to turn back time, however briefly?"

"I'd be surprised if they don't," Kreios said. "It's perhaps one of the most dangerous skills he possesses."

"I don't know if I'd say that," Sariah protested. "I'd say it was one of the most awesome. You turn back time that briefly, you can't break things too much, but there's a lot of wrong you can right before the world gets away from you."

Something in her words caught me, but I pushed on. "But he didn't do that. He didn't make any attempt to cover his effect on our arrival here. He wanted us to be caught, while not looking like we were trying to be caught."

As I spoke, I reached my hand into my pocket, but instead of my fingers first encountering my trusty deck of Tarot cards, they brushed across the thin sheet of a gold celestial paver. I pulled it out, turning it in the faint glow of Sariah's harness light. There were no markings on it, and it didn't so much as give a shiver of recognition of the proximity of the Basilica.

"Not exactly the card I was hoping for," Sariah complained. I rolled my eyes and offered it to her, but she stepped back.

"Vertigo," she said succinctly. "Every time I get near it. Total dizzypalooza."

I blinked in surprise as Sariah looked at the Devil.

"What about you?" she asked.

"I made the attempt back in Las Vegas, under Armaeus's watchful eye." Kreios shrugged. "My heart stopped."

"Jesus," I muttered. I tucked the paver into my other pocket and reached for my Tarot cards.

Three came out easily, but they didn't make me feel all that much better. The Tower, the trusty Five of Wands, indicating a fight was imminent, and Temperance.

"Well, the fight card I probably could have guessed, but what do you think about the others?" Sariah asked, leaning toward me. "I mean this place is practically littered with depictions of angels, but the Tower..."

We all came to the same conclusion, glancing up to the ceiling of the narrow corridor. "The obelisk," the Devil mused. "Why would they position anything so important so far away from the main church? That courtyard is always thronged with people. It would be glaringly unsafe."

"Maybe safety wasn't their primary concern," I countered. "Maybe efficiency was."

I turned one way, then the next. There'd been no more sound from down the long corridor toward the church, but I turned resolutely away from it. "I get the feeling we're going to know pretty soon."

It was another twenty paces before the clean, crisply tiled corridor opened off onto several offshoots, none of them in as good repair as the main hallway.

"Ah, yes, here's the smell of death I love so much," Sariah said, sticking her head down one corridor and taking a deep whiff. "So we've got feeder tunnels that take us to the catacombs, and then this main trail that goes God only knows where. Probably to some mistress's house so the Pope can hook up."

The Devil huffed a laugh. "Ever the optimist. I'm so surprised you haven't found your soul mate."

"You don't need to worry about—"

"Stop," I said, lifting a hand. I reached into my pocket, but there was no discounting what I felt. The thin celestial paver was shaking, the barest tremble, but it was noticeable. I pulled the tile out, and a long low moan sounded from behind us, down one of the corridors that, according to Sariah, led to the catacombs.

"Do I really want to think about what that might mean?" she asked.

I shook my head, stuffing the tile back in my jacket pocket. "Let's go."

We picked up the pace, heading swiftly down the manicured corridor, diligently ignoring any of the offshoots and keeping an ear primed for sounds behind us. After that first door slam, there weren't any. That didn't necessarily make me feel any better. The door slam may have been a mistake, and Ninja Swiss guards could be hotfooting their way toward us.

Another long, haunting moan sent a chill down my spine, and Sariah grunted in dismay.

"Could we get maybe a little more clarification?" she asked, but as I dipped my hand back in my pocket, I knew the card I would pull, and I was right. Judgment.

"Yes, it's coming from the catacombs," I confirmed. "Yes, that's not good."

"Yes," she parroted back to me. "We're about to get attacked by zombies."

"Where have you women been all my life?" Kreios asked.

"You know, I really do want to see this freaking vault, whatever the hell it is," I said. I looked back at him. "I know Armaeus wanted you along for the ride for a reason. Is any of this looking familiar to you?"

"It is not," he said, sounding equally mystified as the corridor narrowed further. "Lies upon layers of lies attend here, but that is the case in any religion. The Catholic Church holds no supremacy over that state. And yet..."

The Devil broke off, and I peered ahead, the corridor illuminated only by Sariah's bouncing harness light until I sent a zip of fire shooting down the space. There was a doorway, and a room beyond.

The Devil glanced up to the ceiling. "It is quite likely we are beneath Saint Peter's Square, which means the obelisk would be directly above us, more or less."

"I'm voting for directly," Sariah said, as we all entered

the room. It was built, and unadorned, with a shallow basin cut into the floor. The indentation was longer than a man's body and maybe four feet wide. Its base was lined with gold.

As with the rest of the corridor, the place was swept clean, but the tiling on the walls now bore a marked resemblance to the patterns I'd seen in Solomon's temple crypt.

"These patterns are consistent, both with what we saw in Jerusalem and the patterns the tiles were making back in Vegas." I waved a hand at the walls. "That can't be a coincidence, but the tiles were never here, supposedly. They were buried like a thousand years before the Basilica was built."

"Divine inspiration?" the Devil offered.

"The magic that ties everything together?" Sariah agreed, but it didn't matter. We were clearly in the right place.

I scanned the floor, but saw only smooth marble. There were no indentations to slip one of the celestial pavers into place. I reached into my pocket to pull the tile out anyway—

Chaos broke out.

I figured it was most likely that the Swiss Guard ninjas would reach us first, or whatever passed for Shadow Court stealth operatives, and I was right. Black-clad men of middling height, the better to race through subterranean corridors, jogged into the room, weapons up. The first shouted harshly at us in Italian, then English.

"Stop! You are trespassing. On the floor!"

"Dream on," Sariah retorted, and I caught the flash of her blade as she whipped it forward, the guard twisting away with remarkable athleticism but still not shooting. He'd probably been given orders not to destroy the chamber.

Sariah had no such hesitation.

"You want a piece of me?" she challenged, but her words

were drowned out by the next party attendees, who flowed into the room not like staggering zombies, but clickety-clack skeletons, their bones pieced together in a hodgepodge way.

"Damn it," I shouted as the tile in my jacket heated up to what felt like five hundred degrees. Rather than grab it, I yanked off my jacket and held it out in front of me as I turned to meet the skeletons' attack, a toreador flourishing my cape.

It did the job. The skeletons raced toward me and then straight into the startled Swiss Guard as I whipped my jacket away, soldiers who clearly had not expected the skeleton crew. Now the guns did go off, which only served to piss off the skeletons more as the bullets zinged around the small space, taking chips out of the walls and damaging the elegant mosaics.

"You're gonna regret that," Sariah howled. "God doesn't like it when you mess up his basement."

Apparently that was a taunt too far, as the guards roared in outrage and began to use their guns like billy clubs, battering back the skeletons. Each successive hit took apart the nearest attacker, like a science fair project gone terribly wrong. As human bones went flying, I noticed something else. My jacket had started smoking.

Careful not to touch the paver itself, I held the jacket upside down and shook it as gently as I could, barely remembering in time to pull my cards out first. The tile broke free. It fell to the floor, stopping short of the surface to hover and spin in tight circles. I reached for it instinctively, but it zipped out of my reach, cycling through the room like a whirling dervish. When it struck bones, they scattered. When it struck the guards, they screamed and collapsed.

The Devil, Sariah, and I plastered ourselves against the walls as the tile finally jerked to a stop at the far left corner of the indentation of gold, then dropped straight down. It struck the indentation and was immediately absorbed. An ominous cracking sound jerked our attention upward. Then there was silence. The tile resurfaced, almost accusingly, as three other indentations appeared in the gold pit.

"They're like landing pads for the Ark of the Covenant thing, yeah?" Sariah suggested. "Except we don't have the Ark."

"We also don't have three additional tiles," the Devil agreed. "But we know where we can find them."

22

I squatted to survey the gold-lined pit. The celestial tile now lay on top of the shallow depression, and as I reached for it, it shifted and willingly went into my hand.

"So I guess we take it with us? I don't feel comfortable leaving it here all by its lonesome, but I didn't think it'd actually let us take it away."

"And speaking of taking it away, where to next?" Sariah asked, scowling down at the men who lay knocked out cold on the ground.

There were four of them, and based on the low moans from deeper in the catacombs, there were also a lot of angry bones trying to sort themselves out.

"You know, that's an interesting question," I allowed. "It feels like if we've come all this way to Rome, we should stick around and see if maybe we can discover something else, yeah? I mean, now that I've been here, I know how to get back, should it ever come down to it. And assuming the obelisk hasn't already blown its stack above us, nobody technically knows what we discovered here."

Sariah made a face. "What did we discover, exactly?"

"A prism of power, capable of raising the dead," the Devil said. "That would be impressive in any era, but it will serve of particular note now, if the Connecteds rise up and unexplained phenomena get laid at their door."

I winced. "You don't think that the influence of these tiles—hell, this one tile—affected any graveyards beyond the catacombs, do you?"

He favored me with a droll smile. "At this point, I no longer know what to think. But to answer your other question, since we've gone to all this trouble, it does seem churlish to leave without saying hello to our hosts."

The Devil waved a hand, and his appearance changed to that of a guard. He turned to Sariah, holding his hand out to her, and she grinned and took it. A moment later, she too had absorbed enough of the Devil's ability that she could create her own glamour as a second guard.

I huffed a short laugh. "Now you guys are showing off. I can't affect that kind of glamour. I mean...right?"

"I would think it might be wise if you did not make the attempt just yet," Kreios said. "It would be more likely that two guards were killed in the altercation, while the other two can now return with the prize of the Justice of the Arcana Council. It might be worth it to see who was interested in recovering you."

I rolled my eyes. "Not to put too fine a point on it, but nobody would believe I was taken out by a couple of palace guards. I don't suck that bad."

"Oh, now look who's putting on her big-boss pants." Sariah laughed.

"I mean it," I protested. "Not to say I couldn't be taken out, but by these guys? Are you kidding me?"

"It is a consideration..." Kreios mused. "And we don't want to reveal that you have one of the celestial pavers..."

"Definitely not," I agreed.

"So maybe you're knocked out, and we found you, but we're completely freaked out because the moment you wake up, we're all fucked. How about that?" Sariah offered. "I'm not carrying your ass, but that's why we've got the big strong Devil here."

"Before we take our leave of these gentlemen, though, a bit of reconnaissance is in order," the Devil said. He knelt beside the youngest member of the group and jostled him awake. No sooner had the guard opened his dark eyes than Kreios leaned close, peering intently into the young Italian's face. I was never sure exactly what the Devil looked like when he went into full-on interrogation mode, but it was effective. The man went sheet white, and his mouth fell open.

"You'll tell me what I need to know?"

"Everything!" the Italian said hurriedly, though it was clear that he was still half-delirious. The information came quick and jumbled, but the gist was clear. These four guards were privy to a newly invigorated SANCTUS, the special operatives division within the church dedicated to stamping out magic in all its heathen forms. But they weren't a part of the Shadow Court, or at least if they were being directed by the Court, this guy had no knowledge of it. He'd served as a member of the Vatican guard for more than ten years, despite his apparent youth. SANCTUS security had known of the disruption in the catacombs, they had surmised that it was likely a member of the magical cabal that was against God and righteousness, and they had been honored to be the ones selected to bring back the unbelievers.

"Were you instructed to kill?" Kreios pressed.

"No weapons were to be used. This is sacred ground," the Italian said in swift, expressive Italian. "But the catacombs were restless, and we have been hearing more disturbances beneath the city."

"The bones have moved before?" Kreios asked sharply, and the man shook his head, clearly confused.

"The dead do not rise without an act of the Father. But there are plenty who move through the catacombs who are not the dead. We have been instructed not to stop them. We have been instructed—"

Some deeply buried synapse finally sparked in the guard's head, and he looked around, his eyes widening as he took in his fallen comrades and the piles of bones. "What infernal magic was this? What happened here?"

At that point, he began babbling insensibly. The guard's usefulness at an end, the Devil whispered the brief instruction for him to sleep, and he slumped down.

"How long should we leave them down here?" I wondered aloud, but the Devil shook his head.

"We will leave a few of the bones that don't seem to be eager to return to their owners, and nothing else. They'll come to in a few hours, barely the worse for wear, and have time to concoct their own story. By then, we will be through the Vatican and out, or in rather worse straits than I think any of us care to be."

"That's what I like about you, always so positive," Sariah drawled.

"Prisoners first." Kreios gestured to me. "No point in carrying you until it's absolutely necessary. These corridors are narrow."

Sariah sniffed with clear derision, but we set out.

Retracing the guards' steps up the corridor proved slightly more complicated than anticipated, because the memory the guard had given Kreios of their trek was overlaid with the shock and disorientation of the attack of the skeletons. But after a few wrong turns, we found ourselves at the door to the entryway to the catacombs.

As we approached, the Devil took out the key fob he had liberated from the first guard. Clicking a series of numbers, he smiled as the door snicked open.

"There is no substitute for good training." He turned to me. "If you would be kind enough to slump, Justice Wilde, we can continue through."

I obliged him, and the Devil swept me into his arms as if I weighed nothing. The door opened onto a small storage area, laden with casks of wine and lockboxes. Electric eyes winked at the doorway, and a scanner swept over our small group, immediately triggering an alarm.

"That better be because of Sara, because my disguise is the bomb dot com," Sariah groused.

The two of them braced, and I tried to look credibly limp as several sets of feet approached. From my position snugged up against the Devil's chest, I could hear the rush of Italian. In short order, the Devil explained that there were two men still left down in the catacombs, attacked and dragged away. But they had proceeded on and had found me in the repository for the Ark of the Covenant. They'd surprised me, managing to knock me out before I could unleash any response.

The guards seemed to believe it, which I thought had less to do with the expertise of the Swiss Guard and more with the hubris of anyone protecting their home territory. Bad enough that I'd gotten inside in the first place; they were more than ready to congratulate themselves on my swift neutralization.

One of the men apparently tapped his communications

device, as I heard the crackle of static and a terse query in Italian. After a short, barely audible conversation, I heard an equally terse directive come across: the guards at the door were supposed to kill me.

Well, that was unexpected.

I braced myself for the sudden shift of energy, knowing that the Devil and Sariah would quickly shuck their disguises to allow them to fight in their natural forms, when a woman's voice broke across the cell phone, sharp and assured. She spoke in flawless Italian, but though she didn't sound quite right, I was sure I recognized her voice, certain I had encountered her before. Either way, her orders were clear and decidedly more encouraging. All three of us were to report to some cardinal's inner sanctum, and I was to be tranquillized for good measure.

"I have what you need," Kreios said in the voice of a middle-aged Italian, presumably the guard he was impersonating. I kept my head pressed against the Devil's chest, heartened by the idea that Kreios himself was handing over the needle intended for my arm. He murmured something soothing to the guard. A second later, I felt the needle strike home.

For the barest moment, panic gripped me. What had Kreios done? Had he actually let some rando tranq me—incapacitated me in some way? Had I been wrong to trust him? Had all of us been wrong? Would I ever be able to trust anyone again?

The Devil shifted his hold on me, tightening his grip to restrain me more securely, and despite my best efforts, my panic spiked.

Kreios's low, rolling laugh sounded through my mind. *"My dear Sara Wilde, you flatter me. If I wanted you to be afraid of me, it would have been a simple enough thing once upon a time. When will you understand that you no longer need to be afraid of anyone but yourself? Now do a better job of faking sleep, or someone may question this good man's skill with the needle."*

Without much choice, I slumped against him, battling the ebb and flow of my reaction. I wanted to trust him; I couldn't trust him. I wanted to trust myself; I couldn't trust myself. Everything was changing; nothing had changed.

Was this what it was like to be the Magician? Endlessly chasing riddles in case one unexpectedly became a truth?

I poked the question out in the general direction of Vegas but got no response.

It seemed to take an eternity to traverse the basement of the Basilica and emerge into the offices of the Vatican, cycling through corridors and flights of stairs until finally, the Devil paused. The sound of the door opening clued me into the fact that we'd finally reached our destination.

As we entered, the Devil shifted slightly, allowing my face more access to the view in front of me. I slitted my eyes open a fraction, and it took everything I had not to stiffen. The woman I'd seen marshaling the Shadow Court at the Palais des Nations, Eleanor St. Claire, sat opposite a small, wizened man in a simple shirt with a priest collar, whose knees bounced nervously across from her, the two of them in casual chairs. There was a couch in the room as well, and Eleanor waved to it imperiously. "Drop her there."

"There is no need for this," the cardinal said quickly. "We know that she is dangerous, we know that she must be eradicated. There is no other consideration."

"Shut up," Eleanor advised him curtly as she approached me. She leaned down, and I channeled every bit of my psychic abilities to continue to give the illusion of slumber.

"She is the rarest creature on this planet," Eleanor

murmured, inhaling as if she could take my essence into her own. "She should be studied, tested, and then dissected. Death is not an option."

"We have *discussed* this," the cardinal whined, and I found myself rooting for the guy, though his preferred ending for me was only slightly more palatable.

"*You* have discussed this," Eleanor said, straightening. "I have not."

She stood away from me, and I felt the pressure of her attention shift, suspecting that she now regarded Sariah and the Devil in their guard glamour. "She was alone? We had reports of three operatives entering the catacombs. Where are the others?"

Still speaking in perfect Italian, Kreios was quick to reassure Eleanor that by the time they reached the crypt, I was the only one there, and I was knocked out. Maybe the others had escaped? They made no mention of the skeletons, but as I lay there thinking, it occurred to me that there were four bodies still lying in the crypt room, which was two more than there should have been. Had the Devil cloaked all four men? Probably. It was what I would have done. But how long would that glamour last?

"She had this on her," the Devil said, refocusing my attention.

I barely avoided stiffening as I heard Eleanor's stunned gasp.

"What is this?" she asked as I remained as still as I possibly could, heartened by the weight of the celestial paver heavy on my chest. Kreios had taken something from me, but it wasn't the tile. Some other illusion? Maybe an illusion of the paver itself?

"I was hoping you would know," Kreios said. "We searched her for weapons and there were none. Only this."

I could hear the rustle of expensive silk as Eleanor spoke again. "Are you familiar with this?" she demanded, apparently addressing the cardinal. "What is it?"

"I don't..." The cardinal broke off. Then he started again, his voice growing more animated.

"See these marks, and these," he said excitedly. What had the Devil given him, dammit? I flicked open my third eye, then jammed it shut again as I was assaulted by the skittering electrical circuits filling the small space. There was something else that I caught sight of—someone else, actually, standing in the shadows of the doorway, whose energy seemed so familiar...

Then the cardinal's next words refocused me.

"These were the inscriptions of King Solomon," he said. "You say you found this on her? Was there only one? Was she doing something with it in the sacred crypt?"

"She wasn't, not by the time we came upon her," Kreios told him. "We searched her after we incapacitated her, looking for weapons. This was all we found."

"Only one." The cardinal breathed out a sigh of relief. "Heavens be praised."

"What? What is it?" Eleanor demanded.

"The footsteps of God is perhaps the best way to describe them," the cardinal said, his voice hushed, and I realized the Devil *had* given up some facsimile of the tile, if not the true paver. "The path He walked in the making and the breaking of creation. It is all that remains of the most powerful act in human history. It is said that He gifted Solomon with these tiles in case there was ever a war that the chosen children of God could not survive. Solomon, in his wisdom, never called upon such power as this, and ancient scripture has it that he dispersed the tiles to all corners of the earth."

"Solomon would give up that much power?" Eleanor challenged. "Why?"

I barely kept from leaning forward as the cardinal continued. "Even the wisest of kings eventually falls. Solomon knew his limits, and more so the limits of those who would follow him. These tiles are not to be trifled with. If there had been more than one, it would be an omen of the end of the world."

Well, that didn't sound so great. Neither did what Eleanor said next. "All the more reason to take her now. Get the clamps."

"Miss Wilde." The Magician's voice rang through my ears. *"It would be wise for you and the others to leave now."*

And Eleanor? I asked. *Should we bring her?*

The Magician paused.

Then it was too late.

23

Even as I opened my eyes, staring straight up for a split second before rolling to my feet, I felt the pull of a heavy weight on my body. I immediately recognized the effects of a psychic dead zone. The Shadow Court had been able to leverage these dead zones when they occurred naturally, but I hadn't thought they'd gotten good enough to wield them as a portable weapon. This wasn't a particularly ideal time for them to get a gold star for effort.

"*Crap,*" I grunted, as I tried to summon fire to my hands and barely managed a flare worthy of a Zippo.

The Devil also hissed out a breath, and I swung my gaze toward him, registering his surprise as he quickly moved back several steps, pulling Sariah with him, most likely to maintain their glamour. None of us wanted to betray our hand completely until we had to, and I glowered at Eleanor as she turned toward me, her flashing brown eyes triumphant and assured.

She was a tall, elegant woman, with a rich fall of mahogany hair, porcelain skin, and a perfect cupid's bow mouth. She held up a strange-looking pair of three-inch tall cuffs, opened to reveal a series of lights glowing cheerfully along their interior. Those cuffs were emitting the deadening energy that I felt dragging down my limbs, and I lurched away as Eleanor lifted them toward me, but could make no further move to protect myself.

"Justice Sara Wilde," she sneered. "The Star told us that your pride would always be your biggest downfall. Good to know she was right."

She stepped toward me, and my vision spun. I twisted away and once again got a sense of someone familiar standing just outside the room. Who the hell was it? And was that person why Kreios wasn't stepping in to help? I tried to reach out mentally to Armaeus, the Devil—even Sariah—but I couldn't focus, not with the dead zone manacles swinging toward me.

I could beat this on my own, I knew I could, but there were so many people, so many souls in this building. I couldn't summon my full power to destroy her stupid cuffs. Too many people would die.

"You know what? Fuck a bunch of dead zones." Sariah muttered to my right. She was too far away to suffer the ill effects of the manacles, and I suspected she was used to her power ebbing and flowing depending on whatever psychic resources she had nearby. She didn't need those resources for what she did next.

She rushed forward, her guard glamour falling away as she reached the field surrounding the dead-zone manacles. Crashing into me and shoving me back from the manacles, she ripped the blades of Justice from her belt and dove for Eleanor.

Eleanor threw up her hands just as a chasm opened up in the center of the polished floor of the cardinal's office. Fire burst up from below, as if Sariah's attack had triggered a portal directly into Hell, and without hesitation, Sariah shoved Eleanor through it, then followed her straight down.

"Sariah!" the Devil shouted and surged after her, only to be rebuffed. He was immortal, I remembered with a jolt. And despite a couple of recent glitches in the system, Hell had a standing policy about that for most of its visitors.

The Devil was having none of it. With a blistering spew of epithets I couldn't quite follow, some of them from languages I suspected had been used before recorded history, he surged forward again, and this time, the gaping maw let him in, only to close immediately behind him, the floor returning to its former pristine state.

"God in heaven," the cardinal breathed weakly, but that didn't solve my immediate problem. Feeling the power of two more dead-zone manacles, I swung around—then stared in horror at the man who held them.

"Mercault?" I managed.

The short, well-dressed, irascibly French, and constantly turncoating head of the House of Pentacles held up the flickering dead-zone manacles like an offering. "I can explain!" he said hurriedly, but I had no time for that. I lurched toward him as he squawked in protest, and disintegrated us both—hoping, praying for a safe space to land.

That space didn't come quickly. A moment later, my third eye flipped opened, and I simultaneously flung myself and Mercault bodily toward Las Vegas and the Magician while I astral projected myself straight into Hell.

It worked—though the effort sapped my already half-dead-zoned energy. The first thing I saw was Eleanor's face, her imperious sneer beneath her thick fall of dark hair and flashing brown eyes replaced by an almost inhuman snarl. Fully inhuman, actually. I stared in horror as the fires of

Hell burned away her visage, revealing smooth metal beneath. *Whoa.*

A voice shouted, sounding as if it were coming from my own throat, but this wasn't me. It was Sariah.

"So *that's* the New World Order you got rolling under your stupid Star? You're going all Terminator on me?" Sariah challenged, moving forward with a speed that made me gasp, though I could only see it in my fractured vision as her knives slashed and tore into Eleanor's body, clanging into metal and circuitry. My mind flashed to the vision I'd seen in the Bright Rock Church birthing center. Was that what Dixie was using the undocumented Connecteds for? This obscene level of augmentation? I shuddered as Sariah roared. "That's all you got, you bitch?"

"Sariah," the Devil warned off to the right of my view, and without turning, Sariah ducked, barely avoiding a horde of demons that exploded from the wall.

"Now we're fucking talking," Sariah crowed, and I saw the Devil lumbering toward her, wielding long jagged swords, his eyes glowing a bright red. For the first time since I'd met Aleksander Kreios, he looked like the Devil incarnate. His head was bright red, hairless, his mouth stretched wide in a gleeful grin. Horns swept up from his temples, and the cruel tips of barbed wings towered over his naked shoulders. The hands that held the blades were immense taloned paws, and a full-on pointed tail whipped around behind him, but there was no disputing the elegant, almost aristocratic shout of pure joy as Kreios leapt into the demon battle.

Then the vision shorted out, and I realized—I was still traveling, my combusted cells scrambled. This was taking too long, I knew, though the attack I'd witnessed had taken place in barely the blink of an eye. I should be at my destination already.

I reached out, struggling for any sense of the Magician, of safety, but it was too far. It was too far! I fell, cartwheeling and flashing in and out of corporeal form, the human whose body I was wrapped around convulsing. It was all happening too fast.

I crashed to earth, releasing Mercault and rolling several feet before landing heavily against a wall.

"Ah...dollface?"

I blinked up as strong hands peeled me away from the wall, and then Nikki was on me, batting out the flames that I couldn't seem to extinguish on my own.

"Sweet baby Jesus on a tricycle, what *happened* to you? And what in the hell is Mercault doing with you?" Nikki demanded. Torsten growled in dismay beside her.

"What are these infernal devices?" the wolf roared, as another voice, one I didn't recognize at first, cut through my haze.

"Lead. Lead boxes—Jonathan, get them now!"

In another thirty seconds, the pressure on my body eased, and I slumped, drawing in the first deep breath in what felt like forever. I was back in the Brombachers' ancestral home, leaning against a wall, my body practically boneless, but at least all of it was together again. Apparently, my tie to Nikki was stronger than any magical misfire, thank all the gods in all the heavens, everywhere.

"What the *hell*," I groaned. My gaze landed on Mercault, who slumped against a chair like a rag-doll who'd gone through the spin cycle one too many times. Annoyance chased away most of my pain, and I narrowed my gaze on the Frenchman. "Is he okay? Wake him up so I can kill him."

"Here you go, honeypie. Let's let Sara kill you." Nikki's

voice was a quiet, comforting coo, and I realized she'd turned away from me to address Mercault. He sat up a little taller at Nikki's address, though his ass was planted firmly on the ground, and small, squinty eyes were stretched wide and full of fear.

Nikki brushed Mercault's hair out of his face, her hands oddly gentle, her voice soothing. "Not a good day for you, hmm? I see it, love chop. I see it. You just couldn't keep your little French fingers to yourself."

Whatever Nikki's sight was affording her of Mercault's memories, it made her voice drop yet further. "Why don't you go ahead and tell us, 'kay? It'll go better for you if you do."

"I can explain!" Mercault bleated, as if he had that particular track on endless loop. He swung his gaze to me. "The Shadow Court disrupted my supply chain, attacked my labs. I got curious—but I was going to tell you! I was."

I sagged back against the wall, strangely cheered by Mercault's lies. Since the first job I'd ever worked for the guy, he'd tried to cheat me. At least something in this world remained predictable. "Sure you were. Lucky for you, I need those manacles you're carrying more than I need to kick your ass. You want to explain what exactly Eleanor St. Claire is?"

"She's a *beast*," Mercault began, then squeaked as, with a subtle move of Nikki's hand, Torsten and every other person standing around us transformed into wolves. Torsten stood as tall as Nikki, his broad shoulders flanking hers from his seated position, the other wolves more compact, but no less fierce.

"Careful, French Fry," Nikki said drily. "Read the room."

Mercault shook himself hard, then seemed to gain more backbone as he met my gaze. "Eleanor St. Claire visited me in Paris, invited me to join the Shadow Court. What could I do?"

"Say no?" I offered wearily. "Display some humanity?"

"Humanity will get you killed," Mercault scoffed. "She used me to gain an audience with Cardinal Milan. She wanted to know the details of SANCTUS, perhaps to invite them to join the Court as well, and I confess, I was curious to see what still existed of SANCTUS. I thought you'd killed them all but the Italians...they are like cockroaches. They don't die easily, or well."

I snorted, then waved him to continue.

"I told her she would have her audience, but only if I came with her. Little did I know you'd be carried in less than three hours later. You are lucky I was there to protect you. I would not have let her dissect you, Madame Wilde. I promise you that."

"Well, that's heartening," I deadpanned. "Do you know what they have planned with their whole world-ending initiative?"

"I do not," Mercault sighed, seeming truly chagrined. Then again, no one could sigh like the French. "But Madame St. Claire truly is a different creature, not merely a loup-garou. She *showed* me her arm—peeling back the skin. She's surgically augmented with artificial limbs, an exoskeleton—even skin that had to be grafted to what remained of her own. She believes herself to be the incarnation of the next level of humanity—half machine, half human." He shuddered delicately. "She is an abomination."

I lifted a hand. "So let me get this straight. She's straight up Bionic Woman, but this Cardinal Milan was still down with taking her calls? I didn't think those guys wanted anything to do with Connecteds."

Mercault smiled. "Ah, but Eleanor St. Claire is not

Connected—she's augmented. That's the difference. And Cardinal Milan is no fool. He sought first to ensure the newly re-formed SANCTUS survived the coming conflagration. Just as I wanted to preserve my own organization above all else."

"Laudable," I observed drily. "But speaking of this conflagration, where are they going to start?" I asked. "Did Eleanor tell you? We already know they've embedded explosives all over the world. Even in Vatican City."

Mercault gave another expressive sigh. "You are not wrong. Cardinal Milan anticipated that the Catholic Church and its buildings of power would fall in the coming coup, would *need* to fall at some level, in order to ensure we were not targeted in the second wave of destruction."

"The second wave?" Nikki asked, but I knew what was coming next, before Mercault even said it.

"Where the governments of the world turn on each other, seeking someone to blame for the terrorist attacks," I prompted.

He nodded. "According to Eleanor, there are as many scenarios as there are stars in the sky. In some, the fighting will end in days. In others, it could last as long as a year. And in all scenarios, there are battles upon battles, fought by people who know nothing of the ultimate war between those who seek to control magic and those who seek to wield it. She was quite passionate about it."

I jerked as an unexpected image flashed into my mind: Sariah staring up, Eleanor standing over her, somehow having managed to get past her blades. Demons screeched and howled all around in the subterranean cavern, and the Devil roared in fury.

The image spun away quickly, and I winced, hoping that

that picture was simply an artifact of my aborted astral-travel detour. But I'd feel it if Sariah was hurt, wouldn't I?

I drew in a breath, ready to launch in again on Mercault, when the Magician's thoughts interrupted me.

"The end is coming swiftly for Eleanor St. Claire, Miss Wilde, but that is not to our benefit—though perhaps it is inevitable. We have stood too long on the edge of war."

I blew out a long breath, understanding immediately what he was saying. *She's the trigger, isn't she? She dies, it all begins? She signed up for that?*

"She did," Armaeus confirmed. *"The Devil has seen her truth, and so have I. For power, glory, and the untold wealth the Star has funneled to her family, Eleanor became a martyr to the cause that she believes is her own, but instead is yet another manipulation by a being as cold and fathomless as the night sky. Come back to me, Miss Wilde. There's more work to be done."*

24

I left Mercault in the care of the Brombacher family, who promised to keep him under lock and key until all the dust settled...assuming the dust settled...but took the dead-zone devices in their lead boxes with me, along with Torsten and Nikki. The Moon and her faithful general both carried a box in case something happened to me midjourney, but this time, we reassembled in Armaeus's inner sanctuary without further incident.

Armaeus wasted no time. He swept forward, pulling the lead boxes out of Nikki's and Torsten's hands, then turned and cast them in front of him, following the movement with his hands. A profusion of slender metal rods extended from the Magician's palms, making my stomach flip a little queasily. Between those rods floated a now-familiar nimbus of power, an infinite loop of energy that dipped, zigged, and zagged.

Under Armaeus's careful watch, the seals on the lead boxes broke, the lids flipping open, while the devices themselves lay securely tucked within their cases.

"Nikola," the Magician beckoned.

A second later, the Hanged Man of the Arcana Council appeared in a burst of electrical sparks, whirling around in front of Armaeus's bookcases in obvious surprise.

"You said you wouldn't *do* that again," he protested. "You said you wouldn't, oh—!" Tesla's attention was affectively grabbed by the hovering devices in their lead boxes. His hands went up, and his ascetic mouth curved into an appreciative O.

"She stole my patent," he complained a second later, though he sounded more awed than irritated. "That conniving Eleanor St. Claire stole my patent."

"So these cuff things work?" Nikki asked, her dramatic eyebrows tenting.

"Of course they work," Tesla snapped. He didn't wait for the Magician to summon him closer, but approached, circling Armaeus with clear fascination. "You can see how, yes? You can see."

"I can't see," the Magician replied, surprising me. "For that, I need the man who first discovered the realms of quantum electricity."

Nikola Tesla straightened, his hands smoothing down the front of his fastidious suit, evening out the panels. He breathed out and flicked his fingers wide, and for the first time, I noticed a set of slender rings on each of his fingers. Had he always worn them? They were thin, a pale silver, and I didn't think so—but I don't know that I would have necessarily noticed before now. The Hanged Man, though he indicated the divine pause in affairs, the change of perspective, never remained in one place for very long. He was always restless, always seeking.

"It is a matter of tapping into the lines that are already there, forming the patterns of the universe that we fail to appreciate."

As he spoke, he moved his hands in smooth and practiced gestures, and as he passed them over each other and apart again, I clicked open my third eye and gasped.

Nikki moved to my side, brushing her hand against my wrist, then blew out a low whistle. "Now that's a seriously unexpected power source."

Pinpoints of light flew around Tesla like fireflies on a summer night, and where they sparked, they served as anchor points for tiny beams of electricity that flowed into the devices.

"They're like those cube things that the Nazis were screwing with, remember?" Nikki asked, tilting her head as she watched.

"Those were far rougher constructs. The daggers of the Shadow Court are a closer comparison," Tesla corrected. "But yes, they all draw on the electrical fields of the quantum realm."

"Electrical," Nikki frowned. "Not magical?"

"What is electricity but magic bent to the will of science?" Tesla countered, still staring with rapturous focus at the spinning devices.

"Right." I made a face. This was all a little beyond my pay grade. "And in this case, the magic serves to nullify the power that it encounters, to blanket it and deaden it, much like the lead prevents the device from reaching us."

"The lead boxes ground magic," Tesla said. "But it is not only these cuffs or even the incendiary devices planted by the Shadow Court that will be affected by any surge in electricity coming from the quantum realm."

I glanced at him sharply, and he stepped aside with a flourish—allowing me to see what I had missed. Caught in the thrall of the Magician's magic, the lead boxes with their dead-zone devices weren't the only items levitating in

Armaeus's study. The celestial pavers, all of them except for the one currently in my pocket, anyway, floated and spun, once again making their prismatic patterns. I shook my jacket open, and the final paver emerged to join its friends.

"What the hell is that all about?" Nikki asked.

Torsten drew closer to her. "This magic I have seen before," he rumbled. "But in Atlantis, every street was once paved with gold."

"The pavers of heaven, brought down to this earth, to amaze the righteous and strike fear in the unbelievers," Armaeus supplied.

"Right," Nikki said. "And the SparkNotes on that?"

"These artifacts of the Christian god can channel power from the quantum realm as well," Tesla said. "If the intention was to impress one's enemies, I should say it was likely successful. Who wouldn't be amazed by the magic, the power of a god such as this? Who would not fall upon their knees and beg to be spared?"

Torsten murmured a low growl beside Nikki.

"Don't answer that, sugar lips," she advised him, and I pursed my own lips together, trying not to smile.

This was incredible, awe-inspiring magic, to be sure. But werewolves were creatures made of magic, as familiar to its workings as we were to the sun rising and setting every day. What if magic was the way of the world?

The devices began to hum, and my attention was once again riveted on the swirling lead cases.

"What does the humming mean?" I asked, newly wary. "Is humming a good thing or bad thing?"

"As with most anything, it all depends on your perspective," Tesla sniffed. "For our purposes, given that these tools are intended to be used against the Arcana Council, it is a good thing. But, as with most discoveries, once it has been let out of the box, it's not going to be easy to stuff it back inside. Even if those boxes are made of lead."

"How many?" I asked. "How many of these clamp units are out there, do you think? Enough to neutralize all the magic in the world?"

"Ah..." Tesla blanched as he considered the question. "Do you think that's yet another layer of the Shadow Court's game, then? To preserve those rarified few who have been deemed worthy of magic, whether because of their race, status, or bank account, while they take these devices, hide them away, plant them, doubtless in the same locations where the explosions are set to take place not only to distract world governments, but to damage—to destroy those with magic..." He trailed off, seemingly overcome with outrage. "How could they contemplate such a thing?"

"Stay with us, glitter boy," Nikki snapped, earning her a glare from Tesla. "Can it be done? Do they have enough of these whozits to make that happen if they've got a direct connection to this electrical source?"

The Magician answered that question. "Based on my analysis of the materials that make up these clamps, the answer is an unqualified yes. Which leaves us with an interesting conundrum. Right now, using the same electricity that fuels these devices, I can overload them, at least these two. Eleanor St. Claire has two additional devices presumably neutralized as well, given their current location in Hell."

"They're still down there?" I asked, instantly guilty for not knowing the answer. I reached out to try to get a fix on Sariah, but with the turbulence of the Magician's and Tesla's electrical play, I got nothing.

"They remain in Hell, yes," the Magician said. "The

Devil has made a Faustian bargain to engage in this battle, however, and I cannot predict its outcome."

"Wait, what?" Nikki turned to Armaeus. "Where's Kreios? I didn't think he could—"

"But he's going to be okay, right?" I asked simultaneously.

The Magician pushed on, ignoring us both to focus on Tesla, his jaw set. "How much of the quantum electrical flow can you control?"

The Hanged Man immediately puffed out his chest, but hesitated.

"I am well aware of your research, Nikola," Armaeus said quietly. "As one scientist to another, I ask you to be clear. What can you do? What can you not do?"

Tesla opened his mouth as if to bluster, then shut it. He beamed at Armaeus, and in his expression, I unexpectedly saw the boy who had run through the farmlands of Croatia chasing lightning storms, the young immigrant without a single patron, taking on the great and mighty business moguls of his day and coming out ahead, if only for a little while. Nikola Tesla was many things, but at his heart, he was a scientist who craved the attention and validation of other scientists, validation that the Magician had given him.

"I don't know the answer to your question," Tesla confessed modestly, tugging on his lapels with his thin fingers. "I know I can channel a great deal of electricity. You could say it was what I was born to do, and you would be right. But this electricity is unstable. The portals that have opened to allow its passage can be unstable as well. I potentially could take it all on indefinitely, but I suspect that's not the case. Far more likely I would be able to withstand a massive surge and then explode into very small pieces."

"Damn," Nikki said. "I'm not sure I like that possibility."

The Magician nodded. "And the probability of that outcome?"

Tesla cast his gaze skyward, looking like every student ever asked an impossible question that he still wanted to answer. "In the event of an explosion? The likelihood of me being able to hold the line as long as it took, one hundred percent." He sketched a short aristocratic bow. "I trust you will do what you can to minimize any delay in assisting me, of course."

The Magician smiled enigmatically and nodded. He opened his mouth to say something in reply, then stiffened. I felt it before Armaeus could speak the words aloud.

"She's dead," I announced, wincing away from the images shooting through my mind, the ripple of magic I could feel all the way from Hell. "Eleanor St. Claire is dead."

"Couldn't happen to a nicer person," Nikki said, but her words were terse, abrupt. "So what now? What happens?"

"The probabilities of Eleanor St. Claire's death being orchestrated in quite this manner were not unexpected, yet it remained one of the least likely catalysts of the battle to come," Armaeus said. "The removal of a central pawn necessitates a reshuffling of those in power."

The words came out in a rush, but not because the Magician was expressing any particular level of stress. If anything, he remained almost preternaturally calm, speaking at his ease. But with every passing word, he spoke more quickly, and while one hand still remained held high as if he were cradling the lead boxes like a master juggler, the other gestured in a wider arc, and suddenly, he was surrounded by a disco tech of glowing numbers, equations, and mathematical symbols. I'd seen him pull this routine before, and I didn't like it any more than I had the first time.

"Speak with your words, not your numbers," I demanded.

The Magician's hand jerked, the numbers and equations spinning off into another frantic dance. "The greatest probability is that the war has begun," Armaeus said. "The devices will be released at the same time as the explosions in the major landmarks and religious and governmental buildings of the world. There is no feasible way to stop the explosions from occurring, no feasible way to stop the powers affected from launching countermeasures, whether to protect their people or merely to preserve their reputations."

"Where countries are impoverished..."

Here he full-on shuddered, as if the information being fed to him was unexpected. I winced right along with him. I was not a fan of the unexpected when it came to Magician-level revelations.

"Societies and communities that are impoverished or cut off from the grid by nature of their remoteness will not be spared," Armaeus continued. "They cannot be spared. They are, in pure Malthusian doctrine, part of the problem. They will be overrun with natural disasters on a much grander scale than were tested previously by the Shadow Court."

"Storms. Floods. Earthquakes," I said abruptly. "So not only is the Shadow Court going to blow up just enough of Earth to set all the governments and their militaries against each other, they're going to unleash Armageddon on people who have no way of protecting themselves and with no advance warning of what they need to do, and follow up both sets of catastrophes with dead-zone chasers to take out any non-Shadow Court Connecteds left behind."

With this, Nikki turned to me, the first evidence of shock

spreading across her face. “Can they seriously do that?” she asked. “And can’t we stop them?”

“We can’t stop all of it.” A new voice rang through the winding bookshelves. Simon, the sharp staccato of his sneakers pounding down the winding pathways of Armaeus’s inner sanctum. He skidded to a stop, juggling two laptops in his arms as he blew out his breath in a rush. “But we can stop some of it. And maybe the right sum of the right parts to make a difference.”

The Magician nodded sharply, the fierce satisfaction of his smile undeniable. “We adjourn to the conference room. Wars weren’t meant to be launched from libraries, not even for the Arcana Council.”

25

With a concentrated burst of magic, Armaeus took Tesla, Simon, and the dead-zone clamps to the Arcana Council conference room, while Nikki and Torsten opted for my slightly crispier route.

"Stay frosty, my friend." Nikki grinned as we rematerialized in the familiar windowed room, and though Torsten stepped away to shake off the last remaining embers that coated his thick head of hair, Nikki paused a second longer, gripping my arm where the tattoo that Death had inked into my skin allowed us to remain forever linked.

"I'm not losing you, dollface, okay?" she told me, as Torsten turned back, then squared up beside her. Her gaze was fierce, her jaw set. "No matter what goes down with all this, I've got your back, front, and every surface in between. You remember that."

"I know," I managed, though I didn't know any such thing, my throat closing up on my words as my eyes suddenly burned. Blinking hard, I offered Nikki the steadiest smile I could, not trusting myself to say anymore, as Simon dumped his laptops on the table.

The room was now ringed with screens between the huge windows that looked out on the Vegas strip and the expanse of desert beyond, the city gleaming with a neon cacophony of lights. None of the screens were lit, for which I was grateful. I didn't mind staying in this cocoon of hope for as long as possible, before all hell broke loose.

"Okay," the Fool began, popping open his laptops and leaning over them with the ease of long practice. "So with the help of the assistant librarians of Justice Hall, I was able to crunch nearly a million cases' worth of data and dump it into the computers. Then I sifted through it with an advanced scanning technology that I will *absolutely* patent, assuming any of us get out of this alive."

Though his last line was said as a joke, the fact that the Fool's face had turned unexpectedly somber made me nervous.

"What did you find?" I asked.

"Whelp, there's been a lot of misery in the world, a lot of misery caused by magical people and a lot of misery visited upon magical people. Basically, it kind of sucks to be Connected. I get why these guys want to rise up."

"Wanting something and doing it are often two very different things," Tesla put in.

"Totally," Simon agreed. "But again, that's a conversation for another day. The bottom line is this. Major disasters in human history afflicting the Connected have paralleled, not too surprisingly, major disasters that have afflicted humankind in general. The difference is the Connected were disproportionately affected. You got your Justinian-era plague, your Antonine plague, a couple of critical floods—not the Great Flood, it should be noted. That one hearkens all the way back to the fall of Atlantis and that's a totally different kettle. But all the way up to and including the black plague, the number one way to wipe out Connecteds was to mask it as the number one way to wipe out a significant portion of the rest of the world. Nobody knew that for every non-Connected person who died, based on my preliminary math, fifty Connected died. Think about that."

"They hid it in plain sight," I said.

"I don't know that in the very early going, they knew what they were doing. It's not like some evil arcane black market person was sitting around saying, 'You know, I think what we should do is hit the world with a very big plague stick and that will knock out the Connected.' But somewhere along the line, people started noticing the correlation. A lot of people died in some of these events, and a disproportionate number were Connected, especially when it came to the plague."

Nikki flipped back a chunk of her platinum-blonde hair. "Bioterrorism at its finest."

"Connected bioterrorism to be more precise, but yeah," Simon said. "And it gets better, or worse, depending on your perspective. Those bombs that went off at Angkor Wat? Dead-zone explosives. We've got some significant loss of Connected ability in the local magical communities, right along with the building damage and emotional disruption of losing such a major cultural and religious structure. I'm talking a lot of people losing their mojo, and the majority of them are too scared to get help. That's not going to be the problem once these other bombs go off, because there's not going to be anybody to help them, especially with the kind of highly sensitive help they're going to need."

"But we can fix them, right?" I asked. "If any Connecteds get hit by one of those psychic dead-zone bombs, can they be healed, their magic returned to them?"

"*You* can heal them, yes," the Magician said, lifting a

hand to briefly quiet Simon. "But events are moving too swiftly for you to take the time for such healing now, Miss Wilde...unless you apply the effects of your healing energy over a large area."

"Like maybe the whole world?" I quipped, trying for a smile. The Magician didn't smile back, but regarded me with the kind of acute scholarly interest that never boded well for me. I could see the probabilities clicking behind his hooded golden-black eyes.

Before I could get any further clarification, Simon plunged on.

"Anyway, let's not solve the problems we don't have yet. My gut feeling is that we're not only gonna be dealing with straight-up bombs, but a fair number of psychic-focused incendiary devices mixed in, and probably some other kinds of crazy crap that we haven't discovered yet that the Shadow Court wants to test out. Because that was the other pattern I noticed. There's evidence of earlier versions of the Shadow Court emerging over the years, groups whose damage was limited to a very small footprint—but that damage matches some of the attacks we're now seeing that are hitting the old Connected families, rural communities, technoceutical market, you name it. If the Justice at the time had been on his or her game enough to take those baby Shadow Courts down completely, I probably wouldn't have noticed any correlation from generation to generation, especially since we had so many gaps where Justice wasn't in the building. But believe me, there are symmetries. This isn't the Star's first rodeo."

"She was trying out different methods of mass destruction," I said. "She didn't see the point in building up a cult following back in the day, but she took advantage of the smaller groups that formed and then let them disperse.

Humans die. It's what they do. Why put your efforts into building a loyal base that could be detected or gain prominence, only to see them become victims and die off anyway?"

"Then how do you explain the actual Shadow Court?" Nikki asked from her position near one of the windows. Her shiny leather bodysuit glowed in the reflection of the Strip's glittering lights. "As far as I can tell, they've been kicking around for centuries, and they're still going strong."

"They're a human construct. Humans also endure." A new voice spoke these words, strong, female, weathered. Gamon, Judgment of the Arcana Council, stepped out of the shadows of the far conference room door, a stiff and snarling Rangi at her side. Rangi still had his hands shackled, and he stared at us all in unapologetic hatred.

"Funny thing happened on my way to killing this asshole," Gamon continued. "His problem wasn't that he wouldn't give up the goods, it was that he never shut up. He also has significant issues with women, power, magic, and anyone with illusions of godhead. He prefers to work out his therapy with his fists, and I was willing to indulge him."

At this, Rangi surprised me by flashing a grim smile. "In all the ages, I have met no male or female who fights so well, and so completely without honor."

"Thank you." Gamon gave a small, satisfied smile of her own. "But the point being, what would happen if there were no Council? Magic would not be balanced. People would die. Information would be lost, arcana that took hundreds, sometimes thousands of years to accumulate. And then the world would start again, whether we wanted it to or not. The human condition would find a way."

"So we should give up?" Simon asked, and now it was his turn to look like he was ready to fight.

"That is one interpretation, but not, I think, the correct one," the Magician said. "I recognize it is not my place anymore to guide the Council, and yet in the Devil's absence..."

"Take the job," Nikki cut in, and both Tesla and Simon nodded in agreement. Armaeus shifted to the side, and his corona of power shifted with him. Rangi stepped forward, suddenly noticing the lead boxes with their infernal devices.

Gamon didn't stop him, and I peered at the chains around his wrists, realizing for the first time that they weren't bound together. Rangi had managed to snap the chain between them and now wore the manacles like some strange badge of honor.

"What manner of magic is this?" he asked. "I sense its wrongness."

"Seriously?" I asked, genuinely surprised. "It's intended to keep down magic. I would think you'd be all in on something that would diminish the power of a god."

"And that's what you get wrong. That's what you *all* get wrong," Rangi shot back, turning around. He pointed into the shadows, and I turned, surprised to see that the High Priestess had joined us in the Magician's conference room. Eshe looked large eyed and hollow cheeked, as if she'd been awakened from a deep meditation that had robbed her of strength and vitality, rendering her beauty less haughty and more fragile.

"Here we have a High Priestess who has the gift of twisted sight, and whose predictions, once discerned, could guide kings, but could also lead them to their death," Rangi said. "She puts her magic out there for others to follow. She gives not one good goddamn whether or not they follow it."

Eshe blinked, clearly surprised to be singled out the moment she arrived, but the attention bolstered her. She lifted a long-fingered, heavily ringed hand, and swept her hair back, the dark mane tumbling over her shoulders.

"My magic is to show the way," she said, her voice clear and resonant. "It is your choice to take the path."

"Exactly," Rangi said. "That is *exactly* what I'm talking about. I don't dispute any of your rights to be a god, if you so choose. I dispute your right to lead humans by nature of your godhead. If you are a good person, or a good fighter, and people rallied to you for those reasons—then lead and be at peace. But if you compel them by force or by magic, you're the lowest creature on this earth. That's what I oppose."

"Thanks for the clarification," Nikki quipped. "But we've got bigger problems than yours on tap this morning, danger boy. We need to focus on stopping a lot of really big explosions from happening. Explosions you helped kick off."

"Whether I started it or not, this war was bound to come," Rangi insisted, folding his heavy, chain-draped arms across his chest. "And in war, there's always a cost. If the cause is true and right, that cost is worth it. My mission was to relieve this earth of an agent who didn't seek to lead by character or by strength, but by fear, coercion, and manipulation. I did that."

I pointed at him, finally getting to ask the question that had been plaguing me. "You drew Viktor out with your attack on Angkor Wat. How could you have known the Shadow Court would send him?"

"I didn't." Rangi's grin was harsh. "That was a bonus. Whoever they sent, whatever agent, he or she had to be strong enough to potentially stop what I was doing. The Emperor couldn't say no to the opportunity to show off once I laid out the path. It was up to him to step on it. And he did."

"How?" Simon asked. "Where'd you get the knife that zapped the life out of him?"

Rangi's lips curled. "Not every enemy of the Shadow Court can be found inside the Arcana Council. There are pockets of resistance to their tyranny I won't betray, but trust me, they're there."

It was all I could do not to dart my glance to the Magician. Surely he was reading Rangi's thoughts, right? The ancient warrior couldn't have enough Connected ability to mask his mind completely. Either way, the Magician remained silent.

Rangi continued, staring around fiercely. "I will help you save humanity from the Shadow Court, even if I won't help you force humanity to follow you."

Gamon rolled her eyes. "Don't try to act like I didn't explain to him that isn't what we're about. He doesn't listen so well."

"Is that not what we're about, though?" the Magician asked quietly, drawing our attention. "Rangi is long-lived, and he has seen enough to know that the Council has fallen victim to its own pride before. Even now, the temptation to kill the members of the Shadow Court outright is strong, instead of merely subverting their desire to rule."

"Yeah, well, I, for one, have no problem kicking some Shadow Court ass," Nikki drawled, and Torsten folded his arms over his chest. The two of them were an unbreakable unit, and the sight filled me with a much-needed upswell of hope.

"The Shadow Court cannot win this battle," Torsten said, his voice gravelly as he stared at each of us. His face was weathered, his eyes hard, but his demeanor remained calm, certain. "Magic must survive within humanity, must grow. It's hidden too long in the shadows."

His words settled over the room. Torsten didn't talk much, so when he did, people listened to him. His six thousand years of perspective counted.

The Magician nodded, then waved an easy hand. He hadn't been idle since Rangi had answered my question about the knives. Whether he'd gathered his intel from the head of the House of Wands or not, a pile of gleaming blades appeared on the long center conference table, making Gamon bark a sharp laugh of satisfaction.

"Tell me that these are what I think they are," she demanded as Rangi strode forward, picking up the nearest knife to study it with his brows bunched together.

"They are," Armaeus said. "Rangi, we owe you a debt of thanks. In sharing this information, you have given us what we need to at least begin the fight. The weapons of your allies are our weapons too, at no cost to them, I promise. But now, the task is clear. We cannot stop the explosions, if Eleanor St. Claire's death is the trigger we believe it to be. Those bombs the Shadow Court has set *will* go off. We can only limit the damage, and give the Connected community a chance to fight back. And so, you must all choose your mountain to protect or to die on—whatever building, city, or group of Connecteds you wish to try to save. But first, Tesla, a question."

Armaeus turned to the Hanged Man, who paid no attention to the glittering knives but still stared at the shimmering dead-zone manacles as if they held the secrets of the universe. Maybe they did. At the Magician's direct address, he refocused on Armaeus, who continued. "These devices are meant to pull the energy from the quantum realm to deaden magic. What if they were instead designed to augment it? What load could they sustain?"

"Unknown," Tesla said, lifting his hands to touch his

fingertips together. "Certainly quite high, but whoever handles them, that individual would also become a conduit and a channel. At a certain point of overload, you can't flip off the switch. The ramifications will be transformational, and by transformational, I mean you will die. You may be blasted into the stratosphere, outright killed if your heart stops, reorganized into an entirely different creature, flung across the world..."

"Understood," the Magician said, but *I* didn't understand—or, better stated, I didn't want to understand. I swung my gaze around the room, taking in the pale, set faces of the Council members. We all knew and didn't want to know.

The Magician shifted his hand, and the lead boxes fell away from their devices. Now, instead of two dead-zone cuffs, there were five, their clamps snapped closed, with flat restraining bands wrapped snugly around them, rendering each clamp into a thick, pulsing orb. Then there were ten of them. He directed them to hover over the bench where the knives rested.

"Take a device with you, and the knives as well, if you like, and go to where you feel you can do the most good," the Magician told the assembled Council.

"There is death in this path," the High Priestess interrupted, but her voice held no strain, only resignation. She glanced around the room, taking in the group. "You note Death herself is not here. She would not countenance the loss of our souls in this pursuit."

"The Hierophant isn't here yet either," Tesla pointed out, but his fingers twitched with excitement, his gaze still locked on the infernal devices that could draw down the power source he'd dedicated more than a hundred years of his life to.

"The Archangel cannot kill a human. And all of us, at one point or another, were human." The High Priestess slid a glance to me, and smiled faintly. "Well, most of us."

Though I was sure she meant the comment as an insult, it made my heart tug hard to the side. I caught myself wondering if I would see Eshe again after the coming battle —and I didn't want to think about that either. She and I had never been friends, but she had helped me when I'd needed it, and I had tried to help her too. I couldn't imagine this world without her in it.

What was going to happen to us? And why did it have to happen this way?

"Are you sure this is the best course?" I asked Armaeus. "That we each take the front bodily?"

"This is *a* course," he confirmed. "A way for each Council member to save that which brings us joy, which is all we can do in the end. The war is upon us, Miss Wilde. Destruction will result."

"But does it *have* to?" I demanded. "We played this game with the gods, and a whole bunch of things exploded. Then you turned back time. You stopped the destruction of London from being something that anyone knew happened. Why is this any different?"

Armaeus regarded me with tented, aristocratic brows. "I turned back time a matter of seconds, which is all I would ever do. To Rangi's point, I'm not a god. No matter how great my powers are, it is not my place to change the fate of the earth simply because I feel it should be changed."

"But doesn't that—"

I shut my own mouth firmly as the Magician's hand lifted and the devices broke free from their nimbuses. One of each flew to the High Priestess, the Fool, and Gamon, while two others disappeared.

"The Hermit," the Magician explained. "He will need them to secure the veil."

My teeth ground together as I glanced away, staring hard at the Vegas skyline for a second. We weren't the kind of dad-daughter duo they made TV commercials over, but dammit, the Hermit was my father. I couldn't quite imagine the world without him in it either.

I swung my gaze to the High Priestess. "Is he going to die?"

She stared back at me, her gaze soft and unfixed, her mouth moving slightly. "He may," she conceded. "So may we all."

"For fuck's sake, this solution *sucks*," I groaned, panic building within me anew. "I don't understand why this is the right way." Anger stoked the fear higher, and I could feel the energy snake along my shoulder blades, my wings desperate to break free. "We don't have Sariah and the Devil here. We—"

Five more devices winked out of existence, and I stared at the space they'd occupied.

"We are all Connected in the end," the Magician offered, though his tone had gentled. "The fight is ours to wage."

"Yeah, but..." Frustrated, I ran my hands through my hair, half pulling it out of its pony tail before roughly yanking it back in place. "You and I have to be able to help too. You've just allocated the last of the dead-zone cuffs. What about us?"

"It is not the designs of man that we must wield." He turned and gestured to the thin golden pavers that hovered behind him. I hadn't realized he'd transpo'd them to the conference room too, but of course he had. Now they too were sparking with the energy that Tesla had called into being. "Cardinal Milan said the arrival of those artifacts foretold the ending of the world, and so they may. But no mortal can make those predictions with full confidence."

I closed my eyes, struggling not to shout back at him in pure frustration. Armaeus was so calm—they all were, even Simon. Did they not understand what was potentially going to happen here? Did they not get that I needed them all to stay safe? To stay whole? That they were the only family I had left in this universe, and I couldn't bear to lose even one of them?

Armaeus didn't hesitate as I flailed, but turned back to the group. "Do you all make your choices? Will you all fight for humanity, a humanity that may no longer be in balance when all is said and done?"

No one spoke. No one needed to. They pulled the devices from the air, weighing them in their hands. The Magician stepped up to Simon. "Where do you want to go?"

Simon grinned back at him. "I've got a full-on ArcanaCon of gamers assembled in Munich. I think those are my people." Without another word, the Magician nodded, and the two of them winked out of existence.

I wheeled around, surprised to see that the High Priestess had moved close to me.

"I was there when you first learned to astral project, and then to help you bodily transport yourself across the realms," Eshe said quietly. "I've seen a great many things in my time: the decay of the world I love, and the hope for its rebirth, a hundred times over. Take me to Egypt, Justice Wilde. And don't tell the Magician where I've gone. But keep him safe."

I stared at her, struggling to swallow the emotion that leapt up within me. "Eshe," I whispered, the word half-strangled, and she gave me a soft smile.

"Trust yourself, Sara. I see the love you have for him. It is a love that transcends space and time. Hold on to that. Always hold on to that."

I nodded hard, blinking back hot, stinging tears. Without saying another word, I wrapped my arms around her, and we were gone.

26

By the time I got back, the screens around the Arcana Council conference room had multiplied—and someone had flipped on the power. Now they were three rows deep and extended around the entire space, each fixed on a different potential target and representing every major city in the world and a few notable landmarks as well.

London, Paris, Geneva, Chicago, New York, Rio, Moscow, Kyoto, Tokyo, Dubai, New Delhi, Sydney. It had been less than three hours since Eleanor St. Claire's death in Hell, but the images on the screens remained eerily peaceful, some bright with the bustle of day, some barely clearing dawn. On any other day, their postcard-perfect views would have made me smile.

Now the images filled me with dread. How much different would they look in only a few short hours? How much time did we really have?

Only Gamon and Rangi remained in the conference room. She glared at me as I crackled into a corporeal state, the last remaining embers winking out.

"Exactly *what* am I going to do with him?" she demanded, hooking a thumb at Rangi.

"What can you mean?" Rangi protested. "You don't think I could fight alongside you, me and all my men? Have you ever seen the fighting power of—"

"Can it, Spartacus. You want to die, I'm happy to let you," Gamon said, rolling her eyes. But she still looked unhappy as she met my gaze. "Bigger problem. Who the hell should I save?"

The question caught me off guard—mostly because I was wondering the same thing.

"Eshe felt she would serve best in Egypt," I offered, then I realized with a jolt who else had disappeared. Nikki had left…without saying goodbye to me. I'd known why she did it, but it still left a hollow pain deep in my gut. *Stay safe, beautiful Nikki…*

I could almost hear her bright, confident laughter as I refocused on Nikki, curving my hands into fists to stop them from bursting into flame. "Where did Nikki go? Or Tesla?"

"Nikki went back to her wolves, but Tesla? New Jersey," Gamon said. "Apparently, even though his original factory was torn down, like, at the turn of the last century, there's something about the energy of the place that appeals to him. He's unstable, you ask me. Far too ready to push his electrical toys to max capacity and go poof just to see how it all turns out. I don't want to be anywhere near him when he blows, I can tell you that. Simon said he was going to Munich, and who knows where the Hierophant and Death will end up. Probably together, though."

"Gods and their minions," Rangi humphed. "I'm surprised an angel of the Christian god was ever allowed to walk the earth so casually. It can be their undoing."

"What do you mean?" My gut tightened at his words as I

remembered the Archangel's expression—the change to his entire body—as he watched Death shepherding the souls of the fallen in Jerusalem. Color had suffused every inch of him, from his burnished skin to his multihued wings.

"Humans have always been an angel's greatest temptation." Rangi shrugged. "They seek to teach, to share the grace of their Father, but humans trip them up. They begin to want what they can't have, to crave the anger, the passion, the endless restlessness that makes humans what we are. It's a slippery path."

"Yeah, well, Michael's a cold fish if I ever saw one." Gamon remained staring at me. "Doesn't change my problem, and we gotta roll, Sara, if I'm going to do any good at all. Half the world is already on fire."

I didn't agree with her assessment of Michael, but that was neither here nor there. I forced the next words out as steadily as I could. "Do you have family you want to save? Friends?"

Gamon's dark eyes gleamed as she gave a soft, rueful laugh. "You know me better than that."

"Who are the fiercest warriors you've ever fought with or against?" Rangi asked abruptly, and Gamon flicked him a glance.

"The Mossad," she said without hesitation. "Not that they don't have their issues."

"So we go there." He nodded. "We'll need fierce warriors who can help the survivors stay alive when all this is done."

I blinked, but as soon as the smile began forming on Gamon's face, I didn't wait any longer. I pulled them both into my embrace and disintegrated, reappearing in a back alley that practically vibrated with radiant heat. Bombs and mortars sang overhead, the sound of fighting nearby.

Rangi peered around. "These warriors are here?"

Gamon huffed a laugh. "The thing with the Mossad, you don't know where they are until they want to be known."

"Right," I agreed. "But we're in Jerusalem, close to Temple Mount, because I knew how to get here. I think there's probably going to be some action here—and maybe action worthy of the Mossad. It's not that far from Tel Aviv, and given the bombing..."

"Oh, they're here," Gamon finished for me, peering down the street as another round of gunfire burst out. "I can feel them."

"Okay, then. Be careful," just as with Eshe, I hated the emotion that rose within me, especially given Gamon's cool expression and Rangi's fierce excitement. "You die and I'm going to chase you down in Hell and kill you all over again."

Gamon shrugged, her face impassive now, though her eyes were dark and steady on mine. "I thought that was kind of the order of the day."

I shoved her so hard, she stumbled back a step, surprise sparking in her eyes. Then I turned to Rangi and poked a finger at him. The heavy-shouldered Island giant met my gaze, his face fanned by the stiff, hot breeze that snaked through the streets of Jerusalem, his black eyes alight with battle fever. "You keep each other alive. We're going to need you, dammit."

Then, not trusting myself to say anything more, I set myself on fire.

As I shot across the planet, I tried my extended sight again—and to my mounting horror, I could see the world joining me in my miniature self-conflagration. Explosions burst up in Rome, Paris, New York, Chicago, the energy signature frying my third eye as genuine fear snaked through me.

"Miss Wilde," Armaeus murmured in my ear, and I rushed to return to the Arcana Council conference room.

"What's going on?" I blurted, as soon as the last bits of burning Sara guttered out.

"The tiles, Miss Wilde," Armaeus said. He gestured, and I turned to see that the celestial pavers were all up off the conference room table, practically quivering with pent-up energy. "They seek their natural resting place, to complete the task for which they were created."

"But they'll bring about the end of the *world*, Armaeus. You said it yourself—you called it the unmaking. If you can't turn back time to fix anything we break, how is the unmaking of *anything* a good plan?"

To my surprise, a flash of pain shot across Armaeus's face, more unnerving than anything that had come before. "Miss Wilde, I think more of you than you ever have of yourself or that you ever will. It is the reason why I am allowing this particular version of the plan to move forward. When Sariah took the High Priestess's vision and worried about the Devil killing me, she forgot that the High Priestess does not always give accurate or exact information. Eshe's vision was twisted and threaded back on itself, to be delivered in the only way it could have been in order for it to be received by the person it was ultimately intended for, which was me."

The Magician lifted a hand, and a new bank of screens appeared, lining the walls of the conference room near the floor. The first few images I recognized. The Louvre, the British Museum. Several others flashed into focus: the library of Trinity College in Ireland, the Met, the Rikjsmuseum.

"What the hell is that about?" I asked, my attention arrested. "They're targeting museums?"

"Museums and famous libraries that are dedicated to

providing access to history to the masses," the Magician said. "How do you ensure that any particular group of people don't get ideas to move ahead of their station? You limit their access to knowledge and restrict their education. Even if we stop the Shadow Court...their damage will live on if these locations are destroyed."

"They're all going to blow up?" I asked weakly, knowing the question was foolish. Armaeus wouldn't be showing these places to me unless these were targets of the Shadow Court.

"It is a one-hundred-percent likelihood," he agreed. "In some cases, once again, the impact on the surrounding ordinary human populace will be minimal. Of course, some of these institutions will have people roaming the halls—staff, guests, students in some cases. But the greatest loss will not be human life. It will be human progress."

"Okay." I blew out a breath. "Why are you showing this to me?"

"Because when I asked the other members of the Arcana Council what was most important for them to save, for myself I had really only two answers. The first, of course, was—"

"Knowledge," I said automatically.

"You," he said, making me blink, I jerked my gaze to his, and naked pain racked his expression.

"Miss Wilde," he began, then stopped for a moment, swallowing before starting again. "Sara, I have come to understand that there is no life for me without you, and all the knowledge of the universe cannot counteract that simple truth. First, you must be saved."

"Armaeus," I began, but he quirked a brow, his usual smile returning.

"However, should events fall the way I anticipate, there

is a ninety-seven-point-three-percent chance that you and I both will make it through the coming conflagration unscathed. It was the best I could do while still ensuring the safety of humanity." He gestured to the screen. "With that in place, the second most important target for me to save was, as you say, knowledge. For that, I will need to devote singular attention to these locations."

He gestured again, and a dozen orbs appeared, more of the infernal devices that had been modified to channel quantum electricity to augment their wielder's power. "While I attend to that, you must attend to that which matters most to you."

I gave a short, grim laugh. "Well, I hate to break it to you, Armaeus, but that doesn't include blowing up the planet."

"Doesn't it? Who are the most important people on this earth that you wish to save?"

"How can you ask me that?" I groaned, a fresh wave of pain curdling through me. "Armaeus, I don't want *anyone* to die by my hand. I've spent most of my adult *life* trying to ensure they don't die, and I haven't really been all that great at it."

He shrugged, not letting me off the hook. "So, who would you champion, then—who have you always championed?"

"The Connected," I said, my voice harsher than I wanted it to be. "All of them. Both the strong and the weakest among them. Anyone who has psychic abilities or believes they might develop those abilities. I want them to understand their power, be able to hold their heads up and know they're special and powerful, able to make magic by the sheer force of who they are. Not drugs, not science. But tapping into the energy of the world around them. I'd help them be safe, and their children to be safe, but that's not possible if they're all *dead*."

"Which is exactly why you are the only member of our number who can do what must be done." Armaeus pointed behind me, and I turned with surprise to see I'd attracted my own following, not of people, but the slender celestial tiles. They had left the space above the conference table and now hovered behind me, dipping and flipping in rapidly changing patterns—circles, stars, radiant sunbursts.

"Go to where the Ark of the Covenant was to find its resting place," the Magician said as I stared at the tiles. "You will not have long to wait. With your intention to save as much of humanity as you can, you will not fail."

He exhaled a long, shuddering breath. *"The effort you make will be their salvation, Miss Wilde."*

I whipped around to realize he was only speaking in my head, that he was no longer in front of me. I spun in a full circle, my gaze shooting everywhere around the room, but there was only me and the tiles left in the empty space.

"Armaeus!" I shouted. But there was no reply.

The pavers drifted toward me, stacking up one upon the other until they had coalesced into a small, tight pile, no bigger than a deck of cards. I reached for them just as the images on the screens around me changed, making me jerk my hand back and stare, disbelieving, from one image to the other. The digital clock above the highest row of screens read 7:00 a.m.

It was dawn in Vegas.

Explosions ripped through every country on Earth and shook the monitors in the Magician's conference room.

"Oh no," I whispered as the sounds and images detonated across my senses. "Oh, no, no, no."

27

The Palace of Westminster exploded first. It wasn't a devastating blast, merely one side of the building bursting outward, looking like a quick cut from any of a dozen Hollywood blockbusters. That didn't make it any less harrowing.

Next up was the Capitol building of the United States, the dome shooting high into the sky. The sight was so ludicrous, I couldn't take it in, and my gaze sheered away from the image, as if I by unseeing it, I could make it less real.

The statue of Jesus in Rio de Janeiro toppled from its mighty perch a moment later, scattering the crowds of people that had flocked to pay homage to it. It was barely after noon in Brazil, and I watched the enormous hundred-foot statue fall in slow motion, my heart wrenching as each bit of it broke off against the mountain and completely shattered when it struck the streets below.

Past the screens of the conference room, out the windows, I saw one, two, three electrical explosions piercing the sky, skittering and jittering so brightly that my third eye flinched. I stumbled toward the bank of windows and watched in horror as every casino that served as a base for an Arcana Council member blew its top. The Stratosphere exploded upward, then Treasure Island—and I gripped the windowsill and barely held on as the top of the Palazzo burst into a fiery, smoking ball.

"Mrs. French," I whispered, my thoughts flashing to the boys in the library. Would they be harmed? Were there people in those other penthouse levels? There had to be. Why hadn't I warned them? Why hadn't I warned *anyone*? Unable to breathe for a second, I staggered back around, only to see more explosions on the screens.

"You have to stop this," I shouted aloud at the still-absent Armaeus, my eyes now swimming with tears. "You can *stop* it."

"We all must do our part," the Magician answered in my mind, but his voice carried a note of desperation I didn't miss. He had made his calculations based on certain expectations of me. But in the end, he didn't know what I would do, or what I could do. Either way, it was time for me to move.

I reached out and wrapped my hands around the tightly packed celestial tiles, tucking them into my jacket as I flashed out of existence.

I burst up from the heart of Vegas, my breath catching as I surveyed the destruction from a new and infinitely worse angle. Was what I was seeing actually happening, or was my fear playing tricks on me, showing one of a hundred possible futures?

If so, this future was defective and it needed to be sent back. The multicolored screens of the Devil's residence above the Flamingo were now a hollowed-out crater. Pieces of the Foolscap glass menagerie tumbled off across the desert, while the aerie that had been my father's perch had completely disappeared. The billowing smoke of the casino explosions obscured any real vision of the state of the Strip beneath—and when I blinked again, the residences of the Arcana Council reappeared, whole and unharmed...I thought. It was all too jumbled to make out.

I powered away, unwilling to look too closely anymore, and shot eastward toward Rome. Flinching at every new explosion, I found my thoughts turning once again toward my long-time friend Father Jerome and his tireless efforts to save the most vulnerable members of the Connected community. He had died before achieving that goal, but he'd never stopped believing in it. I didn't want him to have died in vain.

As I hurtled halfway around the world, I saw other things too, my third eye giving me telescopic views of the Council members fighting to counter the surging energy of the Shadow Court's psychic dead-zone bombs.

Nikola Tesla stood in front of a spindly, mushroom-shaped tower that did not at all fit the gentrified neighborhood that surrounded it, as if he had summoned the structure out of the past. Hell, maybe he had. His hands were up, his head tilted back, and he was exultant as he cried out, drawing down the electricity of the multiverse to finally vindicate his predictions.

As I passed over him, lightning crackled in the sky, and in the distance, far-off booms sounded from Times Square in New York City.

I jerked my gaze forward again and sped on. More Arcana Council members or the results of their actions glowed like beacons everywhere I looked.

A corona of power surrounded the Louvre in Paris, through which I could see fires bursting and then immediately guttering out.

Simon raced down the streets of Munich, at the head of a roaring, frenzied group of men and women, all of them holding their fists aloft as the capital district caught fire.

The beautiful, elegant Hagia Sophia in Istanbul boiled over with flames, only to shimmer back into safety a moment later. The same image repeated itself across Europe and Asia, and even farther. Though I couldn't see him, the Magician was doing his part to save whatever knowledge he could; knowledge that would keep the Connecteds safe, their magic protected when all the fires had finally died away.

I thought I heard the cry of the High Priestess in far-off Egypt, her words formless and ancient, the haunting melancholy of her chant stirring the souls of her acolytes from all four corners of the globe.

And finally, in Jerusalem, unexpectedly waist-deep in demon gore, Gamon and Rangi slashed and thrashed alongside other dark-clothed figures wielding blades. Two bright bursts of light exploded beside Gamon, and I saw Danae and Qadir, and then two other unrecognizable figures bursting up out of the ground as if from the bowels of Hell itself.

I nearly stopped. I wanted to stop. But I didn't need the Magician's voice in my head to remind me that time was short.

I doubled down on my trajectory for Rome and Saint Peter's Basilica. I didn't bother with the Vatican itself, but targeted the Egyptian obelisk in Saint Peter's Square. I plummeted through concrete and bedrock until I reached the corridor that fed into the catacombs.

Unfortunately, I wasn't alone. No sooner had I begun to materialize with my posse of celestial tiles than I heard the blast of rifles. This time, the well-armed guards of SANCTUS didn't hesitate. Bullets swept through the narrow corridor, riddling my deeply abused molecules. Healing as quickly as I was pierced, I managed to disintegrate once again a breath later, sending Armaeus a snarl of irritation that he hadn't warned me about my welcoming committee. The Magician did not reply.

I arrived next in the chamber of the Ark of the Covenant, still minus the actual Ark, but details.

This time, I hesitated before fully forming, not wanting a repeat of the Swiss Guard swiss cheesing me. But if I couldn't materialize, then neither could my weapons. And that was a problem since the room was bursting with gunmen.

My lungs gave out before I wanted them to, and I felt a crackle of pain across my back. My wings struggled to spread free, to allow me to blast out of this hallowed hole in the ground, but there was nowhere for me to fly. This was where my battle would be fought. This was what I needed to do and where I needed to be.

I burst into full corporeal form and heard the sweep of rifles coming up, but I was done with serving as these asshats' target practice.

"A little *help*," I demanded. Deep within the bowels of the catacombs, an unearthly howl sounded, a rolling chitter of pure delight. It was the skeletons' turn to dance.

No matter how good their ear protection was, the gunmen definitely picked up on the sound of the skeleton army as they clattered through the underground passages and burst into the main corridor.

"You like that?" I shouted as more gunfire erupted, along

with sharp shouts of alarm. While all that was going on, I coalesced the rest of the way, fire blazing from my fingers. I didn't want to kill these assholes, but I also didn't have time to play nice anymore.

Fortunately, the prospect of death by firebolt was more concerning than attacking skeletons. The guards turned and ran, fleeing the chamber of the Ark of the Covenant and giving me the time I needed to drop a curtain of fire in the doorway. Nobody would be entering the chamber until I was ready for them—or, most likely, ever again.

"What do I do?" I asked aloud as I whipped around, pulling the celestial tiles out of my jacket. But if Armaeus could hear me, he wasn't talking. If I was honest, I didn't expect him to help me—not here.

I weighed the celestial tiles in my hand and peeled off four, dealing them out like Tarot cards toward the shallow basin lined with gold. As the one tile had before, the pavers dove into the surface of the basin like it was a swimming pool, then emerged a moment later, looking vaguely pissed off that there was no Ark of the Covenant to support. I knew how they felt.

Blowing out a long breath, I let the other pavers drop from my fingertips. They drifted away from me, and, as they had in the Magician's chambers, immediately launched into their twirling dance of multiple designs. I felt the shift of energy around me and remembered how the pavers had impacted the electrical grids once Armaeus had set them in motion. Would that help our cause or hurt it?

I was tired of not knowing.

Opening every door I could in my mind and my heart, while keeping my attention focused on the celestial tiles, I welcomed Tesla's strange electrical force to come on in and play. It filled the room in an instant, making my entire body vibrate with its power and igniting the pavers, sending them spinning ever faster.

My wings shifting up and catching flame, I reached out a shaking hand to touch the nearest paver, my tap sending it skittering into a new direction. The others followed it, and as I tracked the tiles across the room, my field of vision deepened, expanded. I no longer saw the walls or the floors of the intended resting place of the Ark of the Covenant, I saw the sweeping streets of Rome, the angry, billowing clouds of yet more explosions along the side of St. Peter's Basilica. Then my vision spiraled up and away, soaring over the green and verdant valleys stretching off for miles. As I astrally projected myself higher and higher with all my might, my sight widened further, and I no longer was of the world, but above it.

My wings shivered and stretched to fill the chamber, and I glanced at the right and left, not able to process the maze of electrical currents that raced over, through, and around their span. I couldn't tell where the electrical impulses originated, but they filled me with a heady power, and as I turned and refocused on my astrally projected view, I could see the sweep of darkness spreading across Earth, while other sectors sparked and glowed with brilliant light. I heard a solemn, exultant cry, and my vision narrowed to pinpoints, picking out the cloaked and robed priests of Solomon, spread out to every corner of the world, holding their blessed daggers high. They'd known this battle would come. They too were ready to fight, to wipe the world clean and begin again.

This was the power I could wield with the celestial pavers, I finally understood. This was the fury and righteousness of God I could inflict upon the earth. This was—

"Sara."

The Magician's gasp jerked me back to awareness, and suddenly, I could see him too. He stood in the center of an empty, abandoned church, its roof long since removed, thick foliage covering its walls. The countryside around him was lush and full, and I got the immediate sense of France, though I had nothing to base that on other than the sheer beauty of his surroundings.

A dozen of the re-engineered dead-zone devices lay around him, quivering with electricity, but my eyes were only for Armaeus. He was bowed under what looked to be the weight of a thousand worlds, his hair lank, his skin ashen. His eyes were sunken into his skull, and his skin lay flat against his bones, as if all the muscles and sinew beneath had been squeezed dry. For the first time in all the years I'd known him, he looked not only human, but frail. Weary to his bones.

And then I realized—his bones were *vibrating*. Armaeus's body had become a perfect conduit for the same electricity from the quantum realm that was energizing me...only he was dying. In the fullness of my apocalyptic power, I could let him die too. Maybe should let him die, to complete the cycle he had so painstakingly begun.

In a flash, I knew that was what Sariah had seen. Not that the Devil was going to kill Armaeus...I was.

Fuck. That.

"Armaeus!" I jerked my hands up, and all the pavers lifted. Throughout the world, wherever they were buried, every last psychic dead-zone bomb of the Shadow Court that had not already exploded lifted too. For one last, heart-stopping moment, I knew I could end the world.

Then, with my wings spread wide and my blood and bones on fire, as I watched my beautiful, extraordinary

Magician, the beat of my heart and breath in my lungs, become consumed by the same corrosive electrical magic that was ripping its way through me...

I decided to go a different path.

And, for the moment, I left the Arcana Council to theirs.

28

THE HANGED MAN'S LAST STAND

10:00 a.m. EST/7:00 a.m. PST
Day 1
Rahway, New Jersey, USA

Nikola Tesla would save the world. They would write about him in history books—no, *rewrite* the history books, and all the hateful lies that his enemies had spread, taking the credit for his inventions, his patents, his discoveries of the mightiest power in the universe, would be washed away. Never again would he have to grit his teeth and bow to those who did not deserve the glories and accolades he should have received. Because he'd been right.

He'd been *right*.

Tesla threw back his head and shouted to the heavens, an unnecessary but supremely cathartic addition to the scientific process, as the power-dampening manacles-turned-globes whose polarity had been reversed by the Magician sparked and whirled, their internal mechanics creating the necessary conditions to open up pinhole portals to the quantum realm. Through these tiniest of apertures, a type of electricity that bordered on magic flowed, the kind of magic that had never reached its full potential on this earth.

It was going to reach it now.

Above Nikola Tesla, the facsimile of his factory roared to life. It was a factory that electricity had built in truth, not merely in poetry, with razor-thin filaments that, when compressed, might fit alongside a Wheatstone bridge, inside an old wooden box no bigger than a violin case. The perfect conduits to channel quantum electricity. Now those thin strands were linked together with rays of silver-white energy and pulsed with vibrant power.

In only a few minutes, a crowd had gathered, not yet realizing the devastation to come—so many cities thrown into turmoil, so many buildings destroyed. But that devastation wouldn't come for Rahway, New Jersey, nor for the edifices of power in New York City.

Well, not all of them, anyway. Those that had been built through the largesse of Thomas Edison might not fare so well. And why should they?

Nicola drew his hands together, feeling the arcing pain of quantum electricity flow through his body. He had floated in the ether searching for his fabled electrical source for decades, *generations*, until he'd heard the cry of the Arcana Council and returned to Earth to help them bumble their way toward saving magic and those Connecteds who wielded it. They hadn't known he would be the architect of their salvation, but how could he not? You couldn't keep the genius of an inventor under wraps for long.

"There are explosions in the city," someone shouted.

"What are you doing?" another screeched.

The cries of the ignorant and the afraid. Sirens wailed,

but Tesla paid them no mind. They wouldn't catch him unprepared again, mock him, take away all he'd built and hand it over to someone else.

"Behold!" he cried. "Witness the gift that you have been given, the grace you have been shown, and pay attention. It is your turn to shine!"

His voice, magnified a hundred times over with the power of quantum electricity, boomed as far as the Empire State Building. He drew in a deep breath as the crowd pulsed with an energy of its own, rapt with attention. "Do not bow before the overlords who would keep the basic necessities of power from you. You can *all* access this power. It is in the very air around you."

He flung his arms wide, and the heavens responded—gloriously, joyfully—crackling in magnificent splendor, a thousand lightning strikes shooting across the sky. Some in the crowd screamed, others wept, and Nikola Tesla soldiered on.

"Stay back, but only until I'm gone, and then rush forward and take from here every filament and rod. Those who are bold, who seek not to cower and shrink away, will have enough energy to ignite any engine, run any factory, fuel any computer by directing it to be so."

They called him names at that, but the simpleminded always did, but not all these people were simpleminded. In the generations since he'd left this area, the might of the entrepreneur had lived on in Rahway. From here to New York City, the bold and the seekers still congregated, never mind the weather, the corruption, the greed. Because this was a magical place. He'd known it when he'd first come here and had channeled it for his own creations. He'd failed not because of a lack of skill, but merely because of a lack of time. Fortunately, that was no longer an issue.

"Behold!" he shouted again.

He lost track of anything else for a while except the surge of power in his bones, the electrocution of his blood, and the visions that grew before him, a world powered with an energy that could be distilled within the very humans who were now brave enough to wield it. A world that no longer enslaved the weak and the poor because they too had just as much right to thrive as the young boy he had once been, running across the open fields of his homeland of Croatia, chasing a lightning strike.

The pain jumped, the magnificent, impossible pain, too much for one frail human form to handle. Even his.

"Live!" he exhorted the people around him. "You must, finally, *live*."

He convulsed, his molecules overflowing with electricity, with power, with the transformation that he'd always sought to share with the masses. And it was working—he knew it with every white-hot fiber of his being, every shivering synapse of his overloaded brain. It was working, and soon his factory would produce the greatest electrical accomplishment ever conceived—personal power sources for the masses.

Nikola Tesla had come too soon for this earth, but he was leaving right on time.

29

JUDGMENT & THE HEAD OF THE HOUSE OF WANDS

5:00 p.m. IST/7:00 a.m. PST
Day 1
Jerusalem, Israel

There was no glory in death. Fighting, however, was pure holy fire.

"They do not fall back," the nearest Mossad operative shouted at her, not in desperation, merely in observation. Coldly, almost clinically, seeking advice, wanting answers. The Mossad did not stand on ceremony when it came to battle strategy and took their information however they could receive it. With that, they could destroy their enemies with as much speed and practicality as possible.

"They're demons," Gamon shot back. "Our job isn't to kill them. We can't. We just have to hold the line until those who can kill them join us."

"Then we fight." If anything, this dire assessment of their ability to succeed on their own served to galvanize the fighting cabal surrounding her.

Rangi fought at the other end of the street. Several large, swarthy warriors battled alongside him. While she'd been interrogating him at her stronghold, he'd been more than happy to share with her the extent of his abilities, which included summoning his men with an ancient spell given to him by the gods. He'd used that as another segue to spew about his highly specific hatred of the pantheon. He didn't mind exercising the power they'd graciously shared with him. He minded being forced to bend to their will.

The guy never shut up.

Gamon fought on, pausing briefly to glance up as a comet streaked across the sky, easily discernible in the darkening afternoon sky. The city was on fire, but it was going to get worse before it got better, and then there might be nothing at all. As long as she fought skillfully to the end, she could die content.

What seemed like hours passed, the demons falling back slightly at the assault of their human opponents, but never giving ground in any significant way. Each time the Mossad or Rangi's men advanced, the horde would retreat only long enough to regroup and attack again. Gamon understood why. For all their fury and might, her fellow warriors were human. They would not, could not, last forever, and the demons knew it.

As she tore and slashed, she noted new explosions all around her, the Shadow Court's bombs bursting into the sky, and she redoubled her efforts. If she could feel the drain on her psychic energy, how much worse would it be for the ordinary Connecteds? How could they stand such an onslaught?

They could, because they had to.

She had endured being captured and then restrained by enemies. She had subjected plenty of her own enemies to the same. But then she'd met Sara Wilde, a warrior whose tenacity was equaled only by her epic inability to pull the trigger on any gun she aimed. If anybody needed Gamon around to dispense Judgment where it was necessary, it was this particular Justice of the Arcana Council.

The smile Gamon allowed herself was poorly timed.

A demon struck from the right, waving a sickle that she realized belatedly was a claw. Gamon ducked to the right, but she wasn't fast enough. She took the slicing attack to her shoulder, damn near ripping off her right arm. She fell, disoriented, only to hear the roar of a male warrior beside her. One of the Mossad? One of—

"Clumsy female!" Rangi shouted in her ears, and she felt herself being dragged away from the battle by heavy hands.

He propped her up against a wall and barked out other orders to his men as she batted him away with her one working arm.

"Fight," she insisted. "You must fight."

"No. I choose to follow Justice's orders, not yours," Rangi snarled back. Then he knelt in front of her, his face swimming in and out of focus, and began to pray.

"What are you *doing*?" Gamon groaned, the strength leaching from her to mix with the demon gore that streaked her body, but Rangi's words and face slipped away from her as in the street beyond, a retina-searing light flashed...

30

THE SUN & THE MISTRESS OF THE HOUSE OF SWORDS

7:00 p.m. IST/9:00 a.m. PST
Day 1
Jerusalem, Israel

"We are here!" Qadir, the Sun of the Arcana Council, declared, for all the world to take note and be amazed.

For once, Danae didn't even wince at her traveling partner's exuberant announcement, issued with bright and bold good humor as if he was sure his enemies and allies alike were waiting with bated breath for him to arrive. She was just grateful that Qadir had paved the way for her team of Deathwalkers to pour into the moon-blanketed streets of Jerusalem. Then the Syx, the warrior Demon Enforcers directed by the Archangel Michael, flashed into the space next to her. She hadn't planned on that.

"Why are you all here?" Danae demanded of their leader, a tall, hulking warrior with long dark hair and piercing eyes. "You mean to tell me there are no other demon incursions in the entire wide world?"

"Sure there are," Warrick of the Syx growled back.

"But only the biggest, baddest, *nastiest* demons are willing to throw down in the freaking seat of God," Finn, the brashest member of the demon strike team put in. He grinned and finger gunned her, his oddly bright blue eyes sparkling as his fellow Enforcers turned without speaking and leapt into battle. "Long story short, we're not missing this for anything. Besides, there's always gonna be more demons to fight."

Danae didn't have time to argue, as the horde responded to the addition of reinforcements on the streets of Jerusalem by pouring out from side alleys, leaping off stone buildings. The entire Temple Mount courtyard was besieged, and Danae glared at the thrashing bodies within. How the humans had managed to survive even this long was a miracle.

"Be gone, you vile creatures of the night," Qadir roared, startling her by running toward the demons, his beefy arms wide, as if he was going to scoop up the horde in a massive djinn hug. "My queen shall take you down!"

"Oh, for the goddess's sake." Danae waded forward into the teeming horde, nodding with grim determination as a new portal slashed open beside her, and a short, dark-haired witch and her massive Fae king stepped through. She'd figured this battle would draw attention from the other realms—and she was glad for the help.

Despite all the additional warriors that were coming to their aid, they likely wouldn't save every worthy soul this day, but they *would* permanently dispatch the greatest and most powerful of the demon horde back to the pits of Hell. That was worth something.

Witches could rebuild, she thought as she slashed and tore with her ancient athames. Witches could heal the land

and the souls of those who lived upon it. But certain witches were called to do more than that, to rid humanity of this scourge that swept the earth once and for all.

Her witches would do that, or they would all die trying.

She bent herself to the battle and fought on.

31

THE FOOL

4:00 p.m. CET/7:00 a.m. PST
Day 1
Munich, Germany

Running in Vans sucked donkey balls, but Simon would be damned if he'd stop now.

The bombs that had gone off downtown had been right on top of the hotel where ArcanaCon was being hosted—that couldn't be a coincidence. He'd gotten the word as soon as he'd hit town, and he'd ordered everyone out and on foot. The streets were already choked with cars and cops, and traffic was at a standstill.

Kicking up his speed, he rounded the corner, his destination barely a tenth of a mile away. He hadn't wanted to be dropped straight down into the park, but with all the shock and awe of Shadow Court bomb blasts going on, he should have known discretion wouldn't be necessary. Oh, well. The run to the Biergarten had always been a part of the highest level of ArcanaWar.

"Where ya going?" a woman shouted beside Simon,

drawing his attention to the side. Tall, fair, and green eyed, she rocked bright candy-red hair that she'd pulled back into a braid, her body more curves than angles, and the ferocity of her grin letting him know that she wasn't going to slow down anytime soon. At her side ran a one-eyed husky, bounding and leaping with joy.

He glanced down at the woman's shoes, which seemed to shoot up sparks every time she struck the earth—and goggled. "You're wearing stilettos? How're you keeping up?"

She laughed. "Better than you are, looks like."

They turned the corner, and the Fool's attention was ripped away as new explosions rocked the city beyond—way more than should be necessary for a city that wasn't even the capital of Germany. For whatever reason, the Shadow Court definitely had it in for Munich.

Had they known that some of the best and brightest minds in the world were gathering this weekend for the Fool's hypersecretive ArcanaCon? They had to have. Simon had hand curated every attendee after extensive testing, after hacking into the Magician's thought palace and seeing what was likely to go down. Simon didn't know everything that the Shadow Court was planning, but he knew enough. He also knew he needed to save gamers maybe more than any other group of Connecteds. Because the coming post-magical-apocalypse New World Order would need strategists, innovators...and ballers who knew how to complete OG Naxxramas.

One more corner, and they reached arguably one of Simon's favorite places in the world, the Biergarten Viktualienmarkt. A place for congregation, good food, better beer, and pure joy. Now it was ground zero for his guild—and a whole lot of unwanted tagalong assholes with guns and riot gear. Despite the pseudo-military attire of the assholes chasing Simon's people, they were definitely not the Munich *Polizei*.

How had the Shadow Court known they'd be here, though, to have so many fake police ready to deploy? They must've been keeping tabs on all Connecteds who were gamers. Simon had worried about that, especially given the state of the Court's tech and the fact they had money coming out of their ears. But now he needed to act. Nobody was shooting yet, but he had no doubt that when this all went down, it was going to be dubbed another riot in the streets that the "police" had effectively put down, except the only casualties would be the rioters.

Not if he could help it.

"Systems on!" he shouted, and easily forty tech stations around the Biergarten flared into life, covering the nearly two-city-square blocks with bright lights and screens set up against the smoke-filled sky. The gamers stopped, turned, and stared at the stats boards that flickered above them. Their shouts were immediate and filled with joy. Simon didn't see the redhead among them. He didn't know her gamer tag—hell, she might not be a gamer at all. She might have been in the city just by chance. If so, he hoped she wasn't here. The gamers he'd assembled knew what they were getting into, knew the stakes. Knew they wouldn't necessarily have their strength built back up again to reenter the game if they were knocked out. But he'd done the best he could.

"Weapons," he announced, and one hundred cases shot straight up out of the ground where they'd been buried in shallow graves, springing open as the gamers converged in rapid but orderly fashion, exactly as he'd mapped it out.

Some of the weapons were guns, some were swords, some were handheld gripper sticks that didn't require any finesse other than pointing. Within a space of two minutes, his entire team was armed, just as the special forces dick-heads with their rifles and riot gear reached the Biergarten.

They had never fought guilds that were used to taking out bosses, though.

As the two sides clashed, four of the top gamers who'd reached the coveted level 80 in ArcanaWar, advertised only on the arcane web, took up their positions around Simon, one each at the cardinal points. The Fool dropped to the ground with the psychic devices he'd brought with him from Vegas, scowling at them. Though he'd brought his own portable portal maker, he didn't know this new tech. The Magician had managed to keep it hidden from him. But how? He'd been all *through* Armaeus's database, all through his goofed-up thought palace, all through...

After a moment of consternation, a broad grin stretched across his face.

"Okay, okay, Dr. Strange," he muttered, delighted despite being punked. "You knew I was planning this all along, didn't you?"

The Magician's voice flowed into his mind—cool, calm, and satisfied, the perfect counterpoint to the chaos surging through the Biergarten.

"I knew that you might, and that was enough. This adventure is yours to take."

Whether the Magician turned on some switch that Simon couldn't see, or his own hyperkinetic energy finally affected the devices, they flared to life, making his four guards shout half in alarm, half in excitement.

"Hold steady," Simon said. "I've never done this campaign before."

He wanted more *time*, dammit. Needed it. He had these two hundred souls, volunteers all, and hundreds more he'd left behind. This unique guild had made the cut, but if Simon pulled this off, the rest would be waiting for him and his squad after the first wave of the magic apocalypse had passed.

Screams ripped through the air, male and female alike. Fighting in real life was different from fighting online, even for the best out there. That was why he needed time away—to train his soldiers to fight real flesh-and-blood adversaries. Fight and *win*.

The cries abruptly cut off as a new group entered the battle, and Simon smiled to see the twelve Mongolian priests that made up his honor guard. He'd had them flown in last week, worried this battle might go down. They would help teach the others, he knew; he just had to take the final step. He just had to believe that he could lead this group into the greatest adventure of their lives.

The devices crackled to life, and energy pulsed—*way* more than he'd counted on. It damned near electrocuted him as his own equipment overloaded, hissing and sparking. A portal opened up in front of Simon, revealing a land he'd never seen. He'd sort of expected to lead this team into the same plane he'd entered once before in the mountains of Kathmandu, but this wasn't anything like that. His view was filled with rolling hills, a far-off sea, and a tall, twisting stronghold built into the side of a mountain.

"What the hell is this?" he demanded, his eyes going wide. He didn't expect an answer, but he got one anyway.

"A realm in need of a wizard," the Magician informed him drily. *"Try not to break anything."*

32

THE HIGH PRIESTESS

5:00 p.m. EET/7:00 a.m. PST
Day 1
Giza Necropolis, Egypt

"You must come!" Eshe cried out, but even as she noted the comets that streaked overhead, and recalled the moment, hours before, when the gaze of the half goddess Justice Wilde had swept over the land, the High Priestess knew she had failed.

The elders Armaeus had discovered in this country, the ancient priestesses who worshipped the moon and the sun, did not know the High Priestess of the Arcana Council. They had not been alive when she had suffered and bled as the Oracle of Delphi, and she had been content to keep herself locked up within the Council's varied and shifting strongholds for far too long. First to heal, then to learn, and then to lose herself in the visions that had made her the woman, the demigoddess, the isolated queen she was today.

She had hoped to have more time with her newest acolyte, but in the end, Eshe had wrapped the young woman with all the spells she'd been able to ferret out of the Magician's inner chambers to ensure her safety. Perhaps she would see her again, perhaps not. Her visions had been particularly obscure on that subject.

But now she was summoning an army of elite priestesses strong enough to stand and fight with her—and they were not responding.

Eshe gripped the sacred manacle-turned-orb that Armaeus had entrusted to her and gazed down at the simple offering she'd made to the ancient gods. Dried flowers. Herbs. A scattering of jewels. And, of course, her own blood.

It hadn't been enough.

Eshe sighed, her smile rueful but also almost relieved. "If I must fight this fight alone, so be it," she said softly, surrendering to the will of whatever gods still pierced the veil. "I will use this orb to take all my ability and scatter it into the winds."

Her words deepened as she spoke them, and her heart rate quickened, the hint of new, oracular visions teasing at the edge of her senses. "Give whoever hears my call the strength to continue."

She drew back into the shallow cave she had found to shelter her in her hour of need. These caves hunkered down in the shadow of the great pyramids, built to honor the pharaohs and the gods. She could have returned to Greece, but she'd wanted a sacred place with wide open spaces—both for her potential followers to find her and to provide her enough warning if any enemy drew near.

Enemy. She curled her lip. There had been a moment, the briefest temptation, when she had sensed that Viktor had switched alliances to fall in with the Shadow Court. He had wanted magic for more than the Arcana Council, but only according to his rules, like the Emperor he'd been.

Hers was the province of a wilder power, though, the connection of the mind to the whispers of angels, spirits, and gods. Hers was the province of women too, whom Viktor discounted out of hand. No matter how many visions she'd cast, there'd been no doubt the Shadow Court would be a source of darkness and pain. Their rule might still win out despite all the Arcana Council's efforts, both Eshe and the Magician knew. But all she could do was make the attempt to preserve the magic of this fragile world.

"You must come," she whispered again. "Take what I can give you, take what is rightfully yours. Step into your power and rule those who seek your wisdom. There will be no shortage of need for wisdom in the coming age."

She lifted her hands a final time and gave herself over to the visions that were hammering against her mind...then reached out with all her magic to ignite the deadly orb Armaeus had given her.

Pain swept through her. Fire, storms, hordes of demons scurrying in the darkness, mutated and deformed, but still a threat. Machines of war raging at each other, children in adult bodies blowing up anything they could reach, desperate for the chance to lay waste to a world they no longer revered. Eshe felt the cries of anguish as death blasted through the land. The end came swiftly for some, and in lingering pain for others.

So much death. But in the end, also hope. She had to hold on to that.

Eshe opened her fingers wide, and the whirring orb sparked and crackled, its intensity increasing along with her pain. Then, alone and abandoned, her throat parched, her skin aflame, her tears long since burned away on her cheeks, the High Priestess welcomed the magic that yearned to pour through her and collapsed back to the floor of the cave.

It was dark when Eshe woke again, and for a moment, she thought the world had ended and she had passed across the veil. For the first time since she'd been consecrated to her calling, her mind wasn't filled with an endless murmuring sea.

She lifted a hand and caught the faint sparkle of electrical power deep beneath her skin. She had seen that glow in Sara Wilde's hands, seen it burst into full fire. But that had never been her path. Was it now?

When she dropped her hand, she noticed another glow beyond the entrance of the cave, which was now several feet distant. Pushing herself up, pausing to catch her breath, she stood, then slowly, carefully made her way up to the entrance of the cavern.

She hadn't been wrong. There were definitely lights dancing in the plains beyond. Egyptian military come to take her out? Perhaps. Perhaps.

Eshe's mind was a blank, its voices still muted, its images dimmed. She shuffled on, each step a challenge, but finally, she reached the entrance of her cavern—and stopped.

The plane between her and the great pyramids was filled with two hundred women, maybe more. Each of them lifted palms that cradled a flickering white flame—the same flame echoed in Eshe's own hands. Smaller silver-white flames danced above the crowns of their heads.

When the first of their number caught sight of Eshe, she shouted, a voice of feminine strength, fierce and resonant. She held her flame high, and Eshe caught the gleam of her weathered skin, the long fall of white hair.

"You came," Eshe whispered, though her words rolled out across the open plain as if she had shouted them from the heavens. Tears sparked in her eyes, and she sagged forward, struggling not to fall to her knees once more. "The world has ended, but you came."

"We came," the priestess of white fire agreed. "But the world has only begun."

33

DEATH AND THE ARCHANGEL

9:00 p.m. IST
Day 1
Jerusalem, Israel

Humans were idiots, and Death could say that with confidence because there was a part of her that was still human. It was a small part, but one that she could never stamp out.

She sighed as she scanned the jumble of bodies, gently waving her hand to free the latent souls, then casting them off to find their resting place. Each according to their beliefs, even if those beliefs led them to nowhere and nothing at all. This world had no more need for them.

Lifting her gaze again, she squinted into the smoke. There were so many dead in this place. There always were. How many times had she come to Jerusalem to ferry the dead away? And who would do it once she no longer walked this earth?

She trudged on, then stopped abruptly as a rustle of movement blocked her path. The Archangel Michael came into full and translucent form in front of her. She narrowed her eyes against the brightness of his form. "I figured you'd be back in your tower, praying for salvation for everyone left and the sanctity of those who've passed on."

"I should be," Michael agreed, but there was something different about him, something that struck Death as wrong. He looked at her now with an earnestness that bordered on desperation, and something far more dangerous.

"Do not..." He swallowed, then continued as if each word cost him. "Do not continue your work here this day, Blue."

Her brows leapt at his use of her name. On his lips, it was almost a benediction. His voice was soft and earnest, but she could sense the power within him. She'd never given much thought to it before, but the Hierophant was the powerful agent of an even more powerful god, even if it wasn't a god she followed. Why had he joined the Council?

She lifted a hand to rub her temple, her fingers grazing the shaved portion of her skull where the hair lay flat and straight, then raked through the thick shock of it that swept across her brow. "Why shouldn't I work here?"

"Because this path..." Michael winced, shuddering, and with that shudder, he was transformed, if only briefly. His skin grew warm and healthy, his wings spread behind him in an iridescent rainbow, while deep within him, a heart beat.

Death blinked. That wasn't possible, of course. Angels didn't have hearts, not in the way humans did. So how—

The moment passed. Michael returned to his ghostly pallor, and Death exhaled a breath she hadn't realized she'd been holding. But the Archangel looked no happier. His jaw remained set, his fists clenched.

"This path leads to your death," he said.

He glanced away, then returned his gaze to hers, fierce with resolve. "It is not my place. It is not my duty. It is not my freedom to choose one life over another. But I would choose your life, Blue. I would—"

The movement came so swiftly, Death never saw it. Her gaze was captivated by Michael shifting once more to his superhuman form—his face warm, tan, lined with wrinkles from laughter and smiling in the sun, his hands calloused by the weight of hard work, and his wings once again bursting forth with radiant color. So engrossed was she in the miracle of the Hierophant's transformation, she didn't see the human leap from the shadows of the alley, didn't see the cruel, curving blade slash down toward her neck, angling for her heart.

"*No*," the Archangel roared. He turned and flung his hand out, a fiery blast incinerating the human where he stood.

Time stopped.

Death recovered first, shouting out the Archangel's name as the heavens opened around them and a thousand winds screamed in her ears. Michael had killed a human. He had committed the most grievous sin any angel ever could—and he knew it. He jerked his gaze to hers and gave her a smile that somehow captured every glance he'd ever sent her way, every murmured greeting, every nod of deference.

"Humans are our weakness," he said ruefully, whispering into the raging storm. "But you shall not die this day."

"*Michael*—" Death cried, but the word was snatched from her throat as the earth and sky seemed to fall away from them. A horde of demons burst up out of nothing and swarmed Michael, pulling him from her in a howl of pure, otherworldly glee.

Michael never broke eye contact with her, even as his wings were shredded and his robes were torn. He stared at her as if she were the moon and the sun, the beginning and the end, and Death's own heart thudded hard, a harsh and twisting pain flooding through her, unlike anything she'd felt before.

Then a yawning pit opened wide, and Michael the Archangel was ripped away into darkness, the sky and earth rushing back into place as if he'd never been there at all.

34

THE MOON AND THE STAR

4:30 p.m. CET/7:30 a.m. PST
Day 1
Bern, Switzerland

"I got a bad feeling about this."

Nikki squinted at the pair of orbs resting on the back lawn, where they'd lain since she and Torsten had returned from Vegas. Torsten had taken the extra precaution of staking the ground twenty feet distant from each of the orbs, though Nikki was pretty sure that wasn't going to help much should the things decide to blow.

"How do they work?" Torsten asked again. "Why don't we know how they work?"

Nikki shrugged. "I'm thinking we'll get that memo when the time comes, and not before. Go ahead and pull those stakes, though. I don't think anybody from the Brombacher family is dumb enough to go anywhere near those orbs, and we don't need to worry about the clan."

"Agreed. I just felt like I should do something."

She grinned at him, and lightly punched his shoulder. "It's one of your best qualities."

Nikki allowed herself a moment to watch him as her faithful second-in-command strode quickly around the perimeter of the back lawn. It had been a few days without snowfall, and the yard was sheltered from the wind, though the grass was dormant and beaten down. As lightly as he moved, despite his big body, once Torsten removed the stakes, there was no sign he'd been there. It was too damn cold snugged up next to the Alps, even when you weren't directly in the wind and snow, but she liked it, she decided. She got a kick out of anywhere she went with Torsten and the pack. All of it was so new to them, it was like seeing the world reborn.

She knew that in other places, bombs would be going off, but not here, she didn't think. The Star had believed her job already finished with the Brombachers. The Star hadn't counted on Nikki finding the family and turning them to her cause.

"Mistake. Big mistake." Nikki grinned and tossed her snow-white hair, channeling her inner Julia Roberts.

"Do you think so?"

The Star appeared in a cascade of glittering lights, a mini meteor shower zipping down against the darkening afternoon sky. She had adopted her Dixie form, complete with a tight white shimmering minidress, a pink scarf, white cowboy hat, and pink boots. What Nikki had come to know as the Dixie uniform. She even used the same Lowcountry drawl that Nikki had found so charming when she'd first arrived in Vegas—only her eyes were wrong. Deep, fathomless, empty. Frankly, Nikki preferred the Dixie contacts.

"I got to tell you, you fooled me from the start, sugar butt," Nikki drawled right back, forcing herself not to dart her gaze around the lawn. Her pack would be out there, along with the wolves of the Brombacher clan, including Wilhelm and Augustus. They had pledged to defend her, the bristling Torsten beside her most of all...but she couldn't let them die on her watch. They'd only just started to live again.

She also wasn't going to let Sara down. Whatever game the Star was playing, Nikki knew Sara would be at the center of it...but why had she come here instead of attacking Sara head-on? There had to be a reason, and that reason had to be a trap.

If Nikki could get close to the Star, maybe she could read her thoughts or at least her memories. Then again, she'd *thought* she'd been doing that with Dixie all these years, and she sure as jumping Jesus hadn't seen this coming.

"You were easy to fool," the Star agreed as she watched Nikki with her unearthly gaze, her smile condescending. "All broken and defiant, peddling your sob story about the kids you left behind. Pathetic."

Beside her, Torsten growled, and Nikki narrowed her eyes. Her wolf didn't know her story, and he certainly wasn't going to learn it from this bitch. She took a casual step forward.

"Uh-huh. Well, you didn't pick an easy path of it either, having to suck it up and play love goddess to all those drunk and naive tourists who thought getting married in your cheap-ass chapel was the perfect capper to their Vegas trip. How long have you been doing that schtick, and how *were* you not bored out of your mind? Because you damned well were boring me."

It was a blind shot, but it landed anyway. In a flash, the Star fully shed her Dixie regalia and stood before Nikki in a long white satin gown, white boots, her hair no longer showgirl blonde but flowing over her shoulders in blue-white splendor.

"That's a hell of a costume change," Nikki allowed. "I got an opening in my show. You should check it out."

"You have no more power than I possess in my little finger, and they elevated you to the Council without a second thought," the Star seethed.

Nikki bit back a quick grin. God love pride. It was always so handy.

"Well, why do you care? You're more powerful than any of them, right? Why should you give a damn who they put on their Council? I mean, sure, they thought you were just a sweet little dumbass horoscope reader, but that's what you wanted them to think. You did your job really well."

"They should have *known*," the Star countered, intoning the words with haughty grandeur, slow and resonant. "Illusion is their province, magic their playground. They should have recognized the magic I had and begged me to join them."

"Well, maybe they just didn't give a shit about your magic. They'd gotten along well enough without you for six thousand years, you know?"

All the while she was talking, Nikki continued edging forward, using her waving hands and striking dramatic poses to mask the fact that she was nearing her quarry. Torsten kept pace with her, only a step behind. He was going to be a problem if the Star struck.

With that, Torsten huffed a derisive breath, and Nikki fought the smile. *Whoopsie.* She'd forgotten that the wolves weren't that shabby at mind reading.

Unfortunately, the Star didn't respond to her final barb. She tilted her head and regarded Nikki with the kind of amusement only possible in a six-thousand-year-old being.

The moment lengthened until Nikki couldn't stand it anymore.

"You wanna tell me why you're here twirling your hair and not trying to stop the Arcana Council from taking you down?" Nikki prodded. "'Cause, I gotta tell you, my money's on Sara to get that done."

"Oh, my money is on her too," the Star said with a soft, knowing smile, so calm it was a little unnerving as she spread her hands wide, offering her palms to Nikki. "So much so, I don't need to know what she's doing or where she's doing it. I only needed to find you."

The attack was immediate and brutal. A hundred shooting stars exploded from the Star's hands and buried themselves in Nikki's and Torsten's bodies—as cold as ice and brutally jagged.

Nikki staggered back, her limbs going impossibly heavy as the Star laughed. Beside her, Torsten whimpered, the sound so harrowing, it cut across her pain, nearly blotting it out, but not quite. She sucked in a rough breath, staggering to her knees—and only then did she notice that the orbs that she'd dropped on the lawn, now situated behind the Star, had begun to glow more frantically.

"Sara has created an unbreakable tie to you," the Star murmured, her gaze soft and curious as she watched Nikki struggle. "She can't—won't—let you die. So I just have to wait."

The wolves beyond the perimeter of the Brombachers' wide back lawn began to howl, including two throatier, older cries. Wilhelm and Augustus, the storm and the ice bringers. They were too old to fight this fight, dammit. Nikki gritted her teeth, but Torsten's renewed grunt of pain kept her from calling them off. She had to get him out of here, stat. She had to get all of them away.

The Star cooed as she sent a second wave of star daggers into them, taking Nikki's breath away. "Right now, there's only pain, but soon—"

Nikki didn't give her a chance to finish. Stuck full of icy spikes or not, she totally believed the Star would make good on her threat of immobilizing her to draw out Sara, and she was soul-deep tired of entitled bitches trying to hold her down. She hauled her ass up with a roar as the Magician's enchanted toys exploded with crackling fury behind the Star. Not giving herself time to think, she pushed the Star into the force field they created, and then dove in as well, shoving the goddess back several feet as the curtain of crackling energy closed around them.

"The Star is stronger than the Moon," the Star chided as she danced back out of Nikki's grasp, her voice filling Nikki's mind right along with her ears. "Your magic will never defeat mine."

But Nikki had never planned on defeating the Star with magic. She took a running leap and delivered a roundhouse punch straight to the Star's throat. Her fist connected first with flesh and sinew, and then with nothing at all, the sudden loss of the Star's corporeal form overbalancing her and sending her staggering forward. The wolves were closer now, howling in consternation, but unable to pierce the veil of the electrical field. In the skies beyond the barrier, Nikki could see a rush of clouds boiling toward their clearing, lightning crackling in their depths. Wind roared with fury, battering against the force field, and she thought she heard the pelting of what sounded like rocks against it as well.

"You dare *touch* me?" the Star's cry of rage sounded a little surprised as she re-formed—mostly—and turned on Nikki with raging eyes. She was missing a big chunk of her neck, which was deeply disconcerting, until Nikki finally got it.

"You *can't* be touched, can you?" she taunted, straightening against the pain of the jagged spikes and grinning at the Star. "No wonder Detective Delish dumped your ass. You can't be touched!"

"You lie—" the Star began, but Nikki was now a woman crazed. The sound of hail hammering against the force field all around her, she waded in, fists flying, and kept up a running commentary as she knocked the Star backward with another roundhouse punch. "That was for trying to distract Sara when all she's ever wanted to do was save the fucking world."

Her fist encountered a scattering of stardust, then the Star re-formed with half her face gone. Nikki continued hitting, exploding the Star bit by tiny bit, and ignoring the pain of the dozens of tiny stars piercing her own body. "You can't handle me because I'm more woman than anyone you've ever encountered, I'm fucking female in spades, and until this force field lets us out, I'm going to go female medieval on your starry ass."

Chaos raged both inside the electrical barrier and in the clearing beyond it. The twin powers of storm and ice brought to bear against the force field while she battled within. Some dim part of Nikki's mind knew that the Star couldn't be killed, per se, but she could be destroyed all the same, and so she struck and struck...until all that was left was the last rotten core of the Star, a crystalline beating heart. Nikki scooped up one of the pointier star daggers that had liberated itself from her body and buried it deep as the final remnants of the Star burst into myriad glittering lights.

Energy surged, and Nikki arced back. The electrical jolt from the Magician's infernal devices blasted through her, through the star field, and around and around their electrical cage. Then...the force field exploded. A mighty storm broke over her.

Above the brain-pounding assault of light, sound, and pelting hail, Nikki heard the long, fierce howl of her wolves as she collapsed in a boneless heap on the scorched, storm-pounded lawn. Her sight dimmed and had nearly shorted out when she felt the sharp tug of Torsten's teeth digging into her shoulder, the great wolf dragging her to safety. Because of course he was.

Bumping half-deliriously over the blighted grass, Nikki savored the taste of blood and salt on her lips, the agony sparking through every limb, the queasy roll of her stomach. With the help of her wolves, both the pack she'd inherited and the family she'd made, she had lived to fight another day.

Not even the Psycho Bitch of the Universe could keep a fabulous girl down.

35

THE MAGICIAN

4:30 p.m. CET/7:30 a.m. PST
Day 1
Jumièges, France

A dozen orbs hovered in the quiet church where no human breathed for a half mile in any direction. The Magician had shoved them out the moment he'd arrived. They would come back with their police soon enough, but by then, he would be long gone. Everything would be long gone.

He studied the rapidly shifting images shooting through his mind like Tarot cards caught in the wind. One part of his brain calculated the projected death toll, rapidly ticking up, another projected the loss of knowledge, a third projected the change to the state of magic and technology. The numbers were...twenty-seven-point-three percent worse than he'd anticipated.

The Shadow Court had begun with a solid plan to limit death directly attributable to them other than among the Connected population, with much more major carnage happening after the powers of the world turned on each other, seeking to place the blame on whoever they could and gain retribution for further losses. But human constructs always broke down in the face of greed, war, and racism. Still, this swath of death would tip the balance in ways the Shadow Court hadn't perceived. It would be a bloody and costly battle, and there would be death. So much death.

But eventually, there would be magic again.

Armaeus directed his attention to the far-flung bastions of knowledge and learning that he had designated as the most critical for the coming world, and he gave his all to them, knowing his body could not withstand the effects of the quantum electricity that flowed through the magically altered devices for very long. He gloried in the pain and destruction of his own body bent in the service of this magic. He savored within him echoes of Tesla's own transcendent joy as he experienced something similar, though in his mind, he processed that pain with a far more scientific bent. He heard the High Priestess's cry go up, her haunting melody beginning as she called to her the acolytes who would serve her and the cause of magic. In eighty-five-point-three percent of his projected scenarios, Eshe did not survive the strain of her lonely vigil. That death was hers to choose, of course, for death eventually came to all humans. Even him.

The Magician spread his hands, saw the skin shrink against them, the pure magic beneath struggling to break free. He hadn't lied when he'd told his beloved Sara Wilde that there were only two things he wanted to save in this world. He'd been most specific in fact. He would save knowledge, and he would save her.

To achieve that, he would gladly sacrifice himself, giving

up the last vestige of his magic in the process. He could not live in this world without her, but he could willingly die to ensure she lived on.

Pain lanced through him, making him stagger. The weight of the psychic dead-zone bombs he was suppressing worldwide drew more and more electricity through the orbs. The distance was too great, the power required too high. It would not be long now.

It was the unmaking of the world, and it was finally here.

"*Sara*," he cried despite himself, even as he regretted the rash move. Fool that he was, he could not leave without saying goodbye.

"Armaeus!" Then Sara appeared in his mind's eye, her expression revealing that she could see him too—his ravaged face, his broken body. He didn't care anymore.

It was enough that she was there.

36

JUSTICE

4:45 p.m. CET
Day 1
Vatican City

"You are such a fucking *asshole*," Sara bit out, hauling the half-destroyed demigod she loved so much more than life itself away from his bucolic French countryside and into the bowels beneath St Peter's Basilica. She'd never pegged the Magician to be a martyr, but now he was pissing her off.

Easing Armaeus to the floor, she kept her arms and wings spread wide and called the pavers to her. She didn't pray, she demanded—of the Unmoved Mover who had built these pavers and set them within reach of human hands, of any god who would listen. "There has *got* to be a better way," she raged.

She vaguely noted the tiles of gold spinning off in new directions, creating new patterns. She dug deep, remembering the lessons on a faraway mountain with a small, shrewd-eyed sensei who wouldn't let her off the hook.

Chichiro had taught Sara she could manifest whatever she needed. She could create. And she could also heal.

The energy of the pavers expanded as a dozen more celestial tiles appeared in the subterranean chamber, then yet more. They piled up in the shallow golden impression in the floor, the one-time intended resting place of the Ark of the Covenant. She didn't know where that holy box was, but she could damn well build her own.

The chamber around her shook as the pavers continued filling the room, the ceiling rumbling. She scowled up at that ceiling, knowing the obelisk still soared above. Over eighty feet tall, almost the same height as the statue of Jesus in Rio de Janeiro, the job where she'd first met the Magician. Their relationship was coming full circle beneath the mightiest of edifices made by man in homage to their gods. She would do this, because she could do this.

She thrust her hands up and gave herself over to the celestial power she had amassed.

Energy shot from her, a bolt of fire blasting through the ceiling and surging into the column of the obelisk. She was beneath that obelisk, she was above it, she was everywhere at once, her molecules disintegrating to flow with every ounce of energy she pumped into the world. The obelisk shattered in an explosion that pulverized it down to the smallest pieces, and Sara, in her incorporeal state, extended her reach as far as it would go—far enough, she thought distantly, to cover the entire world.

The moment she did, the remaining psychic dead-zone bombs, every last fucking one of them, reversed polarity and exploded, breaking the world. They had to. She couldn't leave behind a minefield for future Connecteds to encounter, she couldn't let their magic be stripped away. She had to give them a chance.

And in that blast that swept the globe, she saw from far away and somewhere else, her body spread so thin she'd become only a whisper of thought—so, so much was lost... and so much more was born anew. Darkness and magic rushed into the broken places, filling them with crazed, chaotic energy.

Those losses she could endure, Sara decided, while she worked to make sure other wrongs were set right. She couldn't heal a broken building, shattered glass, and exploded machines. But she could heal the humans that the Shadow Court's bombs had wounded, and remake them better than they were before.

She bent to the task. The world was vast and full, and the pain of the afflicted was great. But Sara had learned her lessons well.

At long last, after all these years, she could save the most vulnerable Connecteds of all.

TIME PASSED—MOMENTS, centuries, minutes, millennia.

Finally, it was finished.

The darkness lightened. The sun beat down on her shoulders. Wind ruffled her hair.

Sara stared with bleary eyes at her brown and dusty feet, feeling a trickle of sweat trail down her temple, tasting the salt of the sea on her lips. Surrounding her, spilled out on the dirt path she stood upon, were Tarot cards—the Fool and High Priestess, the Devil and Death, the Sun and Moon. Even Judgment and the Hierophant, though they lay farther away, partially covered by other cards. But where was the Magician?

Heart pounding hard, Sara glanced up, a soft rush of breath filling her throat.

Before her rose a towering cliff that she had first seen in the depths of Hell itself, an illusion originally crafted to deliver her deep and lasting pain. At its summit sat a white-washed villa, a pristine retreat set against the bluest sky she'd ever seen. Dazed and disbelieving, she swept her gaze back to the base of the cliff, where an ocean played, kicking up white foam sprays to patter over her battered toes. Stretching up from the ocean, the dirt and stone-paved path wound up the cliff face, edged with wildflowers, blooming brushes, and her scattered Tarot cards...but still no Magician card among them.

"*No,*" Sara whispered, another bolt of panic unnerving her. She shot her gaze once more to the villa at the top of the winding path—and exhaled a harsh breath.

This time, standing at the top of the path, she saw the man who had become her life, her very breath. The Magician of the Arcana Council watched her with an undeniable intensity, hunger, and another emotion she couldn't quite recognize—but which might have been joy—radiating from him, even at this distance. The wind tousled his dark, curling hair, the sun burnished his bronzed skin, and his simple white shirt and long, sand-colored trousers looked impossibly right on that seaside path. He'd be wearing sandals, she thought, his feet bared to the healing touch of the sun. He was perfect. And he was safe.

"Armaeus," she managed, her voice catching on a sob. For a moment, time stopped, and she could see the entire skein of their history unspooling between them. The first hint of his attention in Rio de Janeiro, on the heels of a successful heist that had brought them into each other's spheres. The awkward, intense attraction that had flared between them almost immediately, twin fires of need and impending doom that...that had finally played out, she supposed.

Sara laughed a little shakily with that realization. The dread she'd felt along with her passion for the Magician had only involved the end of the world as they'd known it.

Through it all, Armaeus had been there. Infuriating her, beguiling her, pushing her...loving her. She hadn't seen it always, hadn't deserved it some of the time, but still he'd stood with her, for her. Knowing everything that might happen, calculating the percentages that they might never reach this pathway in the sunlight, might never feel this renewed flicker of hope that even now flared to life, illuminating an existence of...possibility. Peace. And endless, healing love.

Whether it was for the rest of their lives or just a few hours, the cares of the world had finally been swept away.

She lifted her hand, giving him a wave that felt almost shy, and finally, Armaeus moved.

"*Sara.*"

Graceful and sure, he strode down the paved steps—his body whole, complete, and unmarred by the burns and gashes that had rent his skin in France and spilled his blood. Stopping in front of her, he pulled her into his arms, staring at her with wide, unblinking eyes as tears streaked down his face—tears she knew she matched, drop by blessed drop.

"We did it, right? In the end, we did it?" she asked, her whole body trembling.

Armaeus smiled, a look of pure, fathomless wonder filling his gaze as he shook his head. "No, my love, my powerful Sara. *You* did it."

His lips came down on hers, and she sagged in his arms, kissing him hungrily, deeply, drawing on the well of his magic and releasing the torrent of pain and terror the end of days had sown into their very bones.

On another plane, one separate from her and the Magician and yet held as firmly in their embrace as they were holding each other, there were no more explosions. Power billowed and rolled, the world filled with so much more mayhem and magic than it had been even a day earlier. But the Connected lived. They could choose to embrace their true natures or not, but the choice had not been taken from them by the Shadow Court—or anyone else. Justice of the Arcana Council had done all she could to protect them, prepare them. If they chose to do so, they could finally claim their place in this world.

"Is it enough?" Sara pressed, and Armaeus murmured against her lips, deepening the kiss a long moment before he pulled his head back. His golden-black eyes shimmered with impossible magic, and when he spoke, that power danced within him, a host of tiny, crackling angels on the tips of a thousand spectral pins.

"It is enough," he said. "You are enough."

Sara sighed, her soft gust of breath shifting the rolling mists that had emerged on Earth, thickening them and deepening their power. Magic would survive. Earth would survive. And the weak would have the chance to be strong.

Sinking back into the protective arms of her Magician, Justice reveled in a world where all the things that had ever been wrong were—finally—set right.

EPILOGUE

THE DEVIL AND THE NIGHT WITCH

5:00 a.m. CST
Day 2
New Orleans, Louisiana, USA

"How is it you're so *heavy*? You're the freaking Devil, for fuck's sake. You shouldn't be this *heavy*."

Kreios didn't answer. Sariah hadn't expected him to. Since he joined the fight in Hell, turning into a great horned demon that even gave her pause, he'd been focused with single-minded determination on killing everything in sight.

Eventually, she'd figured out that he'd tapped into the weird electrical clamps that the robot formerly known as Eleanor St. Claire had tried to use to restrain Sara. But at some point during the battle, something had shifted with the manacles. They'd flipped a switch somehow and had started *augmenting*, not dampening, Kreios's power. Then more of the cuffs showed up, bound into tight balls, and that'd given him enough juice to take out Robot Chick for good and start piling into demons like it was his job.

Sariah didn't know what the HR protocols were for the Devil turning on his own horde, but she didn't think Kreios was going to get named boss of the year.

"There you go, buddy. Easy does it," she grunted as the Devil sagged against her. She stumbled past a blown-out storefront and ducked into the shattered door of a bakery that would not be opening today, never mind that it was well past time to make the beignets.

"Where..." the Devil mumbled, his head lolling along her shoulders.

Sariah bit her lip against the surge of relief that flowed through her that he was almost coherent again. She'd never trusted Kreios, not completely, but that didn't mean she wanted him to die down in Hell.

Looking out onto the bombed-out street, murky black in the predawn morning, she wasn't sure their situation had much improved.

"French Quarter," she informed him. "I figured out early on that it had the most gateways into and out of Hell. Occasionally, I would help a few unfortunates who'd pissed off the wrong voodoo priestess get back to the other side—in exchange for some beignets from this place. Definitely a worthwhile trade. When all Hell started, well, breaking loose, this was the only place I could focus on where I knew we could get out. I was hoping there'd be pastries. I was mistaken."

With that, Kreios finally blinked open blood-shot green eyes and peered at her blearily. She breathed out a tiny exhale of relief. His disheveled Mediterranean playboy appearance was back in full play, and that was definitely an improvement, though she didn't like to judge. Down in Hell, he'd turned into a hairless red beast who'd stank of sulfur and blood, and she'd worried he'd stay stuck that way.

"You went from the bowels of Hell below Rome all the way to New Orleans?" he croaked, his voice still ragged. "How?"

"Whattya mean, how?" She rolled her eyes. "You know, for somebody who's supposed to be the overlord of the great down under, your property management skills suck. It isn't all just pools of writhing misery, you know. We had some cool stuff. Including doorways that led to wherever you wanted them to go, so long as you weren't too particular about what you saw along the way. How are you feeling, anyway, since you're up?"

The Devil grunted in dismissal as if the question offended him. He glanced away, clearly replaying the events in the underworld. "Those devices, they should not have reacted that way," he said, his voice stronger now. Sharper. "When they switched polarity, I should not have survived."

"Yeah, well." Sariah grimaced, canting her head to the side to work out the worst of the kinks. "You can thank Sara for that, in absentia. I brushed up against her and sucked some healing mojo off her before we took the deep dive into Hell. Every time you busted apart, I was able to put you back together again and me as well. I think her skill set has pretty well worn off, though, so how 'bout you knock that shit off."

The Devil smiled at that, but whatever he was about to say next was cut off by the sound of shattering glass and angry shouts. Sariah jerked him to a standing position, leaning against the empty shelf that didn't sport even a hint of powdered sugar to take the edge off.

Two teenagers burst into the room. They couldn't have been more than eighteen, and they looked ragged, cut up, with torn T-shirts, scorched jeans, and blackened tennis shoes.

"Are you the Donnellys?" one of them demanded, a tall

lanky kid with mahogany-red hair and whiskey-brown eyes, now wide with terror. "There's nothing left of your office, but we saw you in here. We were sent to find you—can you help?"

"Sure we can," Sariah decided, holding up a hand to slow the kid's roll. "Who sent you, and what do you need?"

The second guy stepped up, a little older and steadier, but still pale with shock. "I'm Joe, and this is my cousin Tommy." He gestured with a jittery hand. "Madame Shanda said this would happen, that the bombs would explode and wild magic would flow through the city. That New Orleans would be broken into light and shadow. It's happening. It's happening right now, and—she told us to find you. We need your help."

"Doing what?" Sariah pressed, grimacing at the potential stupidity of the question, but it had to be asked. The younger kid, Tommy, was staring from the Devil to her, his brown eyes starting to go glassy with shock.

"To *fight*," Joe blurted, his voice cracking as he clenched his hands into fists. His fair hair and pale features rendered him almost ghostlike against the empty pastry cases. "Something bad happened yesterday. Really bad. Shit started exploding—that's happened before, right? No big deal. We just braced ourselves for the assholes, but then this completely fucked-up fog rolled in, and not even the looters would go outside. Half the city's power totally shut down, and wherever there was fog, there was screaming. I mean, our families are in there. We have to *find* them."

Sariah looked over to see Kreios studying her, his eyes once more a clear, vibrant green. One of his perfectly winged eyebrows lifted in challenge. "Do you think they'll have beignets, at least?" he asked, his sensual mouth curving into a smile.

Sariah pulled out one of her jagged knives and pointed it at the boy.

"Show us."

Where do we go from here?

THE WORLD HAS CHANGED DRAMATICALLY in the wake of this war on magic, but Earth will keep on spinning, and the Arcana Council will endure... though in a much different way.

I have been getting regular visits from Death since Michael made the ultimate sacrifice for her...and believe me, you do NOT want to get regular visits from Death. She is determined to make things right, both for the Syx and for Michael, so don't be surprised if she demands her story to be told!

Also, the Devil and the Night Witch are up to no good in New Orleans, but if there's anyone who can be called on to fight for humanity in the darkest corners of a magic-overrun world, it's Kreios and Sariah. They also may insist on their stories to be shared.

If either of the above stories sound good to you, drop me an email at Jenn@jennstark.com or via my contact page at https://jennstark.com/contact-jenn/, and let me know which one you'd like to read first! :) And have no fear, Hugh and Raum of the Syx will get their stories too. The world needs them now more than ever.

As to the rest of the Council, I've left their futures in their own hands...some on this plane, some on others, but if there's one thing I've learned over this Wilde adventure, it's that you can never count the Arcana Council out completely. Even with the world turned upside down...anything is possible with a flip of a card.

SPECIAL ANNOUNCEMENT:

I WILL BE WRITING an extended version of ONE WILDE NIGHT, which will be renamed THE WILDE FILES, that I intend to serve as a new introduction to Immortal Vegas for people who don't know about Sara and the Council (yet!). It will delve a little bit more into the introduction of Sara and the Magician, and include her never-before-shared early assignments for the Council. **I will make that book free as a gift for you, because you are amazing readers.** If you'd like to receive information about that, sign up for my newsletter at jennstark.com (the signup is at the bottom of the home page!). I'll be sending information about it in early 2022.

Above all else, thank you so much for taking this adventure with Sara, and with me. You've made these books possible, and I remain grateful and blessed to be able to share them with you.

A NOTE FROM JENN

The Tower is one of those cards that can be a little unsettling to get in a Tarot reading...and it should be! This card puts you on notice that things are about to change. Read on for a complete description!

ALSO: Interested in learning more about the Tarot, upcoming book releases, short stories in the world of the Arcana Council and other bits of mayhem? Get Connected (heh) and sign up for my mailing list here (https://www.jennstark.com - scroll down to the bottom of the home page!).

THE TOWER

The Tower is a card that has no intention of letting you off the hook. Either you will change, or change will be thrust upon you, with a transformation/revelation/bolt of clarity that will shake the foundations of everything you thought you knew or understood. Despite the severity of the imagery, the Tower is *not* an inherently negative card (unless you don't want to change). Rather, it symbolizes sudden awakening or disruption to the status quo. It's a powerful card that can usher in a bold new stage of your journey, or mean the end of one journey entirely and the beginning of another. Often the cards surrounding the Tower will help guide you as to what specifically will be changing, but take heart: if you stop changing, you stop living. So lean into the Tower card the next time it shows up in your reading, and get ready for a wild (and probably bumpy!) ride.

BOOKS BY JENN STARK

Wilde Justice Series

(series complete!)

The Red King

The Lost Queen

The Hallowed Knight

The Shadow Court

The Wayward Star

The Night Witch

The Untamed Moon

The Shattered Tower

Immortal Vegas Series

(series complete!)

One Wilde Night (prequel novella) - soon to be relaunched as the new book 1 of the series, and renamed THE WILDE FILES

Getting Wilde

Wilde Card

Born To Be Wilde

Wicked And Wilde

Aces Wilde

Forever Wilde

Wilde Child

Call of the Wilde

Running Wilde

Wilde Fire

The Demon Enforcer Series

Demon Unbound

Demon Forsaken

Demon Bewitched

Demon Ensnared

Demon Betrayed (coming in 2022)

Demon Beloved (coming in 2022)

Check out all of Jenn's books at her website, www.jennstark.com!

ACKNOWLEDGMENTS

THE SHATTERED TOWER was an incredible joy to write, and I'm so aware of the gift that writing is—a gift that you, my readers, give to me with every purchase of my books. But being able to take Sara's journey full circle allowed me to relive so much of her past...while preparing for what I hope will be an extraordinary future.

As in so many things, I remain deeply blessed by Elizabeth Bemis for her beautiful work on my books and my site—especially my fantastic series covers. She is one of the most generous and caring people I know. My editorial team of Linda Ingmanson and Toni Lee are beyond brilliant despite my continually ridiculous deadlines, and any mistakes in the manuscript are absolutely and completely my fault, not theirs.

Thanks also go to Judi Soderberg for her careful copyediting—she has never failed me, no matter how insane my turnaround needs are, and I am beyond grateful. From the very beginning, Edeena Cross has gifted me with her careful beta reads, Sabra Harp saves me on an almost weekly basis

—and Kristine Krantz, whose battlecry for the bouncing ball shall forever ring in my ears, has made this journey so much richer for her deep and insightful review of my work.

And, as always, thank you to Geoffrey, who makes it all worthwhile. It's been a *Wilde* ride.

ABOUT JENN STARK

Jenn Stark is an award-winning author of paranormal romance and urban fantasy. She lives and writes in Ohio. . . and she definitely loves to write. In addition to her Immortal Vegas and Wilde Justice urban fantasy series and Demon Enforcers paranormal romance series, she is also author Jennifer McGowan, whose Maids of Honor series of Young Adult Elizabethan spy romances are published by Simon & Schuster; author Jennifer Chance, whose Rule Breakers series of New Adult contemporary romances are published by Random House/LoveSwept and whose modern royals series, Gowns & Crowns, is now available; and author D.D. Chance, whose paranormal romantic fantasy series, Twyst Academy, Monster Hunter Academy, and Witchling Academy, are available at Amazon.

Visit her online at https://www.jennstark.com and sign up for her newsletter at the bottom of the homepage to keep up with all the latest information about upcoming releases, new stories, and special events!

facebook.com/authorjennstark

twitter.com/jennstark

Print ISBN-13: 978-1-943768-92-9

Cover design by Elizabeth Bemis

Made in the USA
Columbia, SC
04 November 2024

45607181R00185